Anthony Gilbert and The Murder Room

>>> This title is part of The Murder Room, our series dedicated to making available out-of-print or hard-to-find titles by classic crime writers.

Crime fiction has always held up a mirror to society. The Victorians were fascinated by sensational murder and the emerging science of detection; now we are obsessed with the forensic detail of violent death. And no other genre has so captivated and enthralled readers.

Vast troves of classic crime writing have for a long time been unavailable to all but the most dedicated frequenters of second-hand bookshops. The advent of digital publishing means that we are now able to bring you the backlists of a huge range of titles by classic and contemporary crime writers, some of which have been out of print for decades.

From the genteel amateur private eyes of the Golden Age and the femmes fatales of pulp fiction, to the morally ambiguous hard-boiled detectives of mid twentieth-century America and their descendants who walk our twenty-first century streets, The Murder Room has it all. **>>>**

The Murder Room
Where Criminal Minds Meet

themurderroom.com

Anthony Gilbert (1899–1973)

Anthony Gilbert was the pen name of Lucy Beatrice Malleson. Born in London, she spent all her life there, and her affection for the city is clear from the strong sense of character and place in evidence in her work. She published 69 crime novels, 51 of which featured her best known character, Arthur Crook, a vulgar London lawyer totally (and deliberately) unlike the aristocratic detectives, such as Lord Peter Wimsey, who dominated the mystery field at the time. She also wrote more than 25 radio plays, which were broadcast in Great Britain and overseas. Her thriller *The Woman in Red* (1941) was broadcast in the United States by CBS and made into a film in 1945 under the title *My Name is Julia Ross*. She was an early member of the British Detection Club, which, along with Dorothy L. Sayers, she prevented from disintegrating during World War II. Malleson published her autobiography, *Three-a-Penny*, in 1940, and wrote numerous short stories, which were published in several anthologies and in such periodicals as *Ellery Queen's Mystery Magazine* and *The Saint*. The short story 'You Can't Hang Twice' received a Queens award in 1946. She never married, and evidence of her feminism is elegantly expressed in much of her work.

By Anthony Gilbert

Scott Egerton series

Tragedy at Freyne (1927)

The Murder of Mrs
 Davenport (1928)

Death at Four Corners (1929)

The Mystery of the Open
 Window (1929)

The Night of the Fog (1930)

The Body on the Beam (1932)

The Long Shadow (1932)

The Musical Comedy
 Crime (1933)

An Old Lady Dies (1934)

The Man Who Was Too
 Clever (1935)

**Mr Crook Murder
 Mystery series**

Murder by Experts (1936)

The Man Who Wasn't
 There (1937)

Murder Has No Tongue (1937)

Treason in My Breast (1938)

The Bell of Death (1939)

Dear Dead Woman (1940)
 aka *Death Takes a Redhead*

The Vanishing Corpse (1941)
 aka *She Vanished in the Dawn*

The Woman in Red (1941)
 aka *The Mystery of the
 Woman in Red*

Death in the Blackout (1942)
 aka *The Case of the Tea-
 Cosy's Aunt*

Something Nasty in the
 Woodshed (1942)
 aka *Mystery in the Woodshed*

The Mouse Who Wouldn't
 Play Ball (1943)
 aka *30 Days to Live*

He Came by Night (1944)
 aka *Death at the Door*

The Scarlet Button (1944)
 aka *Murder Is Cheap*

A Spy for Mr Crook (1944)

The Black Stage (1945)
 aka *Murder Cheats the Bride*

Don't Open the Door (1945)
 aka *Death Lifts the Latch*

Lift Up the Lid (1945)
 aka *The Innocent Bottle*

The Spinster's Secret (1946)
 aka *By Hook or by Crook*

Death in the Wrong Room
 (1947)

Die in the Dark (1947)
 aka *The Missing Widow*

Death Knocks Three Times
 (1949)

Murder Comes Home (1950)

A Nice Cup of Tea (1950)
 aka *The Wrong Body*

Lady-Killer (1951)
Miss Pinnegar Disappears
   (1952)
   aka *A Case for Mr Crook*
Footsteps Behind Me (1953)
   aka *Black Death*
Snake in the Grass (1954)
   aka *Death Won't Wait*
Is She Dead Too? (1955)
   aka *A Question of Murder*
And Death Came Too (1956)
Riddle of a Lady (1956)
Give Death a Name (1957)
Death Against the Clock
   (1958)
Death Takes a Wife (1959)
   aka *Death Casts a Long
   Shadow*
Third Crime Lucky (1959)
   aka *Prelude to Murder*
Out for the Kill (1960)
She Shall Die (1961)
   aka *After the Verdict*
Uncertain Death (1961)
No Dust in the Attic (1962)
Ring for a Noose (1963)
The Fingerprint (1964)

The Voice (1964)
   aka *Knock, Knock! Who's
   There?*
Passenger to Nowhere (1965)
The Looking Glass Murder
   (1966)
The Visitor (1967)
Night Encounter (1968)
   aka *Murder Anonymous*
Missing from Her Home (1969)
Death Wears a Mask (1970)
   aka *Mr Crook Lifts the Mask*
Murder is a Waiting Game
   (1972)
Tenant for the Tomb (1971)
A Nice Little Killing (1974)

Standalone Novels
The Case Against Andrew
   Fane (1931)
Death in Fancy Dress (1933)
The Man in the Button
   Boots (1934)
Courtier to Death (1936)
   aka *The Dover Train Mystery*
The Clock in the Hatbox
   (1939)

Something Nasty in the Woodshed

Anthony Gilbert

An Orion book

Copyright © Lucy Beatrice Malleson 1942

The right of Lucy Beatrice Malleson to be identified as the author of this work has
been asserted in accordance with the Copyright, Designs and Patents Act 1988.

This edition published by
The Orion Publishing Group Ltd
Orion House
5 Upper St Martin's Lane
London WC2H 9EA

An Hachette UK company
A CIP catalogue record for this book is available from the British Library

ISBN 978 1 4719 0972 6

www.orionbooks.co.uk

CHAPTER ONE

As soon as he set eyes on The Haven, Edmund Durward knew that his search was at an end. The Haven was emphatically not everybody's house. It stood in a hollow, overwhelmed by green-black trees of incredible age; creepers were draped round the window frames, darkening the rooms whose low ceilings made them dark enough in any case. The knocker resounded with a hollow clang, proclaiming the emptiness within. For half a mile in every direction there was nothing to be seen but dense woodland, with an occasional black pool whose waters seemed unfathomable. When at length he procured a key Durward found the place inches thick in dust. Cobwebs overspread the furniture, the draperies, the black beams of the ceilings. But when these were cleared away, when the creepers were cut back and life moved here again, it seemed to the man that the house would have a certain macabre charm. Whoever had furnished it had had a vast admiration for the Victorians. The walls were papered in satin stripes with true-lovers' knots and baskets of flowers. There was an abundance of red plush, gilt picture framing, ornaments, hand-painted china, woollen mats and fancy work. The lighting was by oil, water was pumped; knick-knacks by the hundred stood about on little gimcrack tables.

"A lady's house," he decided. "Very suitable for one whose profession is a ladies' man."

He took the place furnished on a quarterly tenancy, rent in advance, and moved in without delay. The solitude had no terrors for him. For the activities he had in mind he could have found no place more convenient. There was some trouble in getting his really vast quantity of luggage down the drive, that was half a mile long and, in bad weather, as sticky as a Christmas pudding. By dint of encouragement and bribery, however, he had the boxes carried up the narrow stairs, the chests of books unpacked and the cases removed to the woodshed.

"I'm going to find that woodshed useful," he said. "There doesn't appear to be a lumber room in the place."

"You take care they're not stolen," the foreman warned him.

Durward laughed. "By the rabbits? I don't appear to have neighbours nearer than three-quarters of a mile. Still, I can keep

1

the place locked. At all events it would prevent tramps sleeping on the premises."

"What d'you make of him, Bill?" one man asked the other as they tramped back to the gate, half a mile of plodding, mainly uphill.

"One of two things. Either 'e's dotty or 'e's a Nazi agent. I'd as soon bet one as the other."

"Nazi agent? 'E wouldn't learn much in the Bottom."

"Good place for a secret radio. Besides, they're cunning, these chaps. That wood 'ud be a treat for parachute landings."

"So long as it's not me on the parachute. Why, you'd be tore to bits on those trees and land in a pond like as not."

The village dubbed him the Mystery Man from the start, and was intensely curious about him. But when they did meet him he seemed not merely harmless but attractive.

"Ah, you wait," said Mrs. Hart, the little cockney who "obliged" him in the mornings. The war had been a godsend to Mrs. Hart. A work-shy husband (he called it air-raid nerves himself) made it necessary for her to labour overtime, but until Hitler's hordes drove people out of London there hadn't really been enough work to go round. Now, however, she could work all day and night, and her husband sometimes wondered aloud why she didn't.

"Give me a bit of rest," he remarked sourly.

"You and yer rest," scoffed Mrs. Hart. "Why, you never do nothing else. I should think you'd get tired of resting one of these days."

"So I will," Hart promised her. "Do a bit of work on you if you're not careful."

"You!" his wife taunted him. She was a little bit of a creature, the size of a cock sparrow, but she had the sort of spirit people talk about on the wireless and the imagination of a detective writer. "Why, I'd be in the next county before you picked up your great lazy 'ulk."

"One of these days," he threatened, but she only laughed.

"You'll never get shut of a woman that works 'er fingers to the bone to keep you in luxury. Proper gentleman you are, aren't you? And that makes me a lady, don't it?" She stuck out her tongue and vanished.

"What's the new man at The Haven like?" Miss Martin asked her a few days after Durward's arrival. Mrs. Hart "obliged" Miss Martin too.

"Film star," said Mrs. Hart briefly. "Oh, lovely. Blue eyes, black 'air, little moustache. Ever such a nice way of talking 'e's got."

"Wonder what he's doing at The Haven," speculated Miss Martin.

"Running away from 'is wife I shouldn't wonder. Or 'arf a dozen of them p'raps. 'E's the kind that's got glammer. Cool What wouldn't I do with an 'usband like that."

"What does he do all day?"

"Writes. Scratch, scratch, scratch, like a mouse. Oh, well, they're all dotty, these writers."

Miss Martin nodded. She and her friend, Miss Grainger, lived in a cottage called The Buddies, and reared everything small and inexpensive that could be persuaded to breed. Cats, rabbits, hens, ducks, there was always an accouchement in progress somewhere on the premises.

"Violet," shouted Miss Martin, who was a short, stout woman wearing the blue-gray uniform with yellow trimmings that marked her a member of a prominent voluntary service. "Are you in your room? I'm coming up."

"For heaven's sake, don't go in," exclaimed Violet Grainger, appearing at the head of the staircase. "Josephine will give birth at any minute, and you know how sensitive she is."

"I hope she'll be sensitive enough to have real Manxes this time, that's all. These kittens with apologies for tails are worse than the usual kind. I've been asking Mrs. Hart about that man at The Haven," she added, joining her friend on the landing. "She says he's a writer and has glamour."

"Mrs. Hart's middle name is the Daily Liar, as you know. I wonder if he realizes what a snake he's taken into his bosom."

"It sounds as though he might be worth cultivating. Perhaps he'd write something for the Women's Institute for us. I'm going to take a rabbit up there this afternoon and see him for myself. Good neighbours, you know."

"He probably came here to escape them."

"Mrs. Hart thinks it was a wife."

"I wouldn't be surprised to hear it was the police. If he is an author, why haven't we heard his name?"

"He probably writes under a *nom de plume*."

"Only people who're ashamed of their work do that."

"He might be modest, if you can imagine a modest author. Anyway, I'm going to smell round and see what I can find out."

Mr. Durward's name was better known to Miss Martin than she realized, and he had certainly just finished writing when she came tramping down the path the same afternoon, swinging a defunct rabbit by its ears. Mrs. Hart having departed at midday, he himself answered the bell. For once, thought the visitor, Mrs. Hart seemed to have told the truth. Durward was a tall, soldierly-looking man, with eyes of a peculiarly deep blue under peaked black brows, a trim black moustache, long narrow hands and feet and a charming, slightly diffident manner. "Oh, good afternoon," he said, regarding the rabbit with some apprehension.

"Thought I'd just make your acquaintance," said Miss Martin, breezily. "Neighbours and all that. Live at The Buddies. You're alone here, I gather. If there's anything we can do . . . shopping at Bridport, f'r instance. We go in every Friday, and if you're busy or short of petrol and care to give us a list . . ."

"You're most kind," ejaculated the rather overwhelmed Mr. Durward. "As a matter of fact, I'm expecting my wife in two or three weeks. . . ."

"H'm. Hope she'll like living in Bell's Bottom. It's supposed to be haunted, you know."

"Oh, she's not superstitious," said Durward thankfully. "Yes, I've heard about the ghost. Mrs. Hart saw to that."

"You're not Irish?" suggested Miss Martin, wondering if this man generally conducted conversations leaning against the door lintel or if there was some more sinister explanation of his reluctance to invite her within. "Well, then, perhaps you won't see her. As a matter of fact, she's only supposed to appear to women."

"Then we must hope my wife won't be bombarded with the story as soon as she arrives." His tone was cool, courteous, charming.

"You've a hope, if you're keeping Mrs. Hart."

"Just until I can make more permanent arrangements."

Miss Martin shook her sturdy graying head. "You won't, not here. Most of the local women wouldn't set foot in the place. You're lucky to have got Mrs. Hart."

"I must try and get someone not a local woman."

"The local women will soon put the wind up her. Oh!" She seemed to remember the rabbit she was carrying. "I've brought a contribution to your larder." She swung the limp fur bundle in his direction. Mr. Durward fielded it neatly.

"How very kind! I suppose Mrs. Hart can deal with rabbit."

"I'll clean it myself for you, if you like."

"Certainly not. I shouldn't dream of letting you do such a thing." He didn't seem very pleased with the rabbit now he had it.

"It's no use looking scornfully at bunny if you're going to stay in this part of the world," Miss Martin assured him in her penetrating voice. "This isn't London."

"I don't come from London."

"More used to the country, I dare say. What's your part of the world?"

But Durward, diffident though he might appear, had no intention

4

of being drawn. "This is a very charming part of the countryside, isn't it? So quiet."

"Oh, we get about," said Miss Martin quickly. "You'd be surprised. I expect you'll be joining the Home Guard. They have manœuvres all the time. I belong to the Pelicans, and we look after the canteen arrangements."

"Actually," said Mr. Durward, "I've had a nervous breakdown. I've got to avoid anything in the nature of energetic movement for a bit."

"Funny," said Miss Martin, "you don't look at all that sort. I'd have said you were as strong as a horse."

"You should ask my wife," returned Durward, with a faint smile.

"I will when she comes. When did you say you were expecting her?"

"As soon as she can get things settled up. She's the business head."

"You write, don't you? I was wondering if you'd help with our Women's Institute. A one-act play, you know. It's so hard to find anything without a royalty attached. Or perhaps you act yourself."

"Not professionally," said Durward, giving her an odd smile. His lips were laughing, but his blue eyes were wary.

"Anyway, we're glad to get any men these days. Are you going to accept bunny?"

"Thank you very much. I wonder if I might ask a favour of you?"

"I'm sure you can. As a good neighbour . . ."

Durward took a letter out of his pocket. "I was just going to post this. It would save me a mile of walking if you'd slip it in my post box as you go by. It's fixed on the fence by the gate. The postman collects my stuff when he leaves the letters, and he'll be coming in about half an hour."

"Of course I'll post it. It's a long tramp for you every time, right up to the gate." She slipped the letter into her uniform pocket.

"A little effort of mine for the *Morning News*," smiled Durward, anticipating the moment when she would examine the envelope for herself.

"Fascinating job, writing," suggested Miss Martin. "Seems queer for a man, but I always say it takes all sorts to make a world. When's this going to be published?"

"In the course of the next day or two."

"I'll look out for it."

"Oh, it won't be signed," Durward assured her. "I'm not famous enough for that—yet."

"I'm sure you will be." Durward smiled politely, but made no reply. "Anyway, I'm glad you've come," she told him heartily.

"Only hope you won't find this place too gloomy. They offered it to us, but I said when I wanted to be buried there was nothing wrong with the churchyard."

"It's been standing empty some time," Durward acknowledged.

"Not surprised. Too much out of the world, too damp, too sinister."

"Perhaps it only wants living in," the man suggested.

"You may be right. At present it feels as though it's been mainly used for dying in."

Again he flung her an odd look, but said nothing. Miss Martin took the hint—and her leave.

"He's got a wife," she told Miss Grainger on her return. "She's coming down in the next two or three weeks."

"Sez he." Miss Grainger prided herself on putting a bit of ginger into things. "I'd like to see her marriage lines. Well, would any wife bury herself away here? No, there's more to this than meets the eye, Evelyn. We may find our pictures in the papers yet."

II

The envelope posted by Miss Martin reached the offices of the *Morning News* the following day, the 4th November, 1940, and the advertisement appeared in the paper's personal column the next morning. It read:

MIDDLE-AGED Gentleman, single, wishes to meet Gentlewoman, aged 35–42, view matrimony. Independent means. Should appreciate quiet country life. No family ties essential. Write Box 702, *Morning News*, London, E.C.4.

It was observed with some interest by a variety of people.

Arthur Crook saw it in the tube on his way to his office in Bloomsbury Street. When he arrived, he pointed it out to his A.D.C., Bill Parsons.

"Might as well file that," he said. "There may be a job of work for us within the year."

Bill looked at the paper and nodded. "Think this might be The Shiner on the warpath?"

"It could be, Bill. It could be. And if it ain't it's his twin brother. How many answers should you think this chap will get?"

Bill raised his black brows. "Couple of hundred?"

"Couple of thousand more like. On my word, Bill, I sometimes wonder what's the sense of the higher education of women, seeing

most of them don't seem able to read. Have they never heard of
Landru or George Joseph Smith or that chap, Dougal, who put
his wife in a moat and made merry with the next girl? Don't they
know no man has to spend good money advertising for a wife
unless he's a wrong 'un? And don't it rouse the teeniest suspicion
when they see he isn't even interested in them till they're beginnin'
to drop off the perch? Think of all the women of fifty-and-the-
rest who're goin' to answer this and say they were forty-one last
birthday. Think of the boom there's goin' to be in hair tintin'
during the next few days, and mud packs and surgical needles.
And you take my word for it, Bill, there'll be another Trunk Mystery
in the next few months, and that's where you and me will come in."

Miss Agatha Forbes read it over her frugal breakfast of tea and
toast and honey. She was forty-six years old and had had a drab
existence to date. Up till the age of thirty-five she had tended
an invalid mother and smoothed life for that lady's irascible husband. From thirty-five to thirty-nine she had listened to other
women telling her how they envied her Dear Mr. Forbes. At any
time during those four years she would willingly have traded Mr.
Forbes for an income of three pounds a week and a room of her
own. Patiently she trailed a line of hopeful widows in front of
the widower, but that gentleman knew when he was well off, and
the widows faded out like last winter's snow. When he died unexpectedly of pneumonia Agatha found herself in possession of three
hundred pounds a year and the furniture, all of which she hated
because of its associations. She remained alone in the suburban
house for another twelve months, partly because the shock of her
liberty numbed her senses, but also because she felt that in some
way she would be defrauding the landlord if she moved out before
the lease had expired. At the end of the year she sold all the furniture and took a two-roomed flat in London that she filled with the
kind of chairs and tables she had always wanted and, to complete
the metamorphosis, had a permanent wave and bought a jar of
rouge, price one-and-nine. She also had her ears pierced and
replaced her gold-rimmed spectacles by the invisible sort that are
so much kinder to the middle-aged face. At the age of forty-one
she discovered there were institutions called Women's Clubs where
solitary and undistinguished females may mingle with amusing
people who have done things, among whom Agatha felt it might
be possible to build up a new life. By good fortune, her vicar's
wife was able to give her an introduction to the secretary of the
Hiawatha, and after a little doubt as to her qualifications her
cheque was passed and she found herself one of the two thousand
members of one of London's most prominent women's clubs. She

7

was, as they say, a good club member, which meant that she bought tickets for every club activity and was prepared to sit on committees and back up the chairman. It was scarcely a gay and colourful existence such as she had sometimes dreamed, but, at least, she could open her diary and see a number of engagements dotting the pages. Also, since the experience of many of her fellow members seemed much the same as her own, she could generally find someone to accompany her to the pictures (at matinee prices) and share her table at luncheon. She began to pay some attention to clothes and to learn what she could and what she shouldn't wear. Coats and skirts in sober colourings were for her, she found, and she had her hair discreetly cut and rolled on her neck. She ceased buying shoes from the sixteen-and-nine tray and paid thirty-five shillings instead; she wore small pearl earrings and her mother's diamond ring, with the result that, whereas when she joined the Hiawatha she was forty-one and looked ten years older, on the morning that she read the advertisement she was forty-six and looked rather less than her age.

She saw the advertisement quite by chance when she turned to the back sheet of the paper to see the text for the day. The text said: "Good luck have thou with thine honour," and immediately underneath was the advice that a middle-aged gentleman, single, wished to meet a lady with a view to matrimony.

"What sort of women answer advertisements like that?" wondered Miss Forbes, turning back to see what the Prime Minister had said about home defence and the duty of the civilian on the previous day. But for once she couldn't concentrate on Mr. Churchill. She wondered why a man whose intentions were sinister should stipulate that his correspondents should be middle-aged. What sort of a man can he be? she demanded. For some reason she could not put the thought of him out of her mind. It was easy to say, as her friend, Grace Knowles, certainly would, "He's a bad lot," but wasn't it possible that there were men who, like herself, were shy, lonely, eager for human warmth and companionship, and lacked the usual facilities for meeting the right sort of mate? She pictured him in his remote country home, wording the advertisement—hopefully? nervously?—impossible to tell. Perhaps it was a joke—but, if so, what did he expect to gain? And when the answers came in, would he open them anxiously, wondering if the right sort of woman had applied?

"I'm the last person to make light of loneliness," she chid herself, "since I know it is like a mist hiding the rest of the world from sight."

For the twentieth time she reread the advertisement. She could not have said precisely when it came to her that she was going to answer it. If it was a practical joke, then no harm would be done, but what if it were genuine? What if Fate were giving her this last opportunity to snatch at romance before the candle went out for good? There was a song Mr. Forbes used to sing at church socials; he had been great on church socials.

> *"Fate gives us all one chance, they say,*
> *She gave me mine that November day,*
> *She gave me mine and I threw it away."*

It seemed to her an omen that the text for the morning should be one about honour. It almost seemed a promise that the advertisement was genuine. Providing herself with a pencil and a government circular on "What to do in an Invasion," she began to draft a reply on the back. She wrote:

"DEAR SIR,—I have seen your insertion in this morning's *News* and, feeling that it may be a case of one lonely person desiring the companionship of another similarly situated, I am answering it and should like further details. I am the daughter of a professional man, unmarried, with a small private income over which I have complete control. I am entirely without relations, which is one of my reasons for wishing to establish myself in a home of my own. I am most domesticated and have experience of cooking, nursing, etc. I enjoy a quiet life and have always wanted to live in the country, so I feel we may have much in common. If I have misunderstood your motive and the advertisement was a practical joke, please disregard this letter but, being myself a person of few friends and having, as I say, no ties, I can feel sympathetically towards one who may be driven by circumstances to seek for a congenial companion in this somewhat unconventional manner. Naturally, we should wish to exchange references. should you be interested enough to reply to this letter."

Laying down the pencil, she read through what she had written. It sounded remarkably like an application for a post of housekeeper, but that, she told herself, was probably what it was. As an afterthought she added the precise amount of her income, and then to show that a dishonourable connection had no appeal for her she wrote, "I am a Member of the Church of England and should wish to be married according to its rites." This final sentence gave her a sudden sense of security, like some fire fighter who, having

9

patrolled for weeks bare-headed, is suddenly issued with a steel helmet.

"I stand to lose nothing," she told herself firmly. "If he puts the letter on the fire—well, I am no worse off. And if he answers it, then I am still free if his proposition fails to appeal. In any case, I can scarcely be more lonely than I am, and every step I have taken since Papa's death has been an advance."

Sealing the letter, she wrote the address in her neat, firm hand.

"God moves in a mysterious way," she reminded herself, affixing the stamp. "Wise ones nor mighty for His work He chooses . . ." No, but people like poor, insignificant Agatha Forbes, starved of happiness for so long, and now, perhaps to reap a belated harvest.

The knowledge of what she had done made her cool and resolved at the committee meeting she attended the same afternoon. As usual Lady Queue-Greene was in the chair, full of talk of "Woman's Share in the War." She had a way of speaking that reminded you of a Pekinese—yap, yap, yap, arrogant pug-nose in the air. Grace Knowles was also on the committee, and she took the chair next to Agatha's. She looked rather like her friend and her private history was much the same, except that she had been tormented by a hypochondriacal mother instead of a selfish father.

"The first thing to be decided," said Lady Queue-Greene, "is the election of a secretary to this new sub-committee. I feel it is most important that we should get the right person. She can, in a sense, make or mar our work. Now then"—she looked at the women gathered round the table—"Miss Forbes, I wonder if you would undertake this duty? I feel sure you would be most reliable."

"Seconded," said Miss Knowles enthusiastically.

"Wonderful to be so methodical," sighed little Mrs. Benson.

"Then we may take that as settled," announced Lady Queue-Greene. "Those in favour. Thank you."

And then Agatha upset all her plans by announcing that she was very sorry but her own plans were uncertain; she might be leaving town, and in the circumstances . . .

"Surely, Miss Forbes, you are not going to allow That Man to drive you out of London?" boomed Lady Queue-Greene. "I always feel that people like ourselves should set an example to the others."

"It's nothing to do with raids," said Agatha quickly, but she saw at once that no one believed her. They thought she couldn't take it. The sudden colour flamed into her pale cheeks.

"As a matter of fact," she said, before she could stop herself, "I—I may be getting married."

The moment the words were spoken she would have given anything to recall them. She—married? Why on earth should Box 702 pick her out of the probably enormous number of women who would answer his demands? Yet hope persisted. All the same, it hadn't been wise to share the secret. She could see the faces round her stiffening with disbelief. There was a breathless, an incredulous hush. Then Grace Knowles whispered, "Oh, Agatha! But you never told me."

"It—it isn't settled yet," stammered Miss Forbes. "It's just that so long as it's in the air, so to speak, I don't think I ought to accept responsibilities I might have to relinquish at short notice."

Lady Queue-Greene leaned her ample bosom on the table. "You don't think perhaps, at your age, it might be imprudent, Miss Forbes?"

"As to that," said Agatha, regaining her spirits, "it might be less imprudent now than twenty years ago. At least, if it is a mistake, I shall have twenty years less to pay for it."

Lady Queue-Greene leaned back once more. "Quite an elderly man, I presume, Miss Forbes?"

"Middle-aged," decided Agatha.

"You'd imagine to hear them talk that most men expected to live to be a hundred and forty," said a woman on the farther side of the table.

Agatha felt as though she'd got into the zoo when all the cage doors were open.

"Naturally," said her ladyship, "you must do whatever you think best for yourself, but, in the meantime, the question of a secretary is most pressing. Now, Miss Knowles—you aren't thinking of getting married?" She smiled playfully. Miss Knowles turned an unbecoming crimson.

"No, no. But it's a responsible position—I'm not sure . . ."

"*I'm* sure you will be splendid," said Lady Queue-Greene. "Miss Forbes, you'll be certain to let us know the date of the wedding, won't you? We shouldn't like to miss that."

"I told you, it's not definite yet," said Agatha miserably. The eyes of the women round her met comprehendingly. Hasn't brought him up to scratch, thought Miss Wharton. Not a gentleman, I'm afraid, decided Grace Knowles. Perhaps she's not really going to be married, speculated Lady Queue-Greene. Still waters run deep. . . .

After the meeting Agatha had tea with Miss Knowles and Miss Wharton, and spent the time parrying their questions. She felt she could scarcely protest that she couldn't answer them because she knew practically no more about the bridegroom-elect than they knew themselves. At a quarter to six she invented an engagement and escaped to a cinema, where she saw a rip-roaring melodrama of a woman who married a man she picked up in the train and was subsequently deposited beneath the kitchen flags.

"Very improbable," Agatha told herself severely, waiting for her No. 14 bus. "That sort of thing doesn't happen in real life."

Fate—and Mr. Crook—could have told her different.

CHAPTER TWO

ARTHUR CROOK'S prediction that Durward would receive two thousand replies was a little wide of the mark, but certainly during the week following the appearance of his advertisement his letter box was crammed with envelopes of every shape and colour, some even bearing a crest on the flap, addressed to Box 702, *Morning News*, London, E.C.4. After each delivery he would shut himself into the living room of The Haven and rip the guts out of his correspondence, as he inelegantly put it. The letters were read once and divided among three piles marked: Impossible, Second Reading and Worth While. Into the first and much the largest of the three went all those letters that made no mention of specific sums. A good many of his correspondents showed an unfortunate coyness when it came to financial details. They said they had adequate provision or that they could bring the savings of a lifetime, without any indication as to what the provision was or the approximate amount of the savings in question. The majority of these, Durward noted, enclosed undated photographs, and were either widows, whose husbands had died testifying to their devotion, or else spinsters accustomed to the care of aged fathers whom they had guided tenderly and inexorably to the tomb. All these letters were subsequently dumped on the fire, where they made a grand flare. In the second were letters that might merit a second reading, and these Durward locked away for future reference. In the third pile were very few letters indeed. The standard correspondents had to reach to achieve this pile was very high. To begin with, their financial status must be adequate. Secondly, there must be no tiresome relatives to interfere between man and wife. Thirdly, they must not be the managing type that likes to look after its own affairs. No, what Edmund Durward was seeking was a lady of means, modest but assured, who would regard him as a mighty rock of support and be only too thankful to let him take care of her interests. Such women are never plentiful, and of the supply the majority get husbands without the medium of a daily paper. Into this pile, therefore, went no more than five letters of which one came from a Miss Forbes of South Kensington, S.W.7.

His task completed, Durward thrust his hands into his pockets and began to walk up and down the room. It was long and low-browed, and the creeper waving outside the glass like so many ghostly fingers gave it a sinister air. There were three little windows, all looking onto a wood. The door opened into a dark narrow passage, carpeted thickly enough to disguise the sound of approaching feet. The furniture consisted of numbers of dark cupboards, Victorian what-nots, and sideboards, an array of closed doors that might, felt the sensitive, swing slowly open at any moment to reveal—what? Emptiness perhaps. Or secrets a generation old. There were photographs of dead-and-gone owners on the walls and bureaus. It would have been an admirable setting for a Victorian melodrama—so much red plush and gilt and ebon picture frame, stiff attentive chairs, veiled windows and low ceilings. In the huge open fireplace a sultry fire was burning; the flames crackled; every now and again a puff of smoke blew into the room. The little windows creaked in the stillness; the creeper knocked steadily, softly, against the panes. Even in broadest daylight the room always seemed in shadow. And outside the back door the darkness stretched like a tunnel to the woods and down to the pond known as Dead Man's Lake, round which stood twelve withered trees known as the Twelve Apostles.

And in the heart of this secrecy and solitude sat the man in whose hands Agatha Forbes's fate now lay.

II

Taking a wife is at all times a responsible affair, and for a man like Durward there were additional points to be considered. He could not, as it were, plunge light-heartedly into matrimony, and such inquiries as he must make and assurances he must receive take time. Moreover, there were two names on the list ahead of Agatha's, which explains why she received no reply to her letter until after the New Year.

It was a gray January morning and Agatha's forty-seventh birthday. When she came down to breakfast she reflected that the gap between forty-seven and fifty seems much more than three years. As once she had dreaded forty, so now she dreaded the next decade. In the forties still sounded early middle-age; but in the fifties was rapidly advancing towards dissolution.

"And when I'm fifty-seven," she told herself scornfully, "I shall say that in the fifties has a hale-and-hearty sound, but in the sixties suggests senility."

No one ever wrote for her birthday, and the only presents she received were those she had bought for herself the previous week. They stood on her table now—a box of writing paper, a felt button-hole, two pairs of stockings and a new pink cushion for her living room. They made a satisfactory array and she had thoughtfully added a birthday card to complete the picture. This morning, recklessly, she intended to have egg and bacon for breakfast as well as the honey. She had just brought the dish in when she heard the unmistakable sound of the letter flap. Hurrying out, she saw an envelope lying on the mat.

"It will be for Miss Fawkes," she told herself, referring to the tenant in the flat below. "My letters are like my telephone calls—they only arrive by mistake."

However, the envelope said quite clearly Miss Agatha Forbes, and the postmark was Bridport. Forgetting even the luxury of the egg and bacon, Agatha carried the letter into the living room and slit it open carefully, so that the envelope could be used again. She looked first of all at the signature. It read: "Yours most sincerely, Edmund Durward."

"It is an appeal for money," she told herself sensibly, turning to the beginning of the letter.

. . . The tea grew strong in the pot, the egg cooled; the rare and oh! so precious bacon congealed. Agatha Forbes stared, closed her eyes and stared again. Half crying, half laughing, she at last remembered her pot of tea. It couldn't be true, she was crazy, someone was playing a practical joke on her. All these possibilities chased one another through her agitated mind. For here it was in black and white, the letter for whose advent she had ceased to watch, the long-delayed reply to her own impulsive letter of the 5th November, applying for a post as wife to a man she had never met.

"I cannot imagine what you must think of me," Durward had written, "but the fact is I had a bad attack of influenza immediately after sending my insertion to the *Morning News*, and it is only recently that I have been able to attend to my correspondence. You may, perhaps, be surprised to hear that the response was considerable, but out of over a hundred letters I instantly selected yours, for it struck that note of sympathy for which I was seeking. I feel that you, like myself, are capable of deep feeling, though a natural reserve prevents this from being apparent to the casual onlooker. I am, as you have guessed, a lonely man seeking companionship and a home life. If you are still interested in my proposition and your circumstances are unchanged, may I suggest your coming here for a short visit to talk things over? I cannot offer you hospitality at my house, as I am at present alone here, but there is a very comfortable little hotel at Sultan Buzzard where I could engage rooms for you. This is a very solitary place, but the country round is most beautiful, and as I have a car you would not feel unduly isolated. We should have pleasant neighbours, and there are amateur theatricals locally, if that interests you. Your best train arrives at 3.25, and I would meet you with the car if you would let me know which day to expect you."

Agatha was surprised to find that her eyes were filled with tears as she laid the letter aside. Such gentleness, such consideration were so uncommon to her experience that she felt no matter what Mr. Durward's appearance or circumstances she could scarcely do less than love him gratefully for the rest of her days. She noticed that he said nothing about his age, and decided he was probably on the shady side of sixty. This, however, did not trouble her. Years ago she had abandoned her hopes of romance and now, when she was no longer young and had never been pretty, it seemed to her that life was offering more than she had ever dared to hope. She wondered whether her correspondent would be disappointed in her when they met, and how a gentleman told a lady who had travelled down from London for the purpose of discussing matrimony that she wasn't up to standard.

She remembered something an aunt of hers had said. "Agatha is so colourless." She felt it was true. Her vitality was like her income. It sufficed but it would cover no sort of extravagance She had a sudden vision of her respectable. unsympathetic parents writhing under their marble cross at Kensal Green cemetery at the realization of their daughter's conduct. She knew quite well that women of her class and upbringing do not answer matrimonial advertisements or accept invitations to the country from unknown men. No, they prefer to moulder in two rooms in South Kensington.

"And, indeed," cried poor Agatha aloud, "for all I know they are right. Suppose I am making a fatal mistake? Suppose he is, after all, a scoundrel, and when I reach The Haven I find myself faced with worse than death?"

Common sense, however, assured her that this fate seldom befalls middle-aged ladies of skinny appearance and no experience, and she sat down to write her reply. Her whole future hung in the balance. With all her heart she wanted to accept the invitation, but the tradition of a lifetime held her back. At last, she was inspired to turn to the personal column of the morning paper. Perhaps the day's text would make up her mind for her. She searched for it. It read: "Whatsoever thy soul desireth I will even do it for thee." Feeling that she had divine sanction for any madness she might henceforth commit, Agatha sat down and arranged to travel to Maplegrove on the borders of Dorset two days hence.

She filled up the interim by getting herself a gray cheviot tweed, three-piece suit and a model black hat that, the misguided saleswoman assured her, made her look saucy, and went to a hairdresser for a shampoo and set and a brightening rinse. This last brightened her hair almost out of recognition, but she reminded herself that you owe it to the world to look your best and that her hair had had a kind of auburn glow in youth, and paid the bill without many misgivings. That night she scarcely dared lay her head on the pillow lest she disarrange the curls and rolls the skilful hairdresser had conjured out of her neat grayish hair. In any case she was too excited to sleep. She spent a busy half-hour before the mirror next morning readjusting the curls, and reached Paddington twenty minutes before her train was scheduled. The station was packed with people, and all the trains were running at unusual hours, but she found a comfortable corner seat and bought a copy of *Vogue* for two shillings as a hallmark of sophistication. The weather contributed a good deal to the buoyancy of her spirits as the journey proceeded. The train ran through pleasantly smiling countryside that seemed to bear little relation to London's gaping wounds. Although it was only January, the sun seemed to colour the sky, and even the black branches of the trees were eager with promise. Winter jasmine flattened itself against a red wall like a pale flame, and in Agatha's heart hope rose like a shining flower. Water ran bluely, some white ducks were like flashes of snow, grass was green after recent rains, and the roofs of cottages showed their mellow red tones against a sky like a glazed china plate.

"I am Agatha Forbes," she whispered to herself. "The same Agatha who was trampled on by Papa for years and years and thought the Hiawatha such an adventure. And here I am on my way to meet a man I don't know, and perhaps when I come back I shall be engaged."

But, for all her courage, as the train neared its destination, her heart began to pound as though it would choke her, her hands holding the fashion magazine shook uncontrollably, her mouth was dry with fear. Fortunately the other occupants of her carriage had alighted at Chard, so she had a little time to compose herself and push one wayward auburn curl under the brim of the flighty fashionable hat before it was time to get her suitcase down from the rack and turn to scan the platform. A number of people had come to meet the train. One of them was an old man with a drooping white moustache and lack-lustre blue eyes. Instantly her heart misgave her. If this proved to be Edmund Durward, might she not be buying a wedding ring too dear? She had been prepared, she supposed, for every kind of peril, but she hadn't visualized this feeble old creature who now began to crawl towards the train, peering short-sightedly this way and that. However, a sturdy young woman in brown tweeds leaped onto the platform and claimed the old derelict, sweeping him away as a robust wave disposes of a piece of seaweed. The next moment a tall, attractive man approached and spoke her name.

"Miss Forbes? I felt it must be you. I'm Edmund Durward, and I can't tell you how glad I am to see you. Right up to the last moment I was afraid you would change your mind. Well, it is something of an ordeal coming all this way to meet a stranger. Is this case all the luggage you've got?"

His voice, the friendliness of his manner, the matter-of-fact nature of his greeting, put her fears to flight. Now she only thought he was too good to be true.

"I have just one or two little things," she murmured, counting the items. Umbrella (in case of rain), book (in case of boredom), biscuits (in case of hunger), aspirin (in case of headache), brandy (in case of shock), gas mask (for patriotic reasons)—yes, she had mislaid nothing.

"Then let's come along. I've got my car." He led the way out of the station. As he swung open the door of the neat green roadster for her to enter, there was a clatter of heels behind them and a voice shouted, "Hallo. I say, Mr. Durward." They both turned. Miss Martin, who had come to meet the train to collect two dogs being evacuated from London on account of the raids, was coming towards them.

"So your wife's arrived at last. How are you, Mrs. Durward? We've all been looking forward to your arrival. In fact," she winked, "you were so long on the way we began to wonder if you were a myth. Well, I hope you'll like the house your husband's chosen. Sooner you than me, that's what I say."

"Don't try and prejudice her," Durward broke in. "By the way, Agatha, this is Miss Martin, one of the neighbours of whom I told you."

"Do you run the amateur theatricals?" inquired Agatha politely.

"We're going to rope you and your husband in for those," Miss Martin assured her. "Had any experience?"

"Only at the Hiawatha. They had an amateur dramatic section. I didn't do very much, just middle-aged aunts and so on."

"Here, none o' that," shouted Miss Martin jocularly, looking as though she were going to slap Miss Forbes on the shoulder. "I'm a middle-aged aunt myself, and I dare say you are too.'"

"Actually," said Agatha, "I am an only child."

"I never asked whether there were any little toddlers," continued the amazonian Miss Martin.

"None," said Durward firmly.

"H'm. Well, when you want a spot of youth you must come

up to us. What do you think of these chaps?" She indicated the dogs she had come to claim, an Aberdeen terrier and a black-and-white quadruped whose mother had clearly chosen something—quite what it was it would be impossible to guess—not in the Kennel Club book. "We call this kind 'the buddies,' after our cottage, you know. Oh, you'll hear a lot of gossip about us in the village, but you don't have to believe everything. Well, so long. We'll be calling upon you any time to collect your subscription to the Women's Institute."

She bundled the two dogs into the car that started with an appalling screech, like an air-raid warning.

"I do hope your first encounter with the natives isn't going to prejudice you," said Durward anxiously, taking his seat at the wheel. "I assure you, she's unique."

"Oh, no," said Agatha, looking a little surprised. "There are plenty like her at the Hiawatha."

Durward looked at her with undisguised admiration. "What character!" he murmured. "In your place I'd have looked out the next return train. That woman paralyzes me. Before I know where I am I shall be acting in her dramatic company. I feel it."

"She has certainly broken the ice," Agatha acknowledged. "Though there was one thing I didn't quite understand. Why did she assume that I was your wife?"

"I'm afraid that's my fault. I told her I was expecting my wife to join me quite soon. I said it really in self-protection. She came to call one afternoon, carrying a dead rabbit and, like most bachelors, I feel at an appalling disadvantage with a masterful woman. I felt that in five minutes she would be organizing my whole life."

"From your advertisement," said Agatha demurely, "one assumed that was what you wanted."

"I want a companion," said Durward in quiet tones. "I've held a roving commission for a good many years, and now I want to settle down. You must realize how solitary I am that I should have inserted that advertisement at all."

"At first I thought it must be a joke," Agatha confessed.

"I certainly didn't expect to find myself driving back to The Haven with a lady within a few weeks. But—the fact is I was desperate. I literally know no one. I've spent practically all my life in the East, and when I retired about a year ago on doctor's orders I thought at once of getting married—only to discover that I knew no one whom I could ask. A younger man, perhaps, would have gone about and met people and trusted to luck, but that was out of the question for me. That advertisement was my last hope."

"It occurred to me that was possible. In fact, that's why I answered the letter. It's not a thing I would have dreamed six months ago I should be able to do."

"Do you know why I picked your letter out of all the rest?" he asked her.

Agatha clasped her hands between her knees. "I can't imagine. I don't think I ever expected a reply."

"It was so sincere. I felt that you, of all my correspondents, understood what loneliness is like, how it can seem to disintegrate the spirit. Oh, don't make any mistake. I'm not looking for a nurse or a housekeeper, but I'm not a young man any more, and the things that please young women are no longer mine to offer. What I have is a very modest establishment in what is perhaps the most remote house in England—and myself. That's why I stipulated for a woman of private means. The kind that simply wants a roof at any price is no use to me. There must be some personal element. Do you think me crazy to talk like this to a woman I've only just met?"

Agatha was more touched than she dared let him see. That she, not a particularly charming woman, nearing fifty, should be able to attract such a man, who could surely take his pick of young girls, staggered and humbled her. It did something else. It gave her, like a gift from on high, an assurance she had always lacked.

"I don't think you any crazier than myself," she replied. "My father would turn in his grave to see me at this moment. He always said I had no more spirit than a pink sugar mouse."

"I'm afraid your father was a very poor judge of character."

"It seemed like fate," mused the guileless Agatha. "Suppose I hadn't looked at the personal column that morning. Nothing at all would have happened. I should have gone on living in my little flat on my little income, with the Hiawatha for the highlights, so to speak, always aware that all my life was lived on the surface." She paused abruptly. "Mr. Durward, I believe you're exercising an hypnotic spell on me. I've never spoken to anyone like this in all my life before. There's never been anyone."

He slowed the car at a corner and put one hand gently over hers. "I hope for the rest of your life there will be me. For myself, I could ask nothing better."

It's a dream, the bemused Agatha told herself, a wonderful, enchanted, intoxicating dream. No man living could really want me as he seems to. It was incredible that an hour ago they had not met.

"In the train," she confessed, "I kept trying to think of ways of starting a conversation, of dispelling our mutual embarrassment.

And now that I'm here I feel as though I'd known you for a long time. It seems so natural. . . ."

"It is natural," said Durward quietly. "And don't think it was only you who were apprehensive. If I hadn't known it wouldn't catch you, I'd have sent a telegram calling the whole thing off. Yes, it's true. I was as terrified as that."

"You?" she exclaimed. "Why should you be frightened?"

"Of asking a strange woman to share one's life? It would alarm the bravest man. Come, Agatha, give me credit for a little sensitiveness. It's different for the young; they've so little to hide. At our age one has one's secrets, one's disappointments, failures, tender spots. That's why I could never marry a young woman now. She wouldn't understand."

The car came to a stop outside a gate set in a wooden fence. "The penultimate stage," he told her, getting out of the car. "Our tradesmen, such as they are, come no farther than this. The drive, or whatever you please to call it, is half a mile long and must, I think, have been laid out by a snake. It writhes the whole way to the house."

He re-entered the car and they began to descend deeper and deeper among the trees. Soon the road leading to the ordinary world seemed a long way off; no sound could be heard here but the noise of rooks and the occasional movement of a wood creature among the leaves. Like something enchanted, Agatha sat waiting for the journey to end. Then, she supposed, reality would assert itself and the dream would be over.

The house itself wore an air of decay that chilled her; the windows stared out at the enveloping woodland like the eyes of an idiot. Suddenly she shivered. Durward produced a key and opened the door.

"Come in," he said. "You can see for yourself what a difference a cheerful and sympathetic companion is going to make to me here."

Agatha came into that room that looked like the setting for a Victorian play, the room in which a few weeks earlier Durward had sat engrossed, opening his letters. He left her there for a moment while he went to see about tea. She made a tentative offer of help, but he rejected it at once.

"You've had a tiring journey and an endless drive on top of it. Rest for a minute and see what a good maid-of-all-work I can be." He went out and she heard his feet ring on the stone-paved kitchen floor. Still feeling like a character in a play she began to examine the room. It exerted an extraordinary influence upon her; it seemed alive, as though the dead-and-gone women who had painted those water colours, used those chairs, dusted and polished the ridiculous, useless tables, waited now to see what her choice would be. She felt their eyes upon her. Suddenly she felt rich and secure. For it had happened at last, the miracle for which she had long ceased to pray. She, Agatha Forbes, middle-aged, timid, resigned, had at last fallen in love. The experience was so overwhelming it blinded her to every other consideration.

Durward came back, carrying a tray holding two breakfast cups and an earthenware pot of tea. There were some enormous plain buns on a hand-painted plate and a pot of black currant jam.

"This seems to have been the best Mrs. Hart could contrive," he said. "Will you pour out, if you're not superstitious?"

She lifted the big pot at once. She hadn't poured out for a man since her father died.

"And now," said her host, taking his cup, "it's your turn."

"Mine?"

"I've told you so much about myself, but though you're sitting in my house, drinking my tea, I know nothing about you but what I've deduced. Tell me, are you really as alone in the world as you sound?"

"So much so that on the way it occurred to me that if there should be an accident, and I were among the killed, there was scarcely a living creature who would ask what had become of me."

"You can hardly expect me to believe that," the man demurred.

"Nevertheless, it's true. Oh, I have a few club acquaintances, but they wouldn't ask many questions. They'd say, 'I suppose she decided to go to the country,' or 'Perhaps with money worth so much less than it used to be she's decided to resign her membership.' "

He smiled at her. "What a gloomy view you take. But how about your relations?"

"I was an only child, as I told Miss Martin at the station, and both my parents were only children too. There may be some distant cousins somewhere but, if so, they've never been interested enough to recognize my existence. You see," she went on, with a sudden baring of her heart, "for so many years it wasn't possible for me to make friends because of home conditions. And when one is older one has lost the confidence of youth."

"I should hardly say you'd lost confidence," he reassured her. "It takes courage of no mean order to do what you've done, and I hope you may never regret it."

"Sometimes when I look back it seems as though I had made remarkably little of my life to date," she acknowledged.

"I can see you're one of those women who think too little of themselves. After all, you've had your affairs to manage. . . ."

She shook her head. "Not even that. I leave everything to Mr.

Murdoch. He was my father's lawyer and naturally I retained him. I have no head for figures, which is one reason why I'm sure Father would have tied up my money so that I couldn't touch it if he'd had any idea he was going to die so suddenly."

"But it's not so tied?"

"Oh, no," said Agatha fatuously. "I get my quarterly cheque regularly from Mr. Murdoch, and I'm free to spend it exactly as I please."

He passed his cup for more tea, then leaned back in his chair, his hands folded behind his head, his expression whimsical.

"Will you immediately walk out on me if I say I agree with your father? Do you really mean that you leave everything in your lawyer's hands? Never make inquiries or ask for documents, I suppose? Do you even know what your money's invested in?"

"Once or twice I have had to sign papers, when Mr. Murdoch changed an investment. No, of course I don't know the details. Why should I? I pay Mr. Murdoch to look after my interests."

"And if he didn't protect them, would you be any the wiser? Oh, I've no doubt he's the soul of integrity, but suppose he died suddenly—was killed in one of these night raids, for instance—can't you see what a temptation you present to his successor? A woman with property about which she asked no questions, of whose details she knows nothing, but who's prepared to swallow anything so long as it's written on headed paper. Really, my dear Agatha, I wonder you haven't been parted from your money long ago."

"That argues in favour of Mr. Murdoch's guardianship," protested Miss Forbes. "Besides, if you are going to spend your life suspecting people you're going to have no fun at all."

"All the same, there's such a thing as being too innocent." He smiled at her. When he did this one corner of his lip lifted from his excellent teeth, giving him a new and slightly predatory expression. "For instance, you know nothing about me. I might be a penniless adventurer out to capture just such a woman as yourself. Do you want to ask no questions, demand no bona fides?"

"I can't believe, if that were true, that you would trouble yourself with such small fry as myself," Agatha told him. "There must be many richer women who would be glad to—glad . . ." She stopped.

"Glad to marry an unknown author of moderate means living in great simplicity in an out-of-the-way country cottage? Agatha, your head's in the clouds. Don't you know what women are like? Don't you know that what they want is bounce and glitter and limelight? Don't you realize that a man whose health isn't of the most robust, and who prefers to live obscurely, is no catch at all to the sort of women you have in mind?"

She thought, "Some woman has hurt him desperately once. That's why he is so bitter." And aloud she said, "Some women prefer a quiet life and domesticity—they wouldn't know how to behave in limelight. And now," she went on quickly, "tell me about your books. I've always been interested in authors."

"We're very three-a-penny really," he said. "My book is a sort of John Buchan effort. What's called a spy thriller."

"I should love that. *Greenmantle* is one of my favourite books. As a matter of fact, I should like to learn to type, and then perhaps I could help you. It would be the next best thing to writing myself."

"An author's secretary! Better, do you suppose, than being the author's wife? Oh, I shouldn't ask you so soon. I should give you time. Why, you've not even seen the house yet. It's small enough, just this room and a bedroom upstairs with a little dressing room adjoining, a kind of cubbyhole where I have my meals, and that's really all. The luggage lives in the woodshed. Oh, and there is a bathroom of sorts, though I'm less optimistic about the water supply and the plumbing generally if we should get a drought."

He took her over the premises. The bedroom was all of a piece with the room downstairs. It had an old-fashioned bed hung with chintz curtains in a charming design of rosebuds scattered on an ivory ground; the long mirror against the wall was spotted with mould, and all the appointments on the dressing table seemed as though they waited for someone who lived here long ago.

"Is the place haunted?" she inquired suddenly.

"I've seen nothing. But suppose it were?" He put a big warm hand over hers. "Wouldn't you want to help to lay the ghost? They're pretty miserable people by all accounts, and you look kind."

Later in the evening he drove her over to The Crown, where she was to sleep, and remained to dine with her. During the meal he encouraged her to speak of her past life, and contrived to make her feel witty and desired. Success went to Agatha's head; she bloomed into happiness until by the time they separated until the next morning she would have given him everything she possessed, temporal and spiritual, at a word.

That night she lay awake until the light was stealing back into the sky. The bed was comfortable, the room airy, but sleep seemed a million miles away. Moment by moment she relived the most enthralling evening of her life.

"Tomorrow," he had said, "I shall ask you for your answer. Ah, you don't know how much depends on that."

(And nor, in fact, did she.)

"You mean, it matters so much to you?" She couldn't believe it.

"It is hardly an exaggeration to say it means my whole future to me."

(And that, again, was true.)

Already she knew the reply that she would give. Her chief fear was that, overnight, the scales would fall from his eyes and he would see her as she was, a middle-aged spinster who had never been kissed since she left the schoolroom. She had spoken of intuitions and telepathy, but when she wondered what thoughts passed through his mind, she was a million miles from guessing the truth. No whisper of the danger in which she stood reached her brain. Nothing cried through the stillness: "Go home, go home, before it is too late." Or warned her that there are worse fates for a woman than life in a two-roomed flat on an income of three hundred pounds a year. No young maiden, obsessed by first love, could have been more dazed, more blind to reality, than this sedate, elderly lady whose fiftieth birthday was just three years away.

Her last coherent thought was: "As soon as I am back in town I shall go to Marshall's and see if they still have that prune-coloured taffeta I admired so much. I thought it was too grand for me, too young, even, but I'm wrong. I've been dressing like an old woman for years. For the rest of my life . . ." Here, at length, she drifted into unconsciousness.

The wind chattered at the windows, somewhere a bird called. The house seemed to turn in its sleep.

"The rest of her life . . ." droned the wind.

"The rest of her life . . ." whistled the bird.

But Miss Forbes didn't hear them. Miss Forbes was dreaming of Edmund Durward and her new, unbelievable adventure.

25

DURWARD also slept little that night. The most delicate part of the transaction still lay ahead. He had learned a good deal of what he wanted to know. Agatha was, practically speaking, alone in the world; she had no money sense at all. She didn't even know whether the capital whence her income was derived was her own. Mr. Forbes sounded the kind of parent who would be delighted to tie his daughter's hands as much as possible, and if Agatha could only touch the income, then she could hardly be regarded as a sound investment. If, on the other hand, the capital was available, he would look a long way before he found an easier road to making money. Whatever happens, he told himself, she must not be allowed to get suspicious. He knew he could marry her as soon as he liked; she had made that clear. But between him and anything she possessed stood the figure of the lawyer. He turned over in his mind one plan after another. Lawyers, he knew, were inclined to be suspicious of men who displayed too much interest in a wife's property. But if Agatha could be persuaded to learn the details and transmit the information to him, that obstacle might be overcome. So, next morning, when he brought her back from The Crown, instead of proposing, as she had hoped, he said seriously: "I've been thinking about us—in fact, I've thought of nothing else all night—and the thing that sticks out, to my mind, is the fact that you don't honestly know where you stand. You'll forgive me if I say you're a woman it would be easy to take advantage of. I imagine you give something to every beggar you pass in the street. Don't you?"

"It seems so dreadful to have a roof over one's head and good shoes and a warm coat, and know there are three meals a day, to say nothing of tea, coming to you for the rest of your life, and then refuse to part with sixpence. Oh, I know what the societies tell you, that it's increasing vagabondage, and if they're in the gutter it's because they find it more paying than honest work, but a lot of them are too old to work, and it's a horrible way of having to pay one's rent anyhow."

Durward nodded and sighed. "I thought as much. You're too soft-hearted for your own good, Agatha. They're bad lots, most of them."

"Even bad lots get hungry and cold, and anyway I don't think there ought to be a premium on virtue. It's its own reward."

"Are you going to be as lavish as that when we're married?

26

I think it's a good thing you have got a lawyer to look after your affairs, or you'd probably be peddling matches yourself by this time. Now, I've been thinking. You must admit I have to do the thinking for two of us. Before we come to any definite agreement I want you, in your own interests, to find out exactly where you stand. Suppose, for instance, your father had said that if you marry you forfeit your income? Should you think me worth that?"

"You know I would," said Agatha steadfastly. "Though I should be sorry if that were the case. I'd like to feel I was bringing something to the common store."

"The fact is, you don't really know the provisions of your father's will?"

"Mr. Murdoch did tell me, but it had all been so sudden, and it seemed so extraordinary that I should have an income of my own, I don't think I quite took in the details."

"That's what I supposed. Now, I think in your own interests you ought to understand your position before you take any irrevocable step. You'd have to see these lawyers in any case to arrange about having stock transferred to your married name, and so forth. I want you to ask them just what your position will be, as my wife. Everything's so uncertain nowadays. After all, I might suddenly lose my money, and you'd be stranded. You have to consider every possibility."

"I shouldn't be afraid to take the risk," said Agatha gently.

"Ah, but I'm afraid to take it for you. You know that, in any circumstances, I want you to come here, but I want you to do it with your eyes open."

"If lawyers are as suspicious as you say, perhaps Mr. Murdoch will try and make difficulties," she faltered.

For the first time suspicions of her sincerity flashed into the man's mind.

"You needn't tell them more than you please," he assured her. "Simply say you want to see a copy of your father's will. That's easy enough. He can't refuse."

"If he asks why?"

"You could tell him the truth—or you could suggest that you were thinking of going into business on your own account—a tea shop, say—though naturally he'd dissuade you from that at the present time. But it would give you the information you want."

"I see." Agatha was silent for a moment. "I don't think Papa would have made any such provision," she said. "It would never occur to him that I should get married."

He slipped his arm round her. "I don't want you later on to feel I took advantage of you. Oh, you think now that such an idea would never occur to you, but we have, I hope, years ahead of us. I want us to start straight. I don't mean that I couldn't make provision for you. Naturally, I shall make a will in your favour, and I'm proposing to insure my life, so that in any case you wouldn't be left derelict. But it would make me feel a good deal happier if I knew that, come what might, you would amply be provided for."

"I'll do what you say," Agatha promised. "But, Edmund, you must let me tell you this. I don't think I'm naturally a very impulsive woman. At all events I seem to have taken a great many years to slip out of my rut, but even if I knew I must forfeit everything by marrying you, even if I knew that the marriage was not going to last more than a year, even then I would take the chance the gods offer me, knowing it would be a million times worth while."

"You should ask more of life," he told her, but she shook her head.

"Don't you understand? During that one year I should have lived as I've never lived since I was born. I know hundreds of women who would agree with me. Just being alive isn't enough. Just breathing and eating and sleeping—one wants more than that. I'd risk all my future for one year, and I want you to know it."

II

Miss Grace Knowles was having an early tea in the lounge of the Hiawatha. While she ate the club's wartime sixpenny allowance —tea and dry biscuits—she thought about her friend, Agatha Forbes. She had rung Agatha's number four times in the last thirty-six hours, and each time Agatha had been out. She hadn't been in the club either, because Grace had questioned Porter at the desk, and he said he hadn't seen her. If Porter hadn't seen a member, it meant that that member had not been in the club. Miss Knowles had just broken her second biscuit when the heavy door swung open and Agatha herself came in.

"My dear! What on earth's happened to you? I've been ringing and ringing . . ."

"I had to go down to the country on—business. Aren't you having tea rather early?"

"I want to go to the new picture at the Classic. It starts at four-fifteen. Why don't you have some tea now and come with me?"

"I can't. I mean, I'll have tea but I can't come to the pictures. I have to see my lawyer."

"Agatha! There isn't anything *wrong?*"

"Wrong? Oh, no."

"I mean, your going to the country and then going to the lawyer. One's so nervous about one's own little bit these days."

"I'm not nervous," said Agatha calmly, giving an order for tea. "But I think it's a good thing to know just where I stand."

"You don't think it's so bad you'll have to give up the club?" whispered Miss Knowles with bated breath.

"I shouldn't think so. But I don't know anything about money or investments, and I thought I'd just find out."

"Anyway, you won't be giving up the flat, will you?"

"It might even come to that."

"Agatha, how dreadful! How can you be so calm? What on earth would you do?"

"Go down to the country perhaps."

"You wouldn't like that."

"Oh, I might. I saw some rather nice rooms when I was away."

"Whereabouts?"

"Near Bridport."

"You'd miss the club activities terribly."

"They have an amateur dramatic society down there."

She chatted tantalizingly to her friend for a little longer, then took the tube to Russell Square and went to see Mr. Entwistle. Mr. Murdoch, she learned over the telephone, had migrated to the country some months earlier. When she arrived she was told that the lawyer was engaged, and was offered a seat by an elderly clerk who looked as though he had stepped out of a Dickens charade. Agatha, looking a good deal cooler than she felt, began to mouth opening phrases for the coming consultation. After about five minutes the door of Mr. Entwistle's room was flung open and a man swept out. The whole place seemed suddenly to rock as though a storm had passed through it; the very air was electrified. Yet there was little in the newcomer's appearance to justify such a change. He was a short, fat man with a square, red face, a bright brown suit that fitted him so tightly it almost looked as though it had been painted on him, a brown billycock tilted over his eyes and a gigantic cigar stuck jauntily in the corner of his mouth. Agatha thought how strange it was that one man could smoke a huge cigar and look like a great gentleman and the saviour of his country, while another resembled nothing so much as a large aggressive pig. The man banged his way out without appearing to notice Miss Forbes's presence and, as the door slammed behind him, she drew her little piece of black fur more closely round her throat.

"Very lively gentleman, Mr. Crook," said the clerk, climbing down from his stool and pattering over to the office.

"Yes, indeed," whispered Agatha, wondering what sort of

connection Mr. Entwistle maintained, if this were a typical client.

Mr. Murdoch's partner proved to be a large, rather abrupt gentleman of considerable girth, with a big, clean-shaved face and a disconcerting glare. He glared at Agatha sternly.

"Sorry, Murdoch's not here," he said, offering a large, well-kept hand. "Hope things are all right for you, Miss Forbes, eh?"

The final syllable startled Agatha so much that she sat for a moment in the chair in which he had placed her, looking like a surprised rabbit.

"And what can we do for you? Not coming to ask how you can increase your income, I hope, at this time of day. Our difficulty is to collect any income at all for our clients. Let's see, what have you got?" He examined some papers on the table before him. "H'm. Not too bad. I don't advise any change. Unless you'd like to sell out some of the Pitt Martins and buy Watson Tye instead. Breweries, you know. They're paying seven per cent and stand at thirty shillings. Still, it's as good as you can hope for these days. Four pound thirteen per cent on your money."

All this was Greek to Agatha. "Naturally I should leave decisions of that sort to you," she said firmly. "What I came for was to know whether I can touch my capital."

One of Mr. Entwistle's eyebrows climbed rapidly. "Thinking of starting out on your own?"

"Suppose I wanted to open a—a private hotel in the country, could I raise the money? Or is it tied up in any way?"

"It's tied up," said Mr. Entwistle. "As a matter of fact, your father left a very peculiar will. Put briefly, you get the income for life, and if you die unmarried the money goes to found a Joseph Forbes Scholarship at his old college. If you marry," he looked at her severely, "the capital can be drawn on by you only with your husband's consent. A most unusual provision, but no doubt Mr. Forbes wanted to safeguard the capital and thought two heads would be better than one."

"Oh, no," said Agatha quietly. "He didn't mean me to have a chance of touching the capital. He never expected me to get married."

"So he thought he'd make it worth your while to take the plunge? Well, Miss Forbes, there's your choice. Single bliss on three hundred a year or the risk of marriage on whatever your shares will fetch."

"And how much is that?"

Mr. Entwistle tapped his teeth with a gold pencil. "A lee-tle hard to say offhand, Miss Forbes. You see, owing to the war all stocks have depreciated. Then the raids have seriously affected a good many industries—gas shares, for instance, aren't worth what they were."

"What's the lowest figure they would fetch?" interrupted Miss Forbes.

"We were getting as much as seven per cent for some of these stocks before the war. Say, roughly, your capital was worth six thousand pounds. That's a very approximate figure, you understand. Now—well, we'd be lucky to get five."

"If I put it at four thousand, that wouldn't be exaggerating?"

"I should think very little of your broker if he couldn't get more than that."

"That is very much what I wanted to know. Thank you, Mr. Entwistle." She began to put on her gloves.

"You are not—er—thinking of getting married at the moment, Miss Forbes?" Mr. Entwistle ventured.

"At the moment," smiled Miss Forbes, "I am thinking of very little else."

"Really. Then—er—I congratulate you. I shall hope to meet your husband."

"If he ever comes to town I'm sure he'll be charmed."

"Is it on his account that you're so anxious to know your financial position?"

"And my own. For instance, it would have been quite typical of my father to have arranged for me to lose everything if I married. He didn't approve of women having money, particularly married women."

"A husband likes to do the providing," smiled Mr. Entwistle.

"Or likes to feel his wife is quite dependent," suggested Miss Forbes. Since her visit to Maplegrove she seemed to have changed; the Hiawatha wouldn't have known her.

"And what is your husband's profession?" the lawyer inquired.

"He's writing a book."

"That's not a profession, that's a luxury. But no doubt he has other interests."

"He's retired," said Agatha briefly. "He has a little cottage in the country and intends to devote himself to writing."

"Romantic old buffer of eighty?" wondered Mr. Entwistle. "Gay, elderly spark in the late sixties after her little bit?" He regarded Miss Forbes thoughtfully. His experience told him that the most difficult of all clients are middle-aged women who have had dull lives and suddenly resolve on a final fling before the tomb closes over their respectable gray heads. Not that Agatha was gray, far from it, but he was pretty sure that anyone who had been Joseph Forbes's daughter for forty years was owed something by life.

"And she means to collect on it," he decided. "Well, who am I to say her nay?" Aloud, however, he warned her, "It's as well to be careful before selling out your securities. Capital's very nice, but it means a reduction of income for every stock you sell. You do realize that?"

"I shouldn't draw out my money just to keep it in a stocking," Agatha assured him, with her pleasantest smile. "But my husband and I might prefer to invest the capital in something else. A business, for example."

"Have you any particular business in mind?"

"I am not married yet," Agatha reminded him, smiling still. "But I must admit it's nice to know that if we need the money we can get it. I wonder if you have a copy of my father's will?"

"Naturally," said Mr. Entwistle, looking a little offended.

"I'd like to take it with me. I haven't much head for business; that's why I've left everything in your hands since my father's death, but it might be useful for reference."

"Did your prospective husband suggest your asking for it?"

"He said I ought to be sure that I shouldn't be the loser by the marriage."

"Still, if he is going to support you . . ."

"I've been independent for seven years," said Agatha sweetly. "I should hate not to have anything of my own."

"You have known the gentleman for some time, perhaps?"

"We have corresponded," said Agatha unblushingly. "I think I am going to be very happy."

Mr. Entwistle coughed, blew a little and plunged courageously into speech.

"I don't want you to think me a wet blanket, Miss Forbes, and you mustn't think I'm being insulting, but we lawyers see a lot of queer things. You admit you don't know this fellow very well—has he, by the way, given any indication of his own means?"

"I shouldn't dream of asking him," said Agatha, really shocked now. "Oh, I can see very well what you're thinking: that he is marrying me for what I possess. But even so, why should you try to stop me? I might easily regard a husband as a better investment than even your brewery shares, and all investments are a risk in wartime. You told me so yourself."

"At all events, you will tell me his name?" Mr. Entwistle suggested.

"I'll send you a piece of the wedding cake," promised Miss Forbes.

After her departure Mr. Entwistle drew his diary towards him. "Miss Forbes called today," he wrote. "We shall hear more of this marriage." When, however, he spoke of the matter to Crook, saying he was gravely perturbed, that incomparable man only remarked, "Very sad, of course, if anything should happen, but no sense gettin' the wind up yet. And it don't do to overlook the fact, Entwistle, that crime's our bread and butter. In a perfect world we'd be on an eternal dole. No, no, you just remember you ain't God and let events take their course. We'll get our cue all right when the time comes."

"I don't like to think of that poor deluded woman," murmured Entwistle unhappily.

"Oh, you never know," Crook comforted him. "It's amazin' what enterprise some of 'em 'ull show, especially when they take to marriage late in life. Hell hath no fury and so forth."

And he hung up the receiver.

III

Mr. Entwistle received his slice of wedding cake earlier than he had anticipated. Agatha had the good fortune to find a tenant for her flat, and two weeks later she and Durward were quietly married by special license at a little country church, with only the pew opener and the vicar's elderly unmarried daughter for witnesses. The latter, taking Agatha's hand, said "I wish you the very best of good fortune, but I believe you have it already." Agatha, reading her heart, said gently, "It has all been very sudden, you know. These things sometimes are."

She meant to convey that perhaps a suitor would arrive for Miss Beecher also, but in her heart she didn't believe it. Miss Beecher would never have answered a matrimonial advertisement in any circumstances whatsoever.

A piece of cake also went to Miss Knowles, who stared at it in disbelief. She simply couldn't accept the fact that Agatha, her best friend, had slipped away in this double-faced fashion and got married without a word to anyone. The rest of the Hiawatha was equally flabbergasted.

"I must admit it seems to me very odd indeed," confessed Lady Queue-Greene fastidiously. "Rushing into matrimony at her age. Somehow she doesn't seem the marrying sort."

"It's a marriage all right," said Miss Wharton. "It was in *The Times*."

"Then I dare say he's quite an old man. It's to be hoped for her sake that he has some money."

"In that case, all she's got to do is butter the stairs," observed another member. "I wouldn't be surprised myself to hear the boot was on the other leg."

"Then he can do the buttering. It's the war, of course. It makes people lose their sense of proportion."

"As a matter of fact, he's probably a wise man who realizes that housekeepers are going to be at a premium for the rest of his days and has had the sense to come in on the ground floor."

It was significant that no one believed Agatha had been married for her charms alone.

CHAPTER FOUR

THE WEDDING took place on a biting morning in January, with a stormy wind driving the smothered clouds across the steely sky. As the happy pair drove carefully down the zigzag path leading to The Haven, Agatha felt a curious shudder run through her.

"Cold, Mrs. Durward?" her husband inquired.

"I am a bit, but that wasn't why I shivered. Edmund, what on earth persuaded you to take this house? The woods are choked with unhappiness. I wouldn't be surprised if there were a dozen ghosts attached to it."

"It's quiet and solitary and no one will interfere with us here," said Edmund tranquilly. "That's very important. I don't like interference."

"I don't think you need fear it. Why, even that indefatigable Miss Martin won't trouble us much."

"Miss Martin makes me feel I should be glad to creep into my grave. It'll be no loss if we don't see a great deal of her. Well, there's one thing, you're seeing the place at its worst. Wait till the spring when the woods are full of primroses and the trees full of singing birds. It'll be lovely enough then."

The front door was opened by Mrs. Hart, who had recklessly ceased to "oblige" another local household in order to be on the premises when the happy couple came in. She was a dumpy little creature, skinny and sallow, aged about forty, with dark, frizzy hair and gold rings in her ears. When she saw Agatha her little black eyes, round and sharp as a canary's, nearly popped out of her head.

"Well, this is a nice day for the ducks, I must say. When I woke this morning and saw the rain dripping like an overflow from a cistern, I felt it 'ud be a better day for a funeral than a homecoming. Still, there's a nice fire and the tea's ready when you want it. . . ." Her little beady eyes ran up and down Agatha's figure. Not a bit what she'd expected, she told Hart afterwards, but it was the quiet refined ones that got all the best men as a rule.

"Don't know 'ow long they've bin married," she said, "but she's still bats about him. Soppy, I call it."

She took up Agatha's box and suitcase and headed for the stairs at a scurrying run like a moor hen.

"I've put a fire in your room too, mum. Welcoming, I call it. And 'ow was London?"

Agatha said London was, as might be expected, wet and cold.

"A bit putting-off for that 'Itler," suggested Mrs. Hart. " 'Ave to look on the bright side. You'll find the country funny at first. I used to say to my 'usbing, 'I'll never stand this.' Such a lot of noise, if you know what I mean. Well, I know there's noise in London, of course, but that's life. This is different. Queer, if you ask me. But then I always did think them as lived in the country 'ad a screw loose, and no wonder. Shall I unpack for you, mum?"

Agatha said "Thank you," but she could manage for herself. Up here everything seemed more cheerful. The fire crackled in the grate, throwing great golden shadows across the ceiling, and the curtains had already been drawn.

"Creepy sort of an 'ouse," suggested Mrs. Hart. "But p'raps it ain't got you yet."

"Do you know its story?" Agatha asked suddenly.

"Oh, it's 'aunted." Mrs. Hart nodded her little head with delight. "You wait. Lady drowned 'erself in the pond in the wood. You can see it from the window. I'll draw back the curtains and you can take a look for yourself."

"No, no," said Agatha quickly. "It doesn't matter."

"She comes up among the trees of a wet night, cryin' somethin' 'orrible. Tries the doors, they say, wantin' to come in."

In spite of herself Agatha shuddered. The wild weather outside, the soughing of the wind in the trees, the creak of the boards, all oppressed her spirit.

"Why does she want to come in?"

"She lived 'ere once, in this very 'ouse. And they say 'er 'usbing drove 'er out, and she went down to the woods and she threw 'erself in the pond. There's folks 'ave 'eard 'er cryin' on wet nights and some see a white figure wringin' 'er 'ands and wailing. And it's said she's put a curse on this place, so as no one will ever be 'appy 'ere again. Of course," she added hastily, "it's only what they say in the village. I don't pay no attention to it myself."

The door opened and Edmund Durward came in. "We're ready for tea, Mrs. Hart. Well, Agatha, and are you going to like your new home?"

"I shall like any place where you are," she said quickly. "But, oh, Edmund, I hope you will never leave me here alone. I think I should go mad."

"Mrs. Hart's been gossiping. But surely, my dear, you don't set any store on that kind of nonsense. It's a charming house and full of character. If it comes to that, there are few houses where people haven't died at one time or another."

"You won't mind if I do a little decorating," she suggested. "And perhaps in the spring we could have some painting done on

36

the outside, so that it would have a less forbidding appearance."

"You don't want to spend our substance glorifying the house for the owner's benefit. We've only got it till Christmas, and we may not be here so long as that."

Well he knew that long before Christmas came she would have left The Haven. But with his blue eyes smiling into hers she could feel no fear.

"You mean, something may have happened before then to make us leave here?"

"Perhaps."

"Your book—it will be a success and we shall be quite rich. Oh, Edmund, I am sure you are right. That is what you meant, isn't it?"

"What else could I mean?" Without waiting for her answer he put his arms round her and kissed her, and instantly she relaxed under his touch. The darkness receded; she forgot the drip of the rain and the vast acreage of the ghost-ridden dark. She knew a kind of ecstasy too great for words.

As soon as tea was over Mrs. Hart appeared in her outdoor clothes and announced that it was time for her to go, "Thank you very much, sir." This last was her cockney way of reminding Durward that she wanted her day's wages before leaving. Durward put his hand in his pocket and produced some silver.

"I've left the supper all ready," she announced, "and you don't 'ave to clear it away. Just the bread and butter, because of Mickey Mouse, but that's all. I'll be seein' you in the morning. Tea in bed, I s'pose. Eight o'clock be all right? Then I'll be sayin' good evening. 'Art's waiting for me at the bend—well, I wouldn't walk up that dark path by meself for all the Queen of Sheba's gold."

"Does she always go at this hour?" Agatha inquired as the odd little figure bobbed out of the room.

"Some days, I'm afraid, even earlier. She's in great demand round here. Servants are difficult to find. I wanted to get a couple to live in—there are excellent rooms over the garage—but so far I've had no luck at all. I did ask the alarming Miss Martin if she could help me—she's such a good neighbour, you see—but she said we were fortunate to have Mrs. Hart—lots of people could get no one."

"As I told you, I'm very domesticated," smiled Agatha. "I really shan't at all mind turning my hand to the cooking."

"Even I have my poor skill in that direction," said her husband. "Oh yes, men aren't nearly so helpless since the womanly woman went out. They have to be able to look after themselves."

She laid a hand affectionately on his arm. "I can't imagine you in an apron."

He put his hand over hers. "You'll learn. Why, Agatha, how incredulous you look. I believe you're afraid one of these days I shall poison you with my cooking."

As he spoke they heard a door slam and then, between the dripping of the rain, little feet scuffling on the stones in front of the house. As she went Mrs. Hart sang, presumably to encourage herself.

> "*Maybe I'm wrong again*
> *Trusting in yew-ew-ew*,"

she intoned in a strong cockney accent. The echoes died away and the house seemed suddenly very still. Edmund put his arms round his bride; under the black moustache the red lips were smiling.

"Alone with her fate," he whispered mysteriously. "Ye gods, what a caption for the press."

II

Agatha had sometimes wondered how she would fill the long days in so remote a spot, but now that she was actually here they seemed to slip by so quickly that it was always time to prepare the evening meal before she realized another day had gone. It would be difficult to say what she did. True, she supplemented Mrs. Hart's rather sketchy notions of cleaning and tidying a house, she sewed, she knitted, she read voraciously the books she brought back from Bridport every Friday. Edmund took her in on Fridays to do the week-end shopping, and they separated to do their individual errands, afterwards meeting for lunch at The Pigeons. Then, Agatha had a great notion of making a garden from the neglected square behind the house. She spent a lot of time digging and forking, and when she was in Bridport she consulted with nurserymen as to what would grow most easily and require least attention. She had made one or two efforts to replace Mrs. Hart, but without success. The registries told her at once that no one would be prepared to live in so solitary a spot, with so few conveniences. After a little Agatha accepted their dicta. Really, she quite enjoyed the preparation of the evening meal. Edmund would put aside his writing and join her in the kitchen, where he taught her to like a cocktail, and together they would baste and mash and dish up, afterwards sitting down comfortably to the meal they had prepared. At the end of a month Agatha felt she had known her husband all her life. The Hiawatha faded into a memory; she had had thoughts of inviting Grace Knowles down for a few days, as much to show off Edmund as anything else, but when she spoke of this, her husband darted her a look of mock horror and exclaimed, "I've bored you so soon? Agatha, I warned you it would be quiet here."

"I didn't mean now, of course," retracted Agatha hastily. "Perhaps in the summer. . . . I do hope there aren't a lot of mosquitoes here. If there's one within a mile it makes for me, and that big pond down in the woods would be an absolute breeding ground for them."

Meanwhile, Agatha made arrangements with Mrs. Hart to abandon most of her part-time employment and work at The Haven from eight in the morning until blackout time.

"You're a brave woman," Edmund told her. "You've made yourself no end of enemies by that gesture. You'd better take care how you go about in the evening or one of these days I shall be finding you with a knife in your back. I suppose you know there's no alternative to Mrs. Hart in this part of the world?"

"Mrs. Hart seemed pleased enough," said Agatha, who was inclined to overpay and overtip employees, after the manner of those who have been kept short of funds most of their lives.

"Saves my shoe leather," said Mrs. Hart, telling her husband of this development. "Good place too, though she's a bit daft, poor thing."

"What made 'im marry such a bean pole?" her husband demanded.

"Oh, she's got a bit. No, she don't talk about it much but I can tell. More than what 'e 'as if you ask me. Still, I will say for 'er she ain't got no side. I never could stand the sidey ones. Why, it says in the Bible I'm as good as 'er, don't it?"

They had been married about a month when Edmund came in one afternoon and put two documents on Agatha's knee.

"Cherish them with your heart's blood," he said. "They represent your charter of liberty from the workhouse in old age."

"What are they?" inquired Agatha, looking surprised as well she might.

"My life assurance and my will. Have you somewhere safe to keep them? I feel they ought to be in your possession."

"Wouldn't they be safer at the bank?" Agatha inquired, looking as though she expected either document to bite her.

"Aren't you interested enough to look at them?" He smiled, but the blue eyes were wary.

"If you think I ought to. They both seem rather gruesome to me."

ANTHONY GILBERT

The life assurance was for five thousand pounds and had only been recently taken out. The will was short and simple, the testator leaving everything of which he died possessed to "my dear wife, Agatha."

"Perhaps I ought to make a will," Agatha murmured. "I never thought about it before. But I suppose my money would automatically go to you as my husband, wouldn't it?"

"Far more likely it would go to swell the funds of the Joseph Forbes Scholarship."

"I should turn in my grave if I thought that would happen. The very next time I am in town, Edmund, I shall go and see Mr. Entwistle. I shall probably have to go up after Easter, partly because I make a point of seeing my dentist every six months and partly because the people who took my flat are making trouble, and I ought to be on the spot. You could manage very well for yourself for two or three days, couldn't you?"

"I don't say very well, but I could manage. All the same, Agatha, if it isn't convenient for you to go to town, you're not absolutely tied to old Entwistle. Any lawyer could draw up a will for you."

"I don't think I should like the construction Mr. Entwistle would put upon that, less on my account than yours. He would be sure to suggest you'd been putting pressure on me. I suspect that Mr. Entwistle is a bachelor. No, Edmund, there's really no hurry. I'm not expecting to drop down dead in the next few weeks. It would be very awkward for you if I did, wouldn't it?"

He turned to her in quick surprise. "I'm not sure I understand."

"Oh, Edmund, you must have read detective stories. The not-so-young wife with a little money marries the fascinating villain, makes her will and is found dead shortly afterwards. Naturally everyone thinks the worst." She laughed and went out of the room. He heard her quick, crisp step on the stair and then the bedroom door close.

"Damnation!" muttered Edmund Durward, who liked his soliloquies to be a shade larger than life; "what the hell did she mean by that?"

As spring drew on, Agatha realized how right Edmund had been to say that she would love the neighbourhood at blossomtime. She picked baskets of primroses that she packed carefully in moss and sent to Miss Randall, the Hiawatha's secretary, for the benefit of the club, and to Grace Knowles for herself.

"You must come down and stay soon," she said. "You will love the place when you get to know it. At first it seems eerie, and very much out of the world, but one gets used to that. There is even supposed to be a ghost here, but she doesn't disturb Edmund and myself. In short, I am happier than I believed any woman could ever be."

Easter came and went; Agatha said nothing more about going to London. She seemed to have forgotten her dentist and she made no further reference to the will. On Easter Sunday Edmund drove her to church at the village of Maplegrove, where she met Miss Martin, though not Miss Grainger whose faith transcended all creeds and couldn't, she explained, be confined to four stone walls.

"You're a nice one," said Miss Martin boisterously. "I thought when you came down we should have two more people in the community instead of one; but, in fact, we haven't got either of you now."

"We're very home-loving people, my husband and I," Agatha explained.

"Don't be a dog in the manger. Some of the rest of us like a chance to see a presentable male now and again. Why don't you come to dinner one evening?"

Edmund surprised his wife by saying, "Yes, I think we ought to go about a bit more. Good neighbours and all that, my dear." He grinned.

"We won't give you rabbit," promised Miss Martin. "I suppose you don't want a kitten?"

But Agatha said quite firmly that she didn't.

Dining with The Buddies was curiously reminiscent of meals at the Hiawatha. When the meal was over Miss Martin took Agatha up to her room "to powder her nose" she said, and asked heartily, "Now then, Mrs. Durward, come clean. What is the mystery about your husband?"

"Mystery? There isn't one."

"What's he burying you both in that pit of darkness for?"

"It's a charming house," said Agatha indignantly. "Both of us like a quiet life. That's all."

"All?" Miss Martin chuckled. "You should hear what the village says."

"You must tell Edmund. I'm sure he'd like to hear."

Miss Martin gave her a dig in the ribs that nearly drove the breath out of her body.

"Would he? You're sly, you know. I realized it the minute I saw you." When they were back in the big higgledy-piggledy room where they wrote and ate and occasionally nursed the sickly young of one of the numerous cats, she turned to Edmund and said, "I feel it's my duty to warn you, Mr. Durward, that you're suspected of indulging in black magic."

"That's very complimentary," said Edmund. "I'm afraid the truth isn't nearly so exciting."

"That's what your wife says, but she's a deep one. Well, if you don't conjure up spirits from the black ponds, what do you do in that woodshed of yours?"

"A little carpentering on occasions when inspiration fails. You must let me give you a book rest or something one of these days just as a guarantee of my innocence."

"Oh, we don't have much time for reading here. A cupboard for keeping the cat's medicines in would be more useful."

"Then I must make you that."

"I'll hold you to your promise," Miss Martin assured him. "But I shan't believe you don't do other and more sinister things in that shed. I've always thought The Haven the kind of house where the most gruesome things have happened."

"You'll terrify Agatha," said Durward with a slight shrug. "Mrs. Hart is panting to hear that the ghost has reappeared, but I tell her all that kind of thing is nonsense."

Miss Martin leaned forward. "I wouldn't be too sure. There are more things in heaven and earth than are dreamed of in your philosophy, Horatio."

"Nothing short of a corpse is going to satisfy that woman," Edmund told his wife as they drove home.

There were some letters in the box, among them one from Grace Knowles, who wrote: "When am I to see the fascinating house and the still more fascinating husband? We shall all begin to think he has a hump back or a glass eye or something if you go on being so coy."

Agatha carried the letter down to her husband. "I really think I must ask her down for a few days," she said. "All manner of rumours will crop up in the Hiawatha if I don't. They'll think I'm a prisoner here or gone out of my mind or something."

"Of course we must have her," said Durward kindly. "Find out when she would like to come. Or look here. Why not go up to town and bring her back with you? You were speaking of visiting your dentist and perhaps your lawyer."

"That's a very good idea," Agatha agreed. "Then I'll tell Grace to come at once. I'd like her to see the woods in blossom. If we wait too long she'll say I live in a slough of despond."

It appeared, however, that Agatha's dentist was away with influenza and was not expected back for about a fortnight, and as she wanted to have Grace down at once she decided to invite her the following week and go back to town with her after Mr. Evans was back in his surgery.

42

Grace came down all of a twitter. There had been a great deal
of speculation at the Hiawatha as to Agatha's reaction to this
astounding marriage, and Miss Knowles was delighted to be their
first visitor. Durward drove his wife to the station to meet her, and
as Grace leaned out of the carriage window she saw the two of them
standing by the ticket collector, looking down the little platform.
It was a warm day and Agatha had left her long coat at home,
and was wearing a pale flowered silk frock that made her look quite
absurdly young when you remembered her actual age. Miss Knowles
felt a pang in her heart. Lucky, lucky Agatha, she thought, to have
found such happiness at her time of life. As for Durward, he seemed
too good to be true, with his handsome face and smiling blue
eyes. He stood just behind Agatha, one hand lightly touching her
shoulder, wearing just that air of proprietorship that a husband
should wear, decided Grace. And how sure Agatha seemed, how
calm, how happy. On the way back the guest rode beside the
driver, while Agatha sat behind.

"It's lovely having you here," she said. "We live absolutely
out of the world, you know, and never see a soul. I'm dying to
hear all the news."

"You mustn't believe everything my wife says," Edmund warned
the fascinated Miss Knowles. "We're not quite so isolated as she'd
have you believe. There are The Buddies."

"The . . . ?"

"Two inestimable unmarried ladies with a great love for the
young. Agatha must take you to see them while you are with us."

"We ought to ask them to dinner, Edmund."

"My dear, I beseech you, make it lunch and I'll have an engagement at Bridport. If anything were needed to prove to me that
the female of the species is more deadly than the male Miss Martin
would supply it. I tell you, that woman would drive me into the
river if I had to live with her for any length of time."

"They're the pair you wrote about, aren't they, Agatha? The
ones who were going to get you to act."

"We really have behaved rather badly about that," Agatha said.
"You know, Edmund, we did promise to help, and we've done
nothing."

"Procrastination may be the thief of time, but he's also a very
useful alibi. I shall never understand this passion for dressing up
and pretending to be something you're not. But perhaps you're
fond of acting, too, Miss Knowles."

"I used to think I'd like to go on the stage, but, of course, my
parents wouldn't hear of it."

"But they wouldn't object to amateur acting, I suppose?"

43

"No. It's quite illogical, isn't it? But if you're on the stage, you're paid. I think that's what they didn't like."

"They needn't have been so finicky. After all, only a very small proportion of actresses are paid. And, in any case, why should they object to money earned that way and not out of coal mines or shipping or various quite dubious enterprises?"

"I think it just wasn't done. I was so thrilled, Mr. Durward, to hear you're an author. I've always thought it must be so marvellous to write books. If only I'd had the talent I'd have loved to write myself. I can think of the most marvellous plots. but I never get any further."

"You must sell some to me," said Durward pleasantly. "You'd be a boon to nine-tenths of the authors I know, who have only words and no plots to fit them."

The car turned into the road leading to The Haven. "You're a bit out of the world, aren't you, Agatha?" Miss Knowles suggested.

"It's lucky neither of us hungers for society. And then, of course, Edmund is so busy, and we haven't very much in the way of servants. You wait till you've had your first dinner with us and see what you think of my husband as a cook."

It was almost more than Miss Knowles could bear. Of course, she was devoted to dear Agatha, who was her best friend, but it didn't seem fair. She had suffered just as much in her home life and was just as lonely. Why should one woman get such a prize and the other be left solitary to the end of her days? She saw Edmund touch his wife's hand as they got out of the car and she felt suddenly as though her heart would burst.

"Where did you meet him, Agatha?" she inquired later. "You were very secretive about him."

"I knew what everyone would say, that I was rash, crazy even to marry a man I had only just met."

"But how did you meet him? One never seems to meet any presentable men these days."

Actually Miss Knowles had never met any men before the war, but it was pleasanter to blame the times for this lack.

"I met him at a railway station," said Agatha firmly.

"Quite by chance?"

"Do you think, Grace, that any of the events that seriously affect our lives are due to chance?"

"He's certainly very attractive," her friend admitted. She was still puzzled and showed it to an almost uncomplimentary extent. "Was he a widower?"

"No. He's spent most of his life out East."

"Ah!" Grace Knowles nodded, remembering the books of

Somerset Maugham. Still, there was no gainsaying the fact that Edmund had remarkable charm and seemed quite devoted to Agatha. Grace had been brought up in a strict Church of England home and still clove to her early faith. She supposed if you could accept some of the miracles you could accept anything, though nothing she had read in the New Testament seemed to her more startling than Agatha's capture of such a man. She had further time for reflection that evening when her host and hostess, having supplied her with magazines and a drink, proceeded to cook the dinner in the kitchen together. Miss Knowles, disregarding the magazines, sipped the unaccustomed Martini and ached with loneliness, hearing murmurs and sudden laughter from the end of the passage. It was absurd really, Agatha behaving like a young girl, but there was no denying the fact that she had shed years since her marriage. Poor Grace began to regret coming to The Haven.

The next morning Agatha magnanimously suggested that Edmund should conduct her guest round the neighbourhood.

"You must show her the woods," she said. "Really, Grace. they are absolutely perfect just now."

"Oh, but Mr. Durward won't want to give up a morning to me," fluttered Miss Knowles.

"We have visitors so seldom—in fact, you are our first—I think I can claim a holiday from work for a day," Durward told her with a smile. "First of all," he said, as they came out of the garden door, "you must see what Agatha has done with the garden. This was barren wilderness when she came. Of course, there isn't very much to show yet, but she visualizes a miniature Kew Gardens by next spring."

"I can't quite see Agatha as a gardener," said Grace thoughtfully. "She never even had window boxes in London."

"Perhaps marriage is bringing out all her latent talents. It certainly flatters my vanity to think so."

"She hasn't any roses," murmured Grace. "I always think roses make a garden."

"We agreed that unless you can give roses a fair show it's far better to leave them alone. And emphatically they're not plants for the amateur."

They strolled slowly towards the woods. "Agatha certainly looks very well," her friend acknowledged.

"I'm glad you think so. I was afraid she would find life here almost too quiet after her London activities, but she makes so many for herself—and so far we haven't sampled the amateur dramatic group."

"We," thought Grace resentfully. When she said "we" it always meant herself and another member of the Hiawatha.

"Her marriage was a great surprise to us," she contributed, with an effort.

"It was a great surprise to me."

"She tells me you met quite by chance at a railway station."

"That's so. I'd gone to meet a woman I had never seen, and I had to pick her out of the crowd. And actually, I picked Agatha. She looked so composed. I felt she wouldn't be insulted if a stranger spoke to her, mistaking her identity. I like a woman to look as though she could tackle life."

"It's very romantic."

"I like to think Agatha feels that way. This is our famous pond. This is where the ghost is supposed to have drowned herself."

"The ghost! Agatha didn't tell me about that."

"She's never seen it. It's a source of great mortification to her. For the first time in her life she finds herself in a house equipped with a ghost and the ghost keeps out of the way. I tell you, there are times when I almost feel inclined to put on a sheet and mop and mow among the trees, just to satisfy her."

"But Agatha's terrified of ghosts," said Grace.

Edmund smiled and shook his head. "I don't think so. I don't think there are many things Agatha's afraid of. That's one of the things that are so attractive about her."

"Yes, of course," agreed Miss Knowles feebly. Her heart burned with rage. Who knew better than she that Agatha would simply pass out if she saw a ghost? They had often discussed it. But because she wanted to stand well in her husband's eyes she was pretending it would be all in the day's work. "Anyone," Grace told herself inaccurately, "can get a husband if she is deceitful enough."

Edmund was still smiling. "Any woman who can marry a man she has only just met and come to live with him in a solitary, haunted house must have courage above the ordinary," Durward elaborated.

"It seems so queer, Agatha being so enterprising," poor Grace burst forth. "When you think she shudders at the sight of a mouse. . . ."

"Ah, but that's a feminine prerogative. All tactful women are afraid of mice. I should be disappointed in Agatha if she didn't jump on a chair and scream for aid. Has it ever occurred to you, Miss Knowles, that if women didn't have these delightful weaknesses, we men would have no opportunities of displaying our prowess? I mean, we should have to do something really courageous and probably dangerous. I consider a fear of mice a most endearing trait in a wife."

By the end of the day Grace was head over ears in love with her host. Her feeling didn't take the form of wanting to get him away from Agatha, even had such a possibility occurred to her, or even wishing he'd kiss her or hold her hand; it was too spiritual for that. It was more like the warm emotion she had felt for the last vicar, now, alas, promoted to higher service. She had haunted the pavement in front of the vicarage in the hope of suddenly encountering him coming in or out, and had invented various excuses for writing to him or ringing him up. She told herself she wasn't jealous of Agatha, but oh! how much easier the situation would have been had Durward turned out to be elderly, bald, or just a pompous prig, eager to monopolize all the conversation.

Grace stayed at The Haven for a week. During that time she did her best to keep her end up by retailing bits of Hiawatha gossip, with which she had come well supplied.

"You heard about Mrs. Mostyn?" she said, with careful off-handedness.

"What about her?"

"She's getting married again."

"I'm always surprised she didn't marry before. She's got heaps of money."

"They say he's much younger."

"I suppose she thinks it's worth the risk."

Grace tried again. "Mrs. Podmore is divorcing her husband. After twenty years. It does seem a bit ridiculous, doesn't it?"

"Perhaps she's fallen in love," suggested Agatha. "It does happen to the most unlikely people."

Grace darted her a venomous look. It was enough to bear that one middle-aged woman should have so much while another had nothing at all, but at least the rich could refrain from stoning the poor.

"People are saying she behaved exceedingly badly," she announced in crushing tones.

"Love makes you do the most extraordinary things," said Agatha gravely.

After that the trivia of Miss Knowles's gossip—such details as that there had been a flaming row between the writers and the theatrical group because the writers had asked a famous actress to one of their monthly luncheons without asking the chairman of the theatrical group if they would object—seemed very small beer indeed.

"Does all this make you regret your humming London past?" Durward asked his wife the day before Grace's return.

"Humming is just the word," said Agatha. "It's like an echo from another world. I can't imagine ever going back to it."

"I hope not," said Edmund dryly, exchanging a glance with their guest. "You can't go back on your bargian like that, even if you do regret it."

"I hope you'd never realize it if I did," smiled Agatha.

It was too bad. Like dangling carrots in front of a donkey, though the simile that occurred to Grace wasn't quite that.

"I'm sorry the ghost didn't appear for your benefit," Edmund added as they rose from the table. "You'll think Agatha married me under false pretences."

"Perhaps," said Grace gloomily, "she is there. Perhaps you don't see her. I expect it takes a special temperament . . ."

"She's going to be a very elusive ghost to escape Agatha's eagle eye," Durward observed. "I can just see my wife putting her through her paces." He dropped his hand for an instant on Agatha's shoulder as he moved to hold the door open for the two of them.

The last day of Miss Knowles's visit was overcast and chilly. Agatha had a headache and suggested that Edmund should take their guest on a famous excursion to a nearby town.

"We can't have it said that she came here and we didn't even show her the castle," she pointed out. "I have a good deal to do and, in any case, I'm not feeling energetic."

"Come with me, Miss Knowles," said Edmund. "We'll have lunch out, shall we, and leave the lady of the house absolutely free? Of course, we see through her subterfuge. She considers us two irresponsible beings. I suspect myself that she wants to prepare a surprise for us, and means to get us out of the way while she keeps all the fun to herself. Still, if you think you can put up with my company for a day . . . we can take the car into the village and get a bus from there. I'm afraid the petrol won't run to an all-day excursion if we're to have any left to get you to the station tonight. Are you sure, by the way, you can't stay till the morning?"

Miss Knowles could have stayed another week, but she shook her head. She told herself there was a limit to even her endurance. No, she would catch the 6.30 train that reached London at 10. There were no night raids at the moment and she would have no difficulty in getting a taxi. Actually, she didn't mean to take a taxi. She only had one small case and a slipper box and she could take these very well by bus. Torn between a most humiliating jealousy of Agatha and a burning delight at the thought of an excursion alone with Edmund, Grace went upstairs to put on her hat. She saw, with irrational resentment, that Agatha had no thought of being jealous of her. So many wives wouldn't let a husband walk as far as the post with another woman, but Agatha was so sure of hers, as well she might be, that she sent him out for the whole day with her best friend.

Durward was waiting when she came down to the hall.

"I've been trying to persuade Agatha to join us," he said, "but she's quite determined. We'll be back by four-thirty at latest, Agatha, and in the meantime promise me you won't overwork. Lie down and try to get rid of that headache."

"I shall be all right. Don't worry over me."

"Who should, if not your husband?" he asked, kissing her good-bye. "Now, Miss Knowles, you'll want a rug, I'm sure. . . ." He tucked her comfortably into the car. "I don't like these heads of Agatha's," he confided as they began the steep slope to the road. "I wonder if the atmosphere of The Bottom has anything to do with them. It's apt to be relaxing. If I thought it was affecting her health, of course I'd take her away at once. I don't want to have her ill. Did she have headaches when she lived in London?"

"A great many middle-aged women have headaches occasion-ally," said Grace in crisp tones. "I often have shocking ones myself. It's nothing to worry about."

"As long as I'm certain of that I won't brood. But Agatha's so plucky. She'll never complain."

He turned the car into the road and parked it at the village garage. "It's rather a pleasant ride," he told his companion. "And there's a famous inn where we must stop for a drink. The panelling is unequalled in this part of the country."

On the whole the excursion was a great success. Grace knew something of agriculture, and frankly enjoyed the excellent lunch and wine that her host provided.

"It's been delightful having you here," he told her on the drive home. "You must come again as soon as your other friends can spare you. And it's so nice for Agatha to have a companion. Now that your first visit is almost at an end, I don't mind telling you I was very much afraid you would unsettle Agatha with your talk of town gaieties."

"The Hiawatha isn't as gay as all that," said Grace a little bitterly.

"Well, not only the Hiawatha, but she was always going places, wasn't she?"

Grace ground her teeth. What stories had Agatha told him? she wondered. Painted a wonderful picture of her romantic London life, no doubt. Who would have thought she had it in her? Why, at the Amateurs, they'd never dared give her any but a foolproof part, she was so bad.

"Well, naturally I wouldn't be able to tell you anything about those," she replied. "Agatha didn't take me."

"I'm sure your engagement book is just as full as hers," said Edmund consolingly.

It was no good. The man was infatuated. They reached home shortly after four o'clock and Edmund went immediately to Agatha's room. A minute later he came softly down the stairs. "She's asleep," he said. "I'll just put on the kettle. This is Mrs. Hart's early day. Will you think me a very poor host if I go down to the village for a few minutes to pick up one or two things and see a man there? I'll be back in plenty of time to take you to the station."

"I thought I might pick some wild flowers to take back to London," suggested Grace. "If there is a basket . . ."

"I'll get you Agatha's, and we can all bunch them when I get back. You'll find the best flowers in the woods beyond the pond, if that isn't too far for you after your long day."

"I'm not quite decrepit yet," said Grace, with a difficult smile. And he laughed and went out.

Grace made no move to gather her flowers. She sat brooding. This time tomorrow she would be back in her one-room flatlet in Kensington. She would be washing the tea things probably, unless she decided to go to the Hiawatha and chance picking up an acquaintance there. But she hadn't many friends, and she hated eating alone except in her own flat. The house was very quiet; the haunted feeling of which she once or twice had been aware seemed very strong. It wouldn't have surprised her to see the door open and a spectre peer in. In fact, the impression was so powerful that for a minute she scarcely dared lift her eyes to the mirror hanging on the opposite wall lest it show her the ghost of Bell's Bottom returned to the source of her grief.

She rose at last, shaking herself scornfully. "If Edmund were here, he'd say, 'Let all the ghosts of Christendom come in. Agatha won't be afraid.' What lies she must have told him, and what a fool he is to believe everything." She went restlessly upstairs and stood looking out of the little dressing room window to the woods of The Bottom. Presently she went quietly downstairs.

She didn't want to disturb Agatha.

❦   ❦   ❦

CHAPTER FIVE

AGATHA woke with a start and lay staring round the dim room. The low ceiling and shadowed windows made it dark at the best of times, but with gray skies and low clouds it looked positively wintry. It was hard to believe that this was the beginning of June. Even a mild fall of rain filled The Bottom with mist and wrapped the house in a shuddering veil. Agatha put her feet to the ground and looked at her watch. It was almost a quarter-past four and nearly time for tea. She went to the door and leaned over the staircase. The house seemed deserted. Then she went into Grace's room, but there was nothing there but the suitcase neatly strapped. It seemed that the couple had not yet returned.

"They're running it very fine," thought Agatha. The notion passed through her mind that Grace wouldn't mind if they did miss the train. It was obvious that she had fallen heavily for Edmund. Not that Agatha blamed her; you couldn't blame any woman. But it made things a trifle uncomfortable. She rejoiced to think that by this time tomorrow she and her husband would be alone once more.

She leaned over the banisters, calling her husband's name and then her friend's, but only echo answered her. She had noticed this phenomenon before. If she stood in a certain place and pitched her voice in a certain way, that faint whisper would come stealing up the stairs. "Ed-mund," whispered a ghost. "Gra-ace." She shivered again. She thought the landing curtains stirred, not as though a wind moved them but as if something were concealed behind their folds. Something white moved and evaporated in the hall below, but when, trembling, she reached the hall, she found a window ajar and the mist flowing in evenly like liquid snow. Hurriedly she shut the window and went to the door. Though she strained her ears, however, she could detect no sound. Closing the door she wandered restlessly into the garden. The fantastic notion came to her that Edmund and Grace had eloped. She walked down the little path she had made to the entrance to the wood, and then suddenly she heard her name. It sounded very faint and far away.

"A-gatha! A-gatha!"

"There's been an accident, someone's hurt," she thought, hurrying down to the little gate that shut the garden from the woods. And then she saw it. There could be no shadow of doubt. The ghost had come back and it had found her alone.

It was standing among the trees, moving uncertainly this way and that when her horrified eyes first descried it, turning to stare at the house with its eyeless sockets. It seemed to be wrapped in a winding sheet, and as it moved a low moaning sound floated on the frozen air. Agatha had never heard anything so appalling. It wrung the heart while it petrified the blood.

"Ah-h-h! Ah-h-h!" The banshee wail came at her like a weapon. She flung out her hands to ward it off. The white figure came a little closer, the wailing rose to a higher note.

"Keep back!" cried Agatha in a voice so charged with terror it no longer sounded human. "Keep back! Keep back! Edmund, Edmund, where are you?"

The figure seemed startled by her cries. It hesitated, swaying a little among the dark trunks of the trees. Then it bowed itself, spreading its white arms and, thus crouched, it began to steal towards the house. It had seemed rather a tall ghost, but now it was hunched and twisted. Agatha flung her hands over her eyes.

"Edmund!" she shrieked again. "Edmund! Oh, God, have pity."

Moving backwards, not daring to take her eyes off the apparition that came ever forward with a dreadful stealthiness, still uttering low, disconsolate cries, her foot caught in some obstruction and she flung out her arms too late to save herself. As she fell, her head came in contact with a piece of stone with which she was making a rockery, and darkness crashed down upon her.

* * *

Edmund, coming from the direction of the garage a few minutes later, found her there and, catching her by the shoulder, tried to arouse her to consciousness. When her head simply lolled against his shoulder he gathered her in his arms and carried her into the house. The ghost, of course, had vanished; there was still no sign of Grace Knowles.

"I must get a doctor," said Edmund aloud. "Where's that fool of a woman? She's not much use, but at least she can sit by Agatha while I go down to the village."

There was a sound behind him; Durward turned sharply. Grace had come in unheralded. He saw at once that she had overheard his unfortunate soliloquy, for her face was pale, her eyes blazing.

"Agatha's had an accident," he explained hurriedly; "she must have fallen and hit her head."

"She's not dead, is she?" inquired Grace.

"Dead? Of course not. But she must have had the devil of a fall."

"Perhaps it isn't the fall," said Grace in the same flat tone. "Perhaps she had a fright."

"A fright? Look here, Miss Knowles . . ."

Grace Knowles laughed suddenly, an abrupt, horrible sound.

"You heard what I said. Perhaps she had a fright, perhaps she saw the ghost, after all. Well, why do you look like that? Weren't you always telling me she wanted to see it? You kept saying she wouldn't be afraid, she wasn't afraid of anything. But now, you see . . ."

Durward had risen to his feet while she was speaking. Now he came close, seeming to tower above her though she was not much shorter than himself.

"What do you know about the ghost?" he said in very quiet tones.

She laughed again as she faced him, taut and burning. "What a hypocrite you are! You meant this to happen, didn't you? You knew that if it did—well, now you see for yourself. She's not the wonderful brave woman you swore she was. She was terrified—wasn't she? Well, answer me!" She seemed scarcely sane. a kind of awful triumph investing her with a desperate courage.

"You mean, it was you—down in the woods—and she . . ." Something white glimmering in the doorway caught his eye. In a stride he had reached it, had stooped to lift it on his arm.

"What's this, Miss Knowles?"

"You know perfectly well what it is. Why ask me? You've eyes in your head like anyone else. It's a sheet. Yes, stare at it as much as you please. You can't change it."

He came over to her. gripping her arms fiercely. "Do you know what you've done?"

"Take your hands away," she shouted at him. "Oh, if anything happens to Agatha it's no use trying to put the blame on me. It's you who're responsible—you, do you hear? I shall tell the doctor so. You can say what you please, but I—you think I'm a fool, don't you? You think you can do what you like with women. You've only got to lift your little finger and any one of us will come. Well, I'm not the fool Agatha is." The crazy, hopeless love she had cherished during the past week curdled into hate.

"Be quiet; you've said enough. I suppose your idea is to break up my home, drive Agatha crazy . . ."

She began to laugh again. He silenced her brutally, his hand over her mouth. "It's a good thing I found you out," he said breathlessly. "On second thoughts, I won't leave you here with Agatha. She'd be safer alone."

He laid a rug over Agatha's unconscious form. If she came round while he was out of the house it would be a pity, but it was a choice of evils. Anything would be better than letting this woman remain with her after what had happened. Grace, after uttering her fierce maledictions, was very quiet.

"We'll be going now," he said in a low. furious voice. "I don't want Agatha to see you again."

Grace made no demur; she was beyond that. Together they left the house.

It occurred to Edmund that this unexpected development had made them run things very fine. As he stepped into the car he glanced at the watch on his wrist. His chief thought now was for Agatha. She mustn't be left alone long or anything might happen. He drove recklessly to the station, handed Grace's luggage to a porter with instructions to put it on the London train, and headed back for the village. In his agitation, he would not even stop to see the train depart.

He had no sympathy for the hapless Grace. She was another of those stupid women who, by falling in love where they are not appreciated, had done her level best to wreck all his plans. It was no thanks to her if she didn't succeed, even now.

In the village he stopped at the doctor's house and was fortunate enough to find Howarth in. The two of them came speeding back to The Haven, Edmund explaining that Agatha had had a shock, followed by a fall, and had collapsed. When they returned they found her still unconscious on the sofa where her husband had laid her. Between them they got her upstairs to bed.

"What happened?" the doctor asked. "She must have struck her head pretty violently."

"She slipped and a bit of rockery stunned her."

The doctor looked puzzled. "She was alone at the time?"

Edmund hesitated. "Well—yes."

Howarth looked at him with some impatience. "Dammit, man, surely you know whether she was alone or not?"

Edmund made his decision. "I'd better give you the facts and you can tell me how much you think it's safe to pass on. We've had a friend of hers, a Miss Knowles, staying here. I expect you know the current rumours about the house—the ghost and all the rest of it. My wife took them all for gospel, but I tried to laugh her out of them. If she did see the ghost, I said, she wouldn't be afraid, she wasn't that kind of woman. I didn't want her to get nervy about it, but apparently I overdid the treatment. This woman we had here—I've just seen her off on the London train— was a neurotic sort of creature, just the type to enhance my wife's fears. I made a point of impressing on her that Agatha wasn't afraid of anything she might see. I didn't want them getting together and frightening Agatha into fits; but I seem to have said it once too often. This woman decided to put it to the test. She wasn't a very happy type. Middle-aged, you know, and not too much of this world's goods, and I suppose in a subconscious sort of way she was jealous of Agatha. Anyhow, she seems to have thought it would be a fine joke to dress up as the ghost and put my wife to the test." He put his hand over his eyes. Howarth said something uncomplimentary about women in general and Miss Knowles in particular.

"The damnable thing is I feel partly responsible. If I hadn't said so often how plucky Agatha was, the idea might never have entered her head. Mind you, she was frightened enough when she saw what had happened, quite hysterical, in fact. Kept on saying it was my responsibility, I was always saying how wonderful Agatha was. . . ."

The doctor nodded. "I know the type. Good thing you've got her off the premises. Look out—she's coming round."

He bent over Agatha and became very professional. Edmund was kept running up and down for the next few minutes, obeying orders, fetching and carrying. After an anxious few minutes Agatha stirred and opened her eyes. The first person she saw was her husband.

"Edmund!" she moaned druggishly. "Why didn't you come?"

"I'm here," he assured her. "It's all right. You caught your foot on a stone and took a nasty tumble."

"Did I? I don't remember."

"You've given us all a nice fright."

"Fright?" The word seemed to call up some memory whose shape she could not as yet identify. "Edmund, there was something . . ."

"My dearest, don't exert yourself. You want to stay quiet now."

But Agatha had begun to remember. "It was the ghost, Edmund. You always laughed at me, but she came—she came as they said she would . . ."

"There's no ghost here, only Dr. Howarth and myself. You're not afraid of us, surely?"

"Not now, not when you're here. But one day she'll come again when I'm alone. I know it They say if you see her it means death. . . ."

Howarth took a hand. "Look here, Mrs. Durward, you've had a nasty shock, but you're all right now. Your husband's here and he's going to stay with you. That's all right, isn't it?"

"It's this house," whispered Agatha, her eyes roaming round the walls with their loops of blue ribbon and true-lovers' knots and baskets of flowers. "I think I've always been afraid of it. It's so dark—so cold. . . . What's the time?"

"A little after six," said the doctor

"You've just missed the news."

"It seems much later than that," whispered Agatha.

"I'm going to get you to take a little drink," said Howarth, soothingly. "Then you can have a nice sleep and everything will look different in the morning."

"It isn't the morning I mind," whispered Agatha earnestly. "It's the evening, the cold, dark evening when the shadows come right up to the door and you can hear feet, and voices muttering, and . . ."

They had some difficulty in calming her. "This is damnable," confided Edmund. "I daren't tell her—yet—it was all a trick. Miss Knowles is her best friend; it would upset her worse than ever."

"It might be best to tell her at that," returned the doctor reflectively. "Oh, not tonight. Give the sedative a chance, and I'll come along tomorrow. The shock may take a day or two to wear off. But if she's going on fretting about this damned ghost, tell her the facts."

"I don't believe she'll ever forgive her friend."

"So much the better. You don't want that kind of woman down here."

The sedative was partially successful. That is to say, Agatha returned to unconsciousness, but it was not complete. Through the dark, strange sounds tormented her. She heard little hands feeling over her door—thud, thud, thud—steps stole up the stairs, a low wail pierced the darkness under her window. When at last she woke, the room was still full of shadows; she dared not turn over lest at her first movement the bed curtains should part and she perceive a white, drowned face looking into hers. Her watch was on her bedside table, but she couldn't put out her hand to take it, lest it encounter a white cold hand, dead these many years, swollen and rotted with black pond water. She lay motionless for what seemed an age. Slowly the light moved across the sky; the curtains fluttered.

"She's coming back," thought Agatha, shaken with dread. Softly she heard the door open, a cold draught of wind blew into the room, stirring the tassels on the old-fashioned dressing table cover. But there were no footsteps; whatever it was that had entered made no sound. Softly the door closed again. "Now," she thought, "it is coming. I shall see nothing, I shall hear nothing, but in an instant there will come a cold touch on my throat, hands will squeeze out my life." Wildly she flung herself back on her pillows, screaming her husband's name.

The next instant all was turmoil and bright lamplight. Edmund came in swinging a hurricane lantern.

"Agatha, what is it?"

"Take care! She came in. I heard her. She thought she made no noise—but I heard her. She's here somewhere."

Edmund swung the lamp to prove that the room was empty. "It was a dream, my dear. No one came in. I've been camped outside on the landing. If anyone had passed, do you think I shouldn't have seen? You've had a bad fall and hurt your head". . .

"You think I'm going mad, don't you, Edmund?"

"Of course I don't. I know what concussion can do to you. I had it once when I was out East—a riding accident."

"I don't want you to go away, I don't want to be left alone."

"I'll stay. Of course I'll stay."

For a little while she was quiet. "Edmund, will you tell me the truth?" she whispered presently.

"Have I ever told you anything else?" He took her hand. It was cold and clammy with sweat.

"Edmund, am I dying?"

"Of course, you're not. Do you imagine I'd have let the doctor go—or indeed that he'd have gone—if it was a serious injury?"

"If I die, Edmund, I want you to have everything I possess. You've been so good to me." She moved restlessly. "I never made that will. That's procrastination."

"Listen to me, Agatha. You're not going to die, and you're not going to give another thought to the will. You want a few days' rest and perhaps a little change. You might like to go to London to see your friends. . . ."

"Only if you come with me."

With infinite patience and gentleness he coaxed her back to sleep. There were shadows under his eyes. His face was pale and drawn. It had been a hard night for him too.

In a day or so Agatha was going about as usual, but it was obvious that the affair had shocked her considerably. She did not sleep, she would perpetually look over her shoulder, she was even nervous of going down the short passage from the living room to the kitchen at night. Edmund tried to reason with her.

"Don't think me a brute, Agatha, but you've got to pull yourself together unless you want to have a nervous breakdown. If you go on like this you'll be sunk. I mean it. Every time a curtain moves in the wind you'll think a ghostly hand has twitched it. Every time the wind rustles a branch against the window you'll think it's the ghost trying to come in; if a blind flaps in the dark, for you it'll be the ghost stealing after you down the passage."

"You don't believe she was there, do you, Edmund? But she was, I swear it. I couldn't have made her up. That crying rings in my ears. It isn't right for even a ghost to know such despair."

"I should be inclined to tell her the truth," said the doctor.

"Nothing can make her condition worse. I don't like the way she's taking it and that's a fact."

So the next time Agatha said, "You don't believe I saw her, do you, Edmund?" he replied, "Yes, my dear, I know you did."

Her face hardened. "You say that to humour me."

"No. Agatha, be brave. You did see something, only it wasn't a ghost. Try not to be too angry with her. It was her idea of a practical joke. She didn't know, she couldn't have known, the effect it would have on you."

"She? What are you talking about, Edmund?"

"Your friend, Miss Knowles."

"You mean that Grace . . . no, Edmund, I'll never believe that. She'd never be so wicked."

"You must remember her passion for amateur theatricals. She just thought of it as a piece of play-acting."

"She didn't. She did it on purpose because she was jealous of me, jealous of my being married to you. I saw that at once. Oh, I didn't blame her. In her place I'd have been jealous too. Anyone would be jealous of being married to you. But to take such a horrible revenge. Because she knew I'd be afraid. Afraid! What a poor word. I was distracted—you saw it yourself, Edmund. And she did that to revenge herself not on me but on life. Edmund, I can never write to her or see her again."

He strove in vain to calm her. "You must compose yourself," he urged. "You will make yourself quite ill. Oh, if you feel like that about Miss Knowles, by all means drop her out of your visiting list. In any case I doubt if she'd be keen to come again for a while. I lost my head pretty completely when I saw her. She probably has a bruise on her arm where I gripped it, and it's no thanks to me if she has any teeth left in her head."

"How did you find out, Edmund?"

"I caught her creeping in, with the sheet that she left in the doorway. What the laundry will think when they see the mud and the bark on it I can't imagine. They'll think we've been camping in the wood."

"I can still hardly believe it," repeated Agatha. "Why, I might have died. But perhaps that is what she intended. If I ever saw such a thing again I should die. I know it. Oh, Edmund, I wish we could leave this house. I'll never be happy here now."

Howarth also urged him to give notice at the end of the quarter. "You can hardly have intended to spend the winter here," he pointed out. "It wouldn't be fair on any woman and certainly not on a highly strung woman like your wife. If anything should happen to that Comic Cuts of yours, you wouldn't find anyone to take her place. And your wife isn't strong enough to do all the work. Why don't you look round while there are still places to be had and get settled in before the bad weather?"

Edmund raised the point with Agatha.

"You mean, leave this house? Oh, Edmund, should you mind very much? We've been very happy here, happier than I've ever been anywhere, but I must admit that I dread the winter. Besides, it would be nice to have one or two neighbours if, for instance, you wanted to go away for two or three days, as you very well might. I couldn't be left alone here, but in a house with people next door everything would be different."

"I certainly don't want you to stay here if it's going to make you ill. And certainly I've almost finished the book. Besides, if the petrol ration is decreased, we may find ourselves very much isolated here. We must go the rounds of the agents, I suppose, though they always try and rent you Buckingham Palace."

"I've been watching the papers," Agatha confessed, "and I've found one or two likely advertisements. Of course, they're probably tremendously overwritten, but one or two might be possible."

He looked at the slips she laid before him. "All for sale, I see. My idea was to rent."

"I don't believe you can rent. All the rented houses are gone. Anyway, house property's a very good investment in this part of the world. We could probably sell it at a profit, if we wanted to give it up after the war."

"Meanwhile, we have to live during the war. House property may be a good investment, but most other investments are at a pretty low ebb. Neither of us appears to have been farseeing enough to buy armament or tobacco shares. I'll get in touch with my lawyer and see what he advises. But don't expect a mansion. A workman's cottage is more in our line."

Agatha, however, with the unreasonableness of her sex, had set her heart on ownership, and not a workman's cottage at that. All her life she had lived in cramped surroundings or at someone else's beck and call. This was her chance and she meant to make the most of it.

As they had foreseen, the advertised houses proved to be quite fantastically unsuitable. There was, for example, The Warren, a noble barn of a place about ten miles away; it stood in its own grounds and what the advertiser described as a finely cultivated garden. The only garden the Durwards could discover was a wilderness, while the rose pergola was a thicket growing over the gate, as dense as a hedge. Added to this, there were nine bedrooms and no bath, sanitation was of the most primitive, water came from a well that probably hadn't been cleaned out for years. The paper peeled off the wall practically under their eyes; there were kitchen quarters as large as many a London flat.

"Cross off The Warren," said Durward. "Now for The Knoll."

The Knoll was a little modern villa, one of a row, with a garage where the dining room should have been, a kitchenette, two or three bedrooms, all cramped and already showing damp patches on the walls, and floor boards warped by last winter's rain. The houses on either side were called Kosikot and Journey's End.

"Cross off The Knoll," said Edmund patiently. "Now for The Old House."

The Old House—but why elaborate? At the end of several days Edmund and Agatha agreed they'd never have supposed there could be so many derelict houses in an area of twenty-five miles. There were cottages with worm-eaten beams and no conveniences at all; there were tumble-down farmhouses; there were mansions the size of small palaces—in fact, they were beginning to despair of finding what they wanted, and even Agatha was thinking that The Haven had more advantages than she had realized when Mr. Ainslie, a house agent and surveyor of Sultan Buzzard, wrote that a house had just come on the market, if the Durwards were prepared to buy. The instant she saw Monks Green, Agatha knew that this was her house. It was the kind of home of which most women dream and that few ever possess. It was a modern house built in a Queen Anne style, well-founded, with good sanitation, main water supply, electricity and telephone. It stood in a garden of some size, some way from a high road, but near enough a rousing little village for Agatha to have some personal life. The fittings were good and well chosen, the garden stocked with flowers and vegetables, the rooms lofty and well lighted. A bus service ran three times daily into neighbouring towns. It was about thirty miles beyond Maplegrove, and its only serious disadvantage was the price. The owner was asking two thousand guineas.

Edmund whistled when he heard that. "I'm afraid we can't rise to those giddy heights," he told Mr. Ainslie.

"I might persuade my client to make it pounds," the agent offered.

Regretfully Edmund shook his head. "Even so, I'm afraid it's above our figure. It's a pity, a great pity. My wife and I both like the place and it's a charming situation, but—there it is."

"It's the sort of house I've dreamed of all my life," whispered Agatha. "Don't you think, Edmund . . . ?"

"My dear, you know what markets are like just now, or if you don't, ask your own lawyers. I thought I had some rather good oil shares. Oil should be doing well now, but I find I can't get what I gave for them. I dare say we shall all be bankrupt soon enough, but there's no reason why we should give ourselves the extra kick down the hill."

"You'd find it an easy house to resell, if it came to that after the war," Mr. Ainslie insinuated.

Edmund shook his head, smiling. "Once we were in my wife would brain me if I suggested such a thing. Now, surely you've something a little less ambitious? Something to rent?"

But Mr. Ainslie said quite firmly that renting a house of the kind they wanted in that part of the world was out of the question. Everything had been snapped up the previous autumn when the London raids had driven a new influx of people into the country.

"Well, keep us in mind," said Edmund. "If anything should turn up, be sure to let us know."

And, smiling (but very thoughtfully on Agatha's part), they returned to their car.

Agatha was very quiet on the journey home. "I'm afraid you're disappointed," her husband remarked, "but, honestly, such a sum is out of the question at the present time. I'm not saying the house isn't worth it—it's a delightful house. . . ."

"It's my dream house," repeated Agatha. "Edmund, I've got to have it."

"My dear Agatha . . ."

"No, don't pour cold water over me. I have the most wonderful idea. Edmund, you're not so frightfully keen on the establishment of a Joseph Forbes Memorial Scholarship, are you?"

He stared. "It's nothing to me naturally . . ."

"There you are, then. If we both agree, I can write to Mr. Entwistle and tell him I want enough of my capital to buy Monks Green. Everybody says house property's a good investment, probably much better than the money it represents. Land and buildings will go on being valuable, however much other stocks may fail. Isn't it a wonderful suggestion?"

"Hold your horses," her husband exclaimed. "You're miles and miles in front of the hounds. Do remember that if you sell out, your income drops to less than half."

"What does that matter? I've got a husband to support me."

He laughed and slipped an arm round her waist. "You shouldn't make remarks like that when I'm driving. I might lose control of the car, and then you wouldn't even have a husband."

"I'm in deadly earnest," she assured him. "Even suppose what you said just now became true at any time, I should have the life assurance—and the house. I could take in paying guests."

"I see you've worked it all out," said Edmund drily. "I'm not sure you're a very safe woman to be married to."

"Don't laugh at me. I do mean every word of this. It's not just a spur-of-the-moment suggestion. I've thought of it ever since we decided to leave The Haven. I always meant to touch that capital sometime. Why should the scholarship have it? And we're never likely to get a better chance than this. Even Mr. Entwistle must agree."

"I doubt it," said Edmund drily. "I fancy I know more about lawyers than you do."

"Even if he doesn't like it, he's got to take my instructions," pointed out Agatha grandly. "He told me my stocks are worth about seven thousand pounds and they bring in roughly £300 a year. Suppose we sell half, that leaves me £150. In an emergency I could scrape along on that even if I were left with nothing but the income and the house. No, Edmund, I've made up my mind. There isn't a flaw anywhere."

As Edmund had foreseen, Mr. Entwistle had a good deal to say. He pointed out to Agatha that, even since her last visit to him, her stocks had depreciated. She held a good many shares in a local gas company in a neighbourhood that had been badly blitzed. The company was passing its dividend and would probably do so for some ti ne to come. To raise the required amount would mean decreasing her income to about £100 a year. He was strongly against such a step. No one knew how the war would progress. If the threatened invasion became reality, their part of the country might be overrun. Monks Green might be levelled to the ground and the ground itself rendered quite valueless.

"What did I tell you?" demanded Edmund, handing the letter back. "Well, Mrs. Durward, what's your next move?"

"Could you drive me down to the village this morning?" asked Agatha coolly. "Oh dear, it'll be lovely to have a telephone and be quite independent."

"Why the village?"

"I want to send a telegram."

"Agatha!"

"It's no use arguing with me. I'm a very meek person really, but when I make up my mind I want something desperately, then I have to have it. And what I want now is Monks Green."

As she had said, Mr. Entwistle really had no choice. He did suggest his client coming to town to discuss the matter, but Agatha wrote that she and her husband were fully agreed, and she was afraid as the position was urgent she hadn't time to come to London. Mr. Entwistle's tentative suggestion of a mortgage she treated with the contempt she considered it deserved. So he, poor man, so much wiser in his generation than she, had she but known it, had no alternative but to take her orders. She and Edmund signed the necessary papers and presently a cheque for two thousand four hundred pounds was sent her.

"That's more than we asked for," said Edmund in surprise.

"I told him to make it a little more. We shall want something for papering and painting, and there's furniture too. The lease of my flat is up at Christmas, and I'm not renewing it. I have some furniture there, of course, but not enough. Oh, Edmund, it's going to be so wonderful furnishing a house for us both."

"I can see I shall have to watch you carefully. You're just longing to plunge."

"I've waited a great many years—you must admit that. And now I want you to take this cheque and pay it into your account."

"My account?" He looked at her, stupefied. "But it's your money."

"Our money—to pay for our house. And it will be easier for you to send the cheque and assume the responsibility with the agents and builders. I know it's absurd, but men still don't like to feel that women are paying for things. Call it my belated wedding present to you. No, Edmund, don't refuse. You've given me so much. This is such a little thing by comparison."

It took her some time to persuade him to accept the money but eventually she was successful.

"Though I shall always think of it as your house," he warned her. "Indeed, without you, I couldn't bear to live there."

"But you do like it?" Her voice was anxious.

"Of course I like it. Agatha, are you sure you wouldn't prefer to sleep on this?"

"I should just hate to sleep on it. Now, Edmund, write to the agents and tell them to put the sale through without a minute's delay. Every morning when I wake up I expect to hear someone else has got it and that would break my heart."

The letter had come by the afternoon post. Edmund sat down to write to Mr. Ainslie, and he and Agatha had just agreed on the letter when there was a bump and scuffle at the door and Mrs. Hart bustled in.

"Time for me to be goin'," she announced. "Any letters?"

"Mr. Durward has one," said Agatha.

"I must just get a stamp," said Edmund. "Wait one minute, Mrs. Hart."

While he fetched the stamp Mrs. Hart announced breathlessly, "I've lef' the cauliflower all ready and I've made an apple pie on

63

a plate, and there'll be jus' enough cheese for a macaroni tomorrow, if you fancy it. It's too 'ard to eat natural, but in a pudding it don't notice."

Her little black beady eyes glittered; everything about her seemed on the alert; her snapping jaws, her inadequate bust, her tightly enclosed assertive behind. Edmund came back with the envelope addressed to Mr. Ainslie and passed it over to her.

"Don't get gossiping with Hart and forget it," he said sternly. "It's important."

She looked calmly at the address. "Changing 'ouses?" she inquired. "Well, I don't blame you. Wouldn't spend the winter 'ere in your place, not for an 'undred pounds a night."

She bustled out; they heard the door slam. Then husband and wife broke into spontaneous laughter. "That's the one thing I'll really miss," said Agatha. "Mrs. Hart's spoilt me for well-trained servants."

Mrs. Hart hurried up the path, panting with excitement, her shiny black bag shaking in her hand, her frizzy black hair stiff with delighted apprehension. Her husband, for once, had reached the rendezvous before her.

"You're late," he said.

"I couldn't 'elp it. You wait till you 'ear."

"If they keep you overtime they ought to pay you extra."

"They didn't keep me. I stayed."

"Whatever for?"

Mrs. Hart cupped one hand round her ear and leaned forward in a suggestive attitude.

" 'Aving a row?" Her lord and master didn't seem much interested.

"Not 'er. Why, she's lovey-doveying 'im all the time. But— you know what?"

" 'Ow can I till you tell me?"

"If you ask me I'll never be surprised to find 'er picture in the paper. Well, I ask you. What did 'e marry 'er for? Not 'er looks. And now she's gone and give 'im 'er money, what good's she to 'im now?"

Mr. Hart, a deliberate sort of person, accustomed to the sort of ease an energetic and devoted wife made possible, considered.

"If that 'appens you'll be out of a job. You take my tip, Liz, and 'and in your notice while there's a lady to 'and it in to."

Mrs. Hart looked at him with incredulous scorn. "What? Me clear out just when things are going to begin to 'appen? You must think me a softie. No, you jus' wait. It's goin' to be as good as the pictures, you mark my words."

CHAPTER SIX

EVERY MORNING Agatha looked eagerly at the letters on the break-fast table for one with the Sultan Buzzard postmark. But each morning she looked in vain.

"How leisurely house agents are," she said. "You would think a house was like a row of pins. They didn't care whether anyone bought it or not."

"Perhaps the owner's in the army," suggested Edmund, smiling at her impatience.

"Even in the army people can answer letters. I begin to think there's a conspiracy on foot to rob us of Monks Green. If I thought I should never live there, I believe I'd die."

He flung her an odd look out of his narrow, smiling eyes. "Your thoughts run a lot on death."

"It's only a *façon de parler*, but surely, Edmund, you could make him hurry a little."

"I'll telephone when I'm in Bridport today. I have to buy some more wood. I'm making you a surprise."

"Shall I guess what it is?"

"You never would. No, don't try. You'll learn fairly soon."

He returned in the afternoon with the news that Mr. Ainslie hoped to have definite information for them in the course of a few days. The owner had been ill and there appeared to have been some muddle about the letters. However, he had been very re-assuring, telling Edmund that there was no one in the market at the moment, and in any case he had earmarked the house for them.

Agatha was so pleased to hear this that she took the local bus into Bridport the next morning to inquire about brocades and hangings, and to hunt around for bits of furniture and em-broideries. Edmund had some ado in preventing her from actually buying material.

"You must preserve your soul in patience," he told her. "Wait till you have the actual measurements. It's only a matter of days."

"It's been a matter of too many days," said Agatha sternly. "Next time I go to Bridport I'm going to see that carpenter and find out about fitting shelves in the library."

He threw her a wry glance. "How you like taking the wind out of my sails. Have you forgotten I'm a bit of a carpenter myself?"

"You mean you—and that's why you wanted the wood? Edmund, how sweet you are to me."

A few more days passed and still there was no communication

from Mr. Ainslie. From being impatient Agatha became downright angry. She felt that Mr. Ainslie wasn't doing his best for them. It took a woman to get things done, she thought. When they went into Bridport the following Friday she resolved to put her own shoulder to the wheel. As usual they separated on arrival, each engaged on his own errands. Edmund bought meat and fish and hunted through the shops for tobacco, and Agatha went to the grocer and Woolworth's and the fancywork shop and the post office for Mrs. Hart's insurance stamps. According to plan, she reached The Pigeons a little before the agreed hour of the rendezvous, and finding that Edmund had not yet arrived, locked herself into the telephone booth provided for the use of customers. Here she gave Mr. Ainslie's number. She was afraid she might miss him, but fortunately he had not left the office for lunch and himself answered her call.

"This is Mrs. Durward speaking," she said. "Of The Haven, Maplegrove. The fact is, my husband and I are getting anxious about Monks Green."

"Monks Green?" repeated Mr. Ainslie, as though he had never heard of the property.

"We are wondering if anything, some obstacle, has arisen. We are anxious to take possession of the house as soon as possible. . . ."

"I don't understand you," interrupted Mr. Ainslie sharply. "I had a letter from Mr. Durward saying he was no longer interested in the house."

"I am sure you are mistaken," exclaimed Agatha, astounded at the news. "Why, he wrote the letter in my presence. That would be the 3rd July. I remember the date perfectly. He said it was a pity we hadn't made up our minds earlier because now we couldn't give notice for The Haven until the September quarter."

"If you will hold on a minute," said Mr. Ainslie, "I will get the letter." She heard the faint sound of a receiver being laid aside. A minute later the voice resumed, "I have it here. As you say, it was written on the 3rd July. He says: 'I have to inform you that, on further consideration, I have decided not to continue my inquiries in regard to the above house. My wife feels it would be too large for her requirements. In view of the international situation and the consequent decrease in value of various stocks, we have decided to remain where we are at present, at all events until the lease of this house terminates.'"

Agatha stood quite rigid and unaware of the fact that she was trembling from head to foot.

The shock had been so great that Mr. Ainslie had to repeat

her name several times before she realized she still had the receiver to her ear.

"Mrs. Durward. Are you all right? Mrs. Durward."

"Yes," she said, speaking with difficulty. "Of course I'm all right. It was just that I was rather surprised. My husband certainly gave me the impression that he intended to buy the house."

"We now have a smaller property on our books," said Mr. Ainslie in cordial tones. "I was writing to you about it. If you could come in this afternoon or perhaps tomorrow morning, I could show it to you. It's quite small and will certainly be snapped up at once, but I'm prepared to give you first refusal. Mrs. Durward," for only silence answered him. "Mrs. Durward, are you still there?"

But Agatha had hung up the receiver, not having listened to a word about the new proposition. Stumbling out of the box she saw a notice—Ladies' Cloakroom—and turned blindly in that direction. Her brain was so confused that at first she could recognize none of the implications of her position. There was no one else in the cloakroom and she sank down onto a chair, breathing heavily as though she had been running. Her first thought was that Mr. Ainslie must be mistaken. Yet what purpose could he have in denying a possible sale for one of his properties?

"But Edmund showed me the letter," she reminded herself. "And I myself saw him give it to Mrs. Hart to post. Why, it was sealed in my presence and then . . . then he went upstairs for a stamp. So that was how he contrived it. I thought it odd because he always carries his stamps in his waistcoat pocket, but I didn't pay any attention at the time. Of course, while Mrs. Hart talked to me, he hastily rewrote his letter—or perhaps he had it all prepared —and then he handed a second envelope to Mrs. Hart. That means that, even after my money arrived, he never meant to buy the house."

She caught sight of herself in the mirror. She looked startled, bewildered, rather pale; but otherwise very much the same as usual. It seemed incredible that the foundations of your life could disappear and leave so little trace on your features. A few words had changed all her existence. Now she knew that Edmund, her Edmund had allowed her to draw out two thousand pounds for the purchase of a house he had never contemplated buying. Presumably he had known she would hand over the money to him, but if she hadn't done so, he was quite clever enough to obtain possession of it without arousing her suspicions. But it hadn't even been necessary for him to be subtle; she had played straight into his hands.

. . . Time passed. Agatha forgot Edmund waiting for her

in the hotel lounge. She was following up her dreadful discovery. It led, she found, to one conclusion and one only. All these months he had been playing her as a skilled angler plays a salmon, waiting for the moment when her money would pass unconditionally into his hands. And now that he had it—what then?

"So the films and the novels are right and I was wrong," she whispered. "He only married me for my money, after all. Now I come to think of it, he made very sure of my circumstances before marriage. Two or three times he spoke of making a will—but how do I know that he had anything to leave? Indeed," she added aloud, her eyes wide and dark with horror, "had I actually made a will myself I might not be here now."

But even with this new knowledge in her possession she couldn't believe that he had married her only to be rid of her. In any case, her death would not help him. She had preserved him from that risk. Of course, there was the remainder of her money, but he might well consider that two thousand four hundred pounds good wages for six months' work. During that time she had made him one or two advances of twenty pounds, contributing them happily to the general upkeep of the house. No, it was money easily earned, and he could walk out of The Haven free as air tomorrow morning and know himself rid of her for life. Well he knew she would never pursue him into the courts. The middle-aged woman fooled by the handsome scoundrel is a theme for scornful mirth rather than compassion.

"Well, what did she expect?" asks the Man in the Street. "Does she suppose he married her for her *beaux yeux* at forty-seven?"

She held up her hands and saw that they were shaking. The room seemed darker than when she had come in. Her forehead was clammy and she felt desperately cold.

"I should have worn more clothes," she whispered. Yet it had seemed quite warm when she entered the hotel. "Perhaps he won't come here, after all," she decided. "He would have to wait, of course, for the cheque to be cleared, but perhaps, when he left me, he drove the car away up to London or somewhere. Perhaps at this very moment he's writing out another advertisement to entice another deluded fool into parting with everything she's got. . . ."

The thought was too much for her. She put her hands to her forehead, had a sensation of pitching through black space, and all the lights went out.

When Durward arrived at the hotel he was met by the manager, who told him in distress that his wife had been found in the ladies' cloakroom in a fainting condition.

"Fainting? My wife?"

"It must be the heat," suggested the manager. "We've got her lying down on a couch. She's been asking for you."

"I'll come at once. As you say, she's probably been trying to crowd a week's activities into a couple of hours, and it's been too much for her."

Edmund found his wife stretched on a couch in the manager's sitting room, with two ladies and the manager's wife fluttering round her.

"Here's your husband, dear," said one of them. "Now you'll feel better."

They parted to let Durward approach. He looked troubled and strained, and his voice was full of anxiety. The two ladies exchanged glances. Some women had all the luck, those glances implied.

"No," said Agatha suddenly, in a low voice.

"This is my fault," said Edmund. "I oughtn't to have let you come out in this heat. But you know what women are like with a new house in the offing." He smiled his attractive smile at the two onlookers.

"I'm sure I felt I could have passed out this morning," said the plumper of the two, a cheerful-looking woman in a red frock sprinkled with white butterflies. "Chronic, this heat. Though when it's cold we all complain enough. No satisfying us, that's what I say, and that's what Hitler's saying now. Well, he'll learn. Now, dear," she turned to the dazed and horrified Agatha, "do you feel you could stand up and your husband'll take you home?"

"No," said Agatha again.

The manager's wife, who had left the group when Edmund appeared, now returned carrying a little glass containing brandy. "Drink this, Mrs. Durward," she said. "You'll feel better then."

Agatha drank it meekly.

"That's right," said the manager's wife. "You just lie there a bit longer till you feel able to move. You've got your car, Mr. Durward?"

"It's in the yard."

"She'll be better soon. How about a nice cup of tea?"

"The very thing," said Edmund enthusiastically.

"No," said Agatha for the third time. Her mind was perfectly clear. She wasn't going home with Edmund today or ever. Never mind about the money, never mind about her possessions at The Haven, just get away, get up to London, go to the Hiawatha, somewhere where he couldn't follow her, somewhere she'd be safe. But unfortunately there seemed to be no liaison between her mind and her body. While she was telling herself that this was her last chance, she felt herself being assisted from the couch, felt Edmund's arm go round her in support, heard his voice speaking consolingly, saw his face, kind and considerate, close to hers.

"What a brute you must think me, not to notice you were looking seedy!" he was saying. "The fact is, Agatha, you have so much spirit you deceive us all."

"Deceive!" she whispered, and the word was almost a cry.

He guided her solicitously through the lounge. The car was waiting in the yard in front of the entrance. He opened the door and the manager himself helped her in. She made one more feeble effort at protest, but no one listened.

"See you next Friday, I hope, Mr. Durward," said the manager. Durward smiled. "I hope you'll see us both."

The car drove off. Agatha uttered a little moan.

In the lounge two men drinking sherry at a small table turned simultaneously to one another.

"Did you see that chap go through?" said the first.

"He looked a bit like Paul."

"He didn't only look like him, I'll swear he was him. Oh, he's older, of course, but the voice, the mannerisms—those are unchanged. I don't think he saw us."

"I wonder what he's doing here."

"What he was doing the last time I saw him, if you ask me. Losing wives for what they'll fetch."

"Take care, Geoff. That's actionable."

"Tell him I said it and give him my lawyer's name and address. He won't come into court. Who do you suppose that one was?"

"The latest, I suppose. Good Lord, I don't like this."

"No, she didn't look in very good shape."

"No. You're right."

"*And* if I'm right she'll look in even worse shape tomorrow. We ought to do something about this."

"But what? It's no good, Geoff. You can't walk up to a lady you've never seen before and say, 'Excuse me, madam, but if you had to choose between the man you call your husband (because he's probably got half a dozen wives tucked away here and there) and a man-eating shark, you'd do well to choose the shark.' Besides, we don't know where they're living."

The manager was crossing the lounge. The man called Geoffrey leaned out of his seat.

"I say, that chap who went through just now with a lady—do you know who he is?"

"That's Mr. Durward, sir."

Geoffrey Dale turned to his friend. "I told you it was the same man, Charley. Funny, isn't it, how you can travel half round the world and suddenly, after a dozen years, you bump up against the man you lived next door to for months. I met Mr. Durward out East," he explained for the manager's benefit.

The fellow's face brightened. "Now I come to think of it, I've heard Mr. Durward speak of being out East."

"That's his wife with him?"

"Yes. They come here every Friday. She's a bit overcome with the heat."

"I suppose you don't know where he's living now?" Dale suggested. "It would be nice to look him up."

"I don't. They come in every Friday by car to do their shopping. That's all I know."

"Pity," murmured Dale. "I shall be in Scotland by next Friday. Oh, well, I just thought I'd ask."

"Certainly, sir. Small world, isn't it?" The manager moved on.

Dale shrugged. "I don't suppose there's anything we could do anyhow. Still, I didn't much like the story of the first wife—if she was the first. That woman was never accidentally drowned."

"A coroner's jury found she was."

"Because Durward—as he calls himself—arranged that they should. Still, you're right. There's nothing we can do. It's this woman's funeral. Which," he added, twisting his lips in a grim sort of smile, "is probably precisely what it will be."

But before he paid for the drinks he drew out a diary and made a note of the date and time.

"Regular Sherlock Holmes, aren't you?" his friend, Bate, suggested.

"Don't laugh, damn you. You never know when a bit of evidence like this may come in handy. I'm going to keep my eyes skinned for a little paragraph in the evening papers in the course of the next few weeks, and what do you bet I don't find it?"

III

Agatha was very quiet on the journey home. Whenever she felt her husband's glance on her face she kept her eyes closed, but when a corner had to be negotiated or they found themselves among traffic she peeped at him from under her slightly lifted lids. How was it, she thought, that never until today had she realized the ruthlessness of those features? The profile was as hard as a stone. And the hands that held the wheel, hands that had supported her from the hotel, that had held her, patted her shoulder, stroked her arm, picked her up when she lay, concussed, by the garden door of The Haven—how strong they were, how relentless! She saw the grip with which they twisted the wheel as a fool of an errand boy suddenly tried to cut between two cars. She thought, "Tonight we shall be quite alone, quite, quite alone. From the instant that Mrs. Hart goes, after tea, until eight o'clock tomorrow morning, there'll be no one within a radius of three-quarters of a mile. And he's got my money safe in the bank. He doesn't mean to take all that trouble for nothing."

Durward suddenly turned to her, saying, "How are you feeling, Agatha? I'm going to pop you into bed as soon as you get home, and draw down the blinds and give you a chance to sleep. Sleep's the best thing for you now."

Sleep's the best thing for you now. What simple words and how innocent they sounded. But who could tell what wealth of meaning they concealed? She thought of the text inscribed on her mother's grave: "So He giveth His beloved sleep." She laughed with a sudden burst of hysteria. His beloved.

Durward looked anxious. "Agatha, are you sure you're all right?"

"Of course I'm all right. It was that woman over there—no, you can't see her now. She looked like a monkey in a hat made of red feathers."

"It always seems to me barbaric to kill anything as beautiful as a bird just for the sake of personal vanity," said Durward in his pleasant voice.

She wanted to laugh again—laugh and laugh and laugh. Ha-ha-ha. Ha-ha-ha. But she mustn't laugh. Probably that was just what he wanted. Why, of course it was. What a fool she had been not to see it before. Then he'd have the right over everything she possessed. He could pack her away into a home—she shuddered, remembering an asylum for poor gentlewomen she had once seen in the country. She remembered the nodding heads, the cowed bearing, and an old face, gray and sly and mad, gibbering from behind a yellowed lace curtain, watching her as she went down the path. She threw up her hand and covered her mouth.

"You're feeling sick?" suggested that solicitous voice in her ear. "We're not far now. I'll just tool her along."

72

It seemed an eternity before they reached The Haven, yet she could have wished the journey a hundred times more slow. At last the car drew up in front of the door, which flashed open to reveal Mrs. Hart, like a little black rabbit out of a conjurer's hat, standing on the step.

"Well, I never!" said Mrs. Hart. "Back early, ain't you?"

"Mrs. Durward fainted. It's the heat. Agatha, my dear, you'd better go straight up."

But she shook her head. "Not just yet. Let me sit in the living room. You put the car away."

"Get Mrs. Durward a cup of tea at once," ordered Edmund.

"Nothing like a cupper tea," agreed Mrs. Hart. "You look bad, mum, and that's the truth."

"It's only the heat," repeated poor Agatha.

" 'Eat? You wouldn't talk about 'eat if you'd bin in this 'ouse all day. Like a morgue this 'ouse 'as bin. Every time I come into this room I look for the corpse. Did you remember the Glitto, mum?"

Agatha shook her head.

"There now, and all them windows looking that downcast. It's dark enough any'ow, without them all looking as if they was in mourning for something—or someone. Let me take off your shoes."

"Mrs. Hart," whispered Agatha, "will you do me a favour?"

Mrs. Hart looked up cautiously. "What's that, mum?"

"I'm feeling really unwell, and this is a very solitary place. Could you possibly, just for once, spend the night here? I'd like to feel I had another woman on the premises. It'll be so tiresome for Mr. Durward if I really am ill, and tomorrow we'll have the doctor in, if I'm not feeling better."

But Mrs. Hart had stepped back, her hands on her bony hips, and was vigorously shaking her head. "I'm sorry, Mrs. Durward. I'd like to oblige, truly I would, but I couldn't sleep 'ere. If I was to see anything I'd go crackers. And it wouldn't 'elp you much if I was to go running round with a carving knife."

"That's absurd," said Agatha quickly. "You wouldn't see anything because there's nothing to see."

" 'Ow about the ghost? You saw it, didn't you? And you're getting out before it gets you, and you're quite right."

"We're leaving the house because it would be too damp in the winter. As for the ghost, that was a practical joke played by Miss Knowles."

"Well, that's what you say now, but I think different. No, I'm sorry, but I can't do it. Besides, 'Art wouldn't agree, neither. Ever such a man for 'is own bed, 'Art is. And it's no use suggesting

73

'im coming as well because 'e's psychic too. Why, 'e can see things even when they ain't there. The things 'e's seen since 'e was married you'd never believe."

It was no use, as all along she had known it wouldn't be. Whatever fate lay ahead for her she had got to meet it alone. She wondered what story Edmund would tell if she were found dead in the morning. She remembered a book she had read wherein a man had stifled a girl by pressing a pillow over her face and then standing the body upright in the chimney. The Haven was just the sort of house for a macabre development of that kind. And how Mrs. Hart would gloat, what stories she would tell of Agatha's unexpected return. The poor creature put her hands over her eyes and was surprised to find that the tears were pouring down her cheeks.

"Come, my dear, you're absolutely overwrought. I blame myself for this. I do indeed. Hasn't that woman brought the tea yet?"

There was Edmund again, kind, considerate, bending over her, his hand on her shoulder. And presently, when Mrs. Hart had gone and they had the house to themselves, perhaps he would come even nearer, his hands would close more tightly. . . . At the notion her imagination spread wings and carried her away from the familiar world of light skies and shallow waters into some dark creation where she was beaten by tempests, blinded by huge rain and sleet. Yet even now she could not wholly accept her peril. Murder's a word in a dictionary, a ghastly fate that overtakes other people, never a thing to be connected with oneself. Why, what an anticlimax it would be, after her patient years in Ealing, her sedate pleasure in her South Kensington home, to die at a murderer's hands in a lonely house in a hollow!

Meekly she drank the tea when Mrs. Hart brought it; meekly she agreed to go up to bed and try to sleep. Sometimes, reading the papers, she had been astounded at the folly displayed by the victim. Surely, she would think, she suspected the man; surely she could have shown some enterprise. Why, she is practically his accomplice. She understood better now. When you knew your helplessness, when hope died, you ceased to struggle. It was like a desperate illness; the will to live left you. You lay still and let your fate sweep over you as a wave washes over a recumbent body on the sand.

Presently Edmund came in, bringing an omelet nicely served, with sprigs of parsley round the dish—Edmund, the artist in everything he undertook.

"My dear," he said, "I've just discovered I have no tobacco. I meant to buy it in Bridport, but your collapse put everything out of my mind. Would you be nervous at being left alone for a few minutes—it's not seven o'clock yet and still quite light—while I take the car up to the village? Bannerman will let me have some under the counter, even though the shop is shut."

"Of course you must go. I shall be perfectly all right. In fact, I'm feeling much better already. By the morning . . ."

"You won't do anything rash while I'm away? Promise."

She shook her head. "I promise." Go, go, screamed her lacerated nerves. It was too good to be true. She heard his feet on the stairs and a minute later the cautious slam of the front door. In an instant she had laid the tray aside and had leaped from the bed. Fate was giving her one last chance after all. Every moment was worth its weight in pure gold. It would take—how long to reach the village? About ten minutes. Then there would be a little longer—say, another ten minutes—to chat to Bannerman; Edmund would be sure to recount the story of her collapse at Bridport—indeed that was probably his reason for going to the village; and ten minutes to get back. She had, in all, about half an hour. She was dressing rapidly while the thoughts passed through her mind. She had no time to pack anything; all she wanted was a chance to escape. She might spend the night in the black wood or in some inhospitable gray field, but anything, anything, her mind shouted, would be safer than this house. She would somehow get to London—fortunately she had money in her purse—she would go straight to Grace. . . . Her hands fell limply to her sides. To Grace! Why, she saw it all now. Grace was a victim too. She had fallen under the spell of that irresistible charm during her first day at Maplegrove. Grace would never have dressed up as the ghost if she hadn't been encouraged, hypnotized almost. Edmund had suggested it, directly or indirectly. And then he had thrown the blame on Grace and hustled her out of the house before she could offer her own explanations. Perhaps even Grace had written and Edmund had suppressed the letter.

But as she stood in the middle of her room, glancing wildly left and right, her mind moved on another step. Suddenly she knew there was no need to hurry. Edmund wasn't coming back. After all, what did he stand to gain by her death? It was far simpler to take the car and go away and never come back.

"But even so I shall not spend the night here alone," she assured herself, pulling down an old black mackintosh that hung on the door. "I should go crazy if I did."

She hurried down the stairs, resolved to leave the house, not by the front door, in case she were perceived and halted by some passer-by, but by the back, where the bolts had not yet been drawn.

It seemed very dark down here, although it was only a little after seven o'clock. The trees in the wood seemed to throw enormous black shadows over the little garden where she had toiled with such delight, and where, her fevered imagination warned her, she might perhaps have lain, had circumstances been very little different. The woodshed loomed dark and menacing on her right. She paused, breathless, one hand on the knob of the door.

"What is it I have married?" she whispered, consumed by mingled curiosity and fear. "What is it that he does in the woodshed? What was he making that was to be such a surprise for me?"

Because he wasn't coming back and because, after this evening, she would never set foot here again a new resolution fired her. Edmund had said he kept the place locked because there were trunks and packing cases there—her own large suitcase among them. But why does a man spend time in a lumber room? And why had he always been so secretive, never allowing her to accompany him thither?

"If I were wise I should go now," she said, "but afterwards what a coward I should feel."

She even thought it possible he was an enemy agent and that the shed concealed a private wireless set.

Stiff with artificial courage, she crept into the living room and opened the drawer of the writing table. She had sometimes seen Edmund toss the key to the back of it. He had been so open about his activities that never before had it occurred to her to probe the mystery for herself. Now she found the key and drew it out.

There was no difficulty about opening the shed. "It is all too simple," she told herself. "Whatever he does, I shall not find the truth here."

She was carrying a small torch and this she switched on, for the interior of the shed was very dark. It was larger than she had realized and contained, as Edmund had told her, a number of trunks, boxes and packing cases. There was also a rough deal table on which he did his carpentering, and a quantity of new wood leaned against the wall. In one corner was a small trug full of garden implements, and a larger spade and fork were propped against the wall. Agatha took an adventurous step inside the shed and began to explore.

. . . She had left the shed and now stood in the dim twilight, so shaken and aghast that she was scarcely sane. She ran a few steps in this direction, a few in that. She pressed her hands over her eyes, then, panic-stricken, because she knew at last the danger that threatened her, tore them away and stood staring into the black woods as though behind every tree lurked something with Edmund's face, Edmund's hands.

"Go quickly, you fool," she muttered to herself. She heard someone laugh, low and excited and wild, and then a rapid patter of words.

"Who are you?" she cried. "What are you? Keep away. I'm armed."

The next instant her eyes widened with terror, her jaw fell open. The front door of the house had closed with its characteristic snap and footsteps were coming down the passage towards the garden door! Now she knew she was lost. Now Edmund would not dare to let her live. But perhaps he would first go upstairs to look for her, and in that moment she could save herself. But Edmund had perceived that the garden door was open. He came to the threshold and looked out with puzzled eyes. He must have seen her there, a wild, dark shadow in a shadowy world.

"Agatha!" he exclaimed.

She could not move, could not cry. Fascinated, she watched him draw the door close behind him and come across the path to the place where she stood. Behind her the door of the woodshed creaked as it swung in the wind. Now she could see his face as a white mask; he came nearer. His expression was strange, almost sorrowful, yet the upper lip lifted in a queer, twisted smile.

"Why, Agatha," he said, and his voice was quite low, quite gentle, "what made you come here? I wanted to spare you this, but you gave me no choice. I'd have let you go if I could, but you've made that impossible. You do understand, don't you?"

"Edmund!" The word seemed to burn her throat. "No—no . . ."

"I didn't want to hurt you," he went on in the same tone. "If you hadn't tried to pry, you could have kept your life. You're your own executioner." And all the time he was coming nearer and nearer as she moved away from him, back into the woodshed and the secret it contained. Now she was right inside, now her foot knocked against the spade, now a queer babble of words streamed from her lips. His hands came out to grasp her, and she screamed, a long, thin shriek of fear. Animals sometimes scream like that in their agony.

"It's no good, Agatha," said Durward gently. "There's no one to hear—except, perhaps, the ghost of Bell's Bottom. And she can't help you because, you see, she's dead too."

※　　※　　※

77

CHAPTER SEVEN

I

THE MAPLEGROVE WOMEN'S INSTITUTE, a small but indomitable body of women who were determined not to allow Hitler to spoil all their fun, was holding its last meeting of the summer to draw up the autumn program. Miss Martin, in the chair, proposed that they should get up some form of entertainment in the early autumn.

"Morale," said Miss Martin, baring her teeth like a bloodhound. "That's what's going to win this war. Shells and bombs and planes—yes, we all know we can't do without them—but it's the spirit that counts beyond everything."

This little speech was a preliminary to suggesting a program of one-act plays to be performed in the Church Hall at the end of September or the beginning of October, the time now being mid-August. Miss Martin, who was going to town the following week, undertook to call at French's and read one-act plays until she found some that were suitable.

"What about the royalty?" demanded Miss Grainger. "That always runs up our expenses."

"We'll ask the authors to forgo their royalty," said Miss Martin unscrupulously. "After all, there is a war on. And I'll ask Mr. Durward if he'll write as well as act. He couldn't charge us anything. I'll go down there this afternoon."

At three o'clock, therefore, The Buddies set out for The Haven. Neither, today, was wearing uniform Miss Martin wore rust-coloured dungarees and let nature have its way with her hair; Miss Grainger wore a worsted suit in green and yellow with a home-made jumper. She sported a mustard-coloured beret and open sandals. The legs of both ladies were bare.

"I wonder how Agatha Durward's getting on without Mrs. Hart," Miss Grainger suggested, as they reached the gate and prepared for the descent.

"It won't be long. Mrs. Hart won't let an appendix hold her up more than a couple of weeks."

"I went to see her in hospital, you know, and she said that the Durwards had gone to London for a short break. I hope we haven't come all this way for nothing."

"He's back. I saw him in his car two or three days ago. He didn't see me, and I suppose he was immersed in love's young dream because, although I hoo-ha'd at him, he drove straight past."

"Agatha said he was a very handy man about the house. I dare say he's managing for himself, if she's not back."

It was, however, soon clear that Edmund was doing nothing of the kind. In response to Miss Martin's hearty tattoo on the knocker, the door was grudgingly opened by a plump, shortish woman of about thirty-eight, wearing a brushed wool jersey of pale blue, fastened with a gold brooch shaped like a Maltese cross.

"Ah!" said Miss Martin, not in the least disconcerted by this unexpected apparition. "Is Mrs. Durward in?"

"Oh!" The apparition opened its mouth and left it open. "Did you want to see her?"

"Do you suppose I walked up here for the sake of my figure?" demanded Miss Martin. "Don't be silly. You must know if she's in or not."

The door of the living room opened and Durward himself came out. "Why, Miss Martin. And Miss Grainger. It's a long time since we met."

"Just what I was saying to Violet this morning. You really must come over and dine with us one night. Is your wife in?"

"I'm afraid she's away."

"Away?"

"Yes. I left her up in London. She had to see her dentist and her lawyer—she's quite a woman of affairs, you know—and one of her friends wanted her to stay, so here I am, a grass widower for the time being. I'm getting well ahead with the book, though. Agatha expects me to have it finished by the time she comes back."

"When do you expect her?"

"Not before the end of the month. It's a wonderful chance for her. She's going to all the plays and having a new permanent wave and spending all her coupons and probably most of mine. . . ."

"And you're left to manage. You must miss Mrs. Hart."

"I've got a housekeeper now. I really don't think Agatha ought to be left alone in this house in the winter and, of course, I can't always swear to be on the premises."

"That was the housekeeper who opened the door to us, I suppose?"

"Daisy, yes. Agatha interviewed her in London and left me to break her in." He laughed, showing his fine white teeth.

Miss Martin's brow creased. She was aware of something odd about this conversation. It seemed strange that in six months she had never been invited inside the house. Brazenly she said as much.

"As soon as Agatha returns you really must come and dine," smiled Durward. "I'm afraid we're hopeless people." He laughed with his usual undeniable charm, his dark blue eyes shining. "We shouldn't make much of a success of communal living, should we? But I really will prod Agatha into being slightly more social this winter."

"What we really wanted to know was whether you'd help us with our W.I. plays."

Durward groaned humorously. "I felt there was something behind this unexpected visit. Miss Martin, have pity on us."

"Why should she?" demanded Miss Grainger without warning. "She's not asking much, is she? In a war?"

"The bare thought of exhibiting myself on a stage gives me goose flesh. But you needn't worry, Miss Grainger. Agatha will push me into it. She's really very keen on acting."

"It'll give her a chance of meeting a few more people. We did hear some rumour about your leaving. . . ."

"We did think of it and, in fact, we may even now. The difficulty is to get hold of the kind of house one wants at the price one can afford."

"I think Mrs. Durward's shown great strength of mind in staying here so long," said Miss Grainger. "The house gives me the creeps."

Durward smiled again. "As soon as she comes back I'll send her to see you. I'm always telling her she ought to get about more. London may have waked her up. She'll probably come down full of ideas for your plays."

"I'm going to London myself next week," said Miss Martin. "Perhaps we could fix a meeting and we could go to French's together. Two people are so much better than one at that sort of thing."

"She goes to stay with a friend at Winchester on Saturday," said Durward smoothly.

"Well, that puts my suggestion out of court. Good-bye, Mr. Durward. You'll soon be hearing from us again."

"You have your car?" he suggested. "Or can I run you up to The Buddies?"

"We haven't lost the use of our limbs yet," said Miss Martin. "Come, Violet."

Sturdily they tramped away.

"I wonder where Agatha got that housekeeper. She doesn't look much good to me," murmured Miss Grainger, giving the ball a gentle push.

"Housekeeper nothing. She's a hussy if ever I saw one. Violet, there's dirty work at the crossroads."

"What on earth are you talking about, Evelyn?"

"Did you notice the jumper that woman was wearing?"

"I thought it quite unsuitable for a housekeeper. She might, at least, wear an overall."

"That was one of Agatha Durward's jumpers," said Miss Martin deliberately.

"Oh? Well, I suppose she gave it to her."

"How could she, if she's still in town? But that's not all. That brooch was one Agatha wore the night she came to dinner. It had belonged to her Aunt Marian in India. There was some story attached to it, and she insisted on telling us. Do you mean to suggest she gave Daisy that too?"

"You mean, she's stolen it? But that's absurd. I mean, it's dangerous. Agatha would find out the moment she came back."

"If she comes back. Besides, do you suppose Agatha's gone to London and left her brooch behind? She told us she always wore it. No, Violet, if you ask me, it was Providence who sent us to The Haven this afternoon."

They reached the gate and came out onto the highroad.

"What are you thinking, Evelyn? You've made me feel quite unsettled."

"I think something's definitely wrong, and as soon as I get up .to London on Monday I'm going to see Agatha's lawyer."

Miss Grainger stared. "Even you, Evelyn, can't do that."

"Can't I? Oh, you needn't be afraid. I shan't create a scandal. I'm just one of Agatha's friends who wants to get in touch."

"He'll probably think you want to make a touch."

"This is no laughing matter. I don't believe Agatha ever went to London at all."

"Then where do you think she is?"

"Ask Edmund Durward," replied her friend in sinister tones.

"Evelyn, this is fantastic. If what you're suggesting is true, Mr. Durward can't hope to keep up the pretence forever."

"He won't be here forever. The next thing we shall hear is that he's found a more suitable house, and he'll vanish, lock, stock and Daisy one moony night, and there'll be no one left to care what's happened to poor Agatha."

"But you don't know who her lawyer is."

"I know his name's Entwistle. She talked about him at dinner that night."

"There must be dozens of legal Entwistles."

"You do enjoy making difficulties, don't you? I shall go to Mr. Crook and ask his advice. That man can smell out a crime before it's been committed. And I shall ring up her club. . . ."

"I suppose she told you which that was the night she came to dinner?"

"You were too much occupied with her husband, Violet, to listen to what Agatha was saying. But, fortunately for us all, I did, and she distinctly said she had acted with the Amateur Group of the Hiawatha. They will know if she's been in lately. I don't mean to leave a stone unturned."

"Or one standing on another, I suppose," sighed Miss Grainger, who knew her Evelyn in this mood.

Miss Martin did not deign to answer her. She gave a sudden chuckle and walked on.

When Mr. Crook heard that Miss Martin was waiting for him, he told his clerk to give him three minutes' grace and instructed Bill Parsons to open a bottle of beer. Unlike many lawyers, he kept a supply on the premises. He said it was more useful than a gun.

"That woman's one of Nature's mistakes," he informed Bill robustly. "She's probably come to tell me that a fox has poached her chickens and she wants to serve a writ on the fox. And she'll expect me to identify the actual animal. And—damn it, Bill— I shall do it."

Miss Martin came striding in in all the glory of her uniform, her basin-shaped felt pushed well back to reveal her broad, shining forehead.

"I've got a job for you," she announced, taking a chair. "No, I won't smoke one of your fags. Never take cigarettes from a man who doesn't smoke them himself. They're sure to be chopped beetle and floor sweepings." She produced her own case and lighter. "Now then, this is something right up your street."

"Murder?" asked Crook dispassionately.

"I wouldn't be surprised."

"Not one of your own?"

"Not yet. No, it's my neighbour, Mrs. Edmund Durward. The fact is, she's disappeared in mysterious circumstances."

"Widow?"

"Wife—or thinks she is. I wouldn't put anything past the man myself. The fact is that, according to him, she left for London rather more than a fortnight ago and he's got another female down there wearing her clothes and her jewels, whom he calls his housekeeper."

"A very ambiguous term," agreed Mr. Crook gravely. "Still, she may only be havin' a grass-widow's holiday in London."

"She's not that kind. Besides, if she is in town, why hasn't she been near her club? They've seen nothing of her. Certainly, it was closed for cleaning the first week she was in town, but not the second. And where's the sense in having a club if you don't use it when you're in London?"

"Perhaps they didn't notice her come in."

"I spoke to the secretary. She says they haven't seen her since she married."

"When was that?"

"In the New Year. And that's another fishy thing."

"There must come a time in every married woman's life when she's been married less than a year," protested Crook.

"You haven't seen Mrs. Durward. Why, the woman's older than I am, years older, and I'm forty-three. What was she doing, getting married to a man like Edmund Durward at her age?"

"You couldn't expect the poor woman to wait much longer," Crook protested.

"She's not the *femme fatale* type," continued Miss Martin, who, like Tennyson's brook, flowed on over all obstacles. "I'd have called her the born spinster myself, and she's obviously infatuated with her husband."

"You don't find that suitable?"

Miss Martin leaned forward. The smoke of her cigarette blew into Crook's eyes.

"What did he marry her for? Why, he could have married anyone, a good-looking chap like that, if he'd been on the level, I mean. No, my way of reading it is that she had money and he knew it."

"You're reading a good lot into a short jaunt to London, aren't you?" suggested Crook. "What do you want me to do about it?"

"Do you know a Mr. Entwistle, a lawyer, of Bloomsbury Street?"

"Piggy Entwistle?" Crook looked pleased for the first time. "Well, suppose I do? Still, I'm a lawyer, not a private detective."

Miss Martin winked vulgarly. "Sez you! Wait till you hear the rest of the story. Do you think a woman like that would send that little so-and-so down to The Haven with her husband and stay in London? And, if he was straight, do you think he'd have her there? That kind was born in a double bed and wouldn't know what to do with a single one."

Mr. Crook, looking shocked, as well he might, at this outspokenness, inquired of his client what she expected him to do about it.

"Ring up your friend, Piggy Entwistle, and ask if he's heard anything of Mrs. Durward during the last fortnight. If he has— well and good. I take everything back. If he hasn't—then the sooner someone starts asking awkward questions, the better."

Mr. Crook looked at her with something between admiration and dislike. "Do you know her unmarried name?" he inquired, lifting the receiver.

"Yes. Forbes. Agatha Forbes. I got that out of the club."

"Your middle name isn't Agatha Christie, I suppose. Hullo? Entwistle? This is Crook here. Isn't Mrs. Agatha Durward, *née* Forbes, one of your clients?"

That was the way Crook always framed his questions. "Rush 'em," he said, "don't give 'em a chance to find their feet."

"Mrs. Durward? Certainly. I hope you haven't bad news of her?"

"I haven't any news of her—that's the point. She's supposed to have left Maplegrove two or three weeks ago to come to town to consult you."

Mr. Entwistle instantly sounded extremely agitated. "Are you sure of this, Crook? Yes, yes, of course you are. But, my dear fellow, this is truly appalling. I always knew there was something odd about that marriage. She was so very secretive. And then selling out those stocks against my advice—dear me, dear me, I believe I always expected something like this."

"I shall expect the telephone to explode if you don't calm down. I gather you haven't seen her?"

"I wasn't even aware that she contemplated coming to London. I did write to her recently suggesting she should consult me before taking certain steps, but she replied that it was not convenient. Dear me, this is most disturbing."

"Did you say she sold out some stocks?"

"Yes. I need hardly say, without my approval. The total amount of the cheque was between two and three thousand pounds."

"And she's had the dibs?"

"Yes. By cheque."

"Can you find out if she ever paid it into her account?"

Mr. Entwistle considered. "She banks at the Westmoreland. The manager of the South Kensington branch is a personal friend of mine. In the circumstances, he might give me a little information on the strict q.t."

Crook winked at Miss Martin. "Any idea why she wanted the money?"

"She wished to buy a house. She could only draw her money if her husband agreed as to the expenditure."

"We'll assume he did. By the way, did she ever make a will?"

"She spoke of it when she told me she was about to be married, but nothing was done, not, that is to say, by myself. As a matter of fact, I didn't feel altogether happy about the affair. You may remember my telephoning you . . ."

"I remember. And I said all things come to him who waits, and we waited and it's come. Quite sure about the will?"

"So far as this office is concerned," repeated Entwistle. "To be candid with you, I didn't press her. I felt she might be more secure if the will wasn't signed. Naturally, I don't know whether her husband persuaded her to make a will with a local attorney. I know he was anxious to learn the provisions of Mr. Forbes's will."

"Well, so would you be, in the gentleman's shoes. I don't say things ain't a bit queer, Entwistle. One of the lady's neighbours is in my office. Mrs. D. hasn't been seen in Dorset for more than a couple of weeks, and she hasn't been seen in London. Of course," he added, turning to Miss Martin, "she may have done a bunk on her own."

"She wouldn't," said Miss Martin decisively. "I tell you, she was crazy about her husband. And if she had gone, she'd certainly have taken her jewellery with her."

Crook turned back to the phone. "Got the address of the place she was going to buy? Right. Well, would you like me and Bill to go ahead?"

"I shall go to the police if you don't," said Miss Martin.

"Get that, Entwistle?"

"I should prefer the police to be kept out of it, if possible." Miss Martin's piercing voice could be as easily heard at his end of the line as if she had spoken direct into the receiver. "Naturally, Crook, you must use your discretion, but perhaps a little preliminary inquiry wouldn't come amiss."

"Naturally," agreed Crook, meaning the bit about discretion. "I haven't got anything else, have I? You do your stuff with the bank manager and let me know what happens." He rang off and turned to his client. "Miss Martin, I'm not sure you haven't picked a winner. All the world loves a deluded spinster."

"You ought to give me a commission," said Miss Martin, stubbing out her cigarette and picking up her "service" gloves. "I don't believe I'll go to French's after all. I've a good mind to try my hand at a one-act play. It's an ideal situation. The Vanishing Wife. And I might ask Durward to play the husband."

"That's called having a sense of humour," commented Crook, midway between admiration and scorn, as his client stamped out. "Ah, well, male and female created He them, seeing further than we. And a damned sight further, we'll hope. Where's the rest of that beer, Bill? I could do with it."

Shortly after lunch Entwistle arrived in person, a large, warm, anxious figure of a man, panting up Crook's innumerable stairs.

"If I die of an aneurism I shall expect you to pay my funeral expenses," he announced. "Why you can't get into a building with a lift. . . . Look here, Crook, I don't like the look of things at all."

"Seen the bank manager?"

"Yes. He hummed and ha'd, but he's thrilled to the bone at the idea of one of his clients being murdered. You would think a man of that age would have some balance, some sense of decency." Mr. Entwistle puffed with resentment and disgust. "Got several things to tell you," he ejaculated. "First, cheque hasn't been paid in."

"Wonder where Durward banks," murmured Crook.

"Second, someone appeared at the bank on the 8th and drew out all Miss Forbes's balance, about eighty pounds."

"And it's now the 12th. When you say someone, who do you mean?"

"That's what disturbs me. We had the cashier in, fellow called Rogers. Miss Forbes always made a point of going to Rogers, used to ask after his family—you know the way women do—but this time she seemed to be trying to avoid him. Barry asked him point-blank if he could identify the caller as Miss Forbes, but he wouldn't commit himself. Said it was like her, but the voice seemed different, as though she had a bad cold, and she kept a dark veil over her face all the time, and wore black gloves, and a sort of black cloak that hid her figure. He told her she was drawing her account dry, and she said hurriedly she'd be paying in a large cheque soon, she'd cashed some securities. Oh, and she asked for the money in one-pound notes and didn't stop to count 'em."

"Give any reason?" inquired Crook.

"Something about it being difficult to cash larger ones in the village. What do you make of that?"

"Elementary, my dear Watson. Whoever it was realized that banks keep tally of fivers and upwards, whereas one-pound notes can't be traced."

"Precisely my own deductions." Mr. Entwistle puffed heavily. "Crook, I'm deeply disturbed. I feel sure things are not all right."

"How about the signature?"

"We examined that. Of course, we'd need an expert to give us his opinion, but Barry seemed to think it might be Miss Forbes herself writing under duress or someone imitating her hand. Oh, one thing more. The date wasn't filled in till the cheque was cashed. That might be significant."

"Like hell it might. Well, Entwistle, on your instructions me and Bill will do our Sherlock Holmes act. I shan't mind a little trip to the country at someone else's expense," he added cheerfully. "It all makes a change."

CHAPTER EIGHT

AFTER THE DEPARTURE of his visitors Edmund Durward wandered from room to room of The Haven in rising doubt and exasperation. As a rule, he mapped out his adventures as neatly and carefully as a schoolboy drawing maps—mountain ranges there, valleys there, rivers there, capital clearly marked. In a lifetime of social buccaneering he had never made a mistake. And now, of all the glamorous, young and enticing women in his life, it was one who had been none of these things who looked like bringing him to grief. He thrust his hands into his pockets and stared out at the woods, as though he expected to see a ghost materialize and come towards him. He'd never meant things to work out like this. As usual, everything had been perfectly arranged. Should it prove necessary to eliminate Agatha—as, despite his assurances to her in the woodshed, he thought would be probable—he had intended everything to be open and aboveboard, including a funeral to which anyone could come who pleased, a doctor's certificate anyone could examine, and no questions asked. The stage had been perfectly set. After all, Agatha had been complaining of giddiness, she had fainted—he had thought that a godsend at the time. The stairs of The Haven were narrow and twisting and the place was undeniably dark. An elderly woman, descending, might easily lose her footing and crash to the flagged hall below. Oh, he had left nothing to chance. And now Agatha herself, by her cursed curiosity, had upset his apple cart.

"The fool!" he muttered, moving away from the window into the hall, where he stared gloomily at the very place where she had been destined to lie; "did she guess? Or just suspect? Or was it only curiosity after all? But no," he decided, "it was more than that. Something happened that last day in Bridport. It wasn't just the heat that made her faint."

Even after that dreadful night, however, he had believed he could save himself. There had been two days of sheer terror, when every footstep had made him start, lest it should be the police tramping up to the door, but Friday night merged into Saturday and Saturday into Sunday, and then Monday dawned and still no police came, and he began to calm down and believe his stupendous luck had brought him safely through yet one more adventure. One of his first activities had been to withdraw the greater part of Agatha's cheque and open a fresh account with a new bank, using a new name, so that if he were hounded from The

Haven he would at least have money behind him. More, he had persuaded Daisy—the Moron he called her—to withdraw her life savings, a sum of no less than a hundred and fifty pounds—from the savings bank and deposit them with him for a business they were to start jointly. Naturally, the business did not exist, but he now had a certain amount of ready money, together with what he had contrived to set aside from other sources, if he had to make a sudden getaway. All the money was in pound notes. His first stumblingblock had been Mrs. Hart, but to her he had explained Agatha's absence by saying she had had to make an unexpected journey to town, where he would be joining her shortly. This would prove sufficient excuse for keeping her away from The Haven for some days until he could make more permanent arrangements. And it had been a divine dispensation that she should be attacked by appendicitis during the following week and removed temporarily from a sphere where she could be counted upon to do as much harm as possible.

And now this meddlesome old hag—by which he meant Miss Martin—had interfered. He had seen at once that she didn't believe his story. If he followed his original plan and left The Haven for some unspecified address, on the excuse that he was joining Agatha who was detained in town (for an operation? on doctor's orders? it didn't matter; he could cook up some adequate story), she was quite capable of dragging in the police. And once the police get their teeth into a case they are like the British bulldog, they never let go. And, Durward told himself grimly, accidental death by falling downstairs, even if the lawyers do get nosy and ask a lot of questions, is several streets removed from death by strangulation. Hell, you can't even pretend strangulation's an accident. And it was the more unfair that he'd never intended to strangle the woman. It hadn't been part of his plan at all. It was just one continuous run of bad luck. He moved back from the hall into the living room.

The plump and good-natured moron he had taken in Agatha's place came and slipped her hand through his arm.

"Whatever's the matter, Eddie? You're like a dog that can't settle."

He turned. "What should you say to a little change, Daisy?"

"What, go away from here when we've only just come? Not that I mind. This place gives me the willies. When do we start?"

"I should have to stay a day or two to clear things up . . ."

The easy-going expression vanished from her face: a hard suspicion now informed it.

"You mean, me go away on my own? And where do you think I could go? I gave up a good job to come down here with you, let me tell you. And the tales you told me before I came. A lovely little place in the country. A lovely little graveyard, if you ask me. I feel as though I were walled up here with the dead."

Durward frowned. It had, perhaps, been a mistake to saddle himself with the woman. Yet, in the past, he had been a great success with this type. They were, as a rule, too unintelligent to be suspicious and too easily fascinated to ask questions. Besides, unlike their better educated sisters, they could be shaken off without dreaming of going to the police. They'd been brought up with a healthy awe for authority. And there was no denying that her little bit of money might prove the turning point in his perilous career. But he mustn't let her get ruffled. He smiled persuasively.

"I just thought you were getting the hump down here. Of course I don't want to lose you. I should hate this place by myself." And that, oddly enough, was true. He was the type of man who can't do without a woman round him. Something psychological perhaps. . . . It wasn't just the money; he needed a foil, and also he needed companionship. He'd like above all things to get out, but Miss Martin had cut away the ground under his feet. It would be madness to bolt now. He remembered Crippen, who had signed his own death warrant by his frantic dash overseas, when, if he had stayed in Hilldrop Crescent, he might have died in his bed full of years and honours. No, he couldn't afford to run and he couldn't afford to antagonize Daisy. Later, when the cloud had passed, he would take her up to town and lose her in a tea shop. It was the oldest trick there was, but it practically never failed. It would mean abandoning The Haven, of course, but then he intended to do that in any case.

He put his arm round Daisy's waist. "Sulking?" he whispered. "You silly little thing. What do you think I brought you here for?"

She giggled. "You are the queerest boy, Eddie. Like a weather-cock. Tell you what, let's get the car out and go into Bridport for the pictures. Do us both a power of good, that would."

All the same, Durward's heart remained heavy. Miss Martin was the type beloved of the psalmist (wasn't it?) who, having put her hand to the plough, wouldn't look back. She was probably ransacking London for traces of Agatha. And when she didn't find any, she'd come hareing back to The Haven to ask more questions. Durward knew. And you couldn't strangle her, and even if you did it wouldn't help. She, being dead, yet speaketh, would be her epitaph. During the five days following her visit he scarcely left the house at all, and was always on hand to collect the letters. He didn't trust Daisy an inch. It wasn't that she was treacherous, but she was a fool, and fools, he knew, do more harm in the long run than knaves. And if another visitor should come to the cottage she was capable of spilling all the beans before she could be prevented.

On the afternoon of the fifth day the anticipated visitor arrived. He was heralded by a tremendous clatter and chugging, and then a little red car came to a standstill near the door of The Haven and a short, plump man in a brown suit emerged. He fitted his absurd little car so tightly that he seemed to peel it off him like a skin. Durward caught sight of him from a window and viewed him without apprehension. The fellow wanted to sell something, he supposed. This was no plain-clothes man nor, from his appearance, would he be a friend of the missing Agatha.

"Common as dirt," he reflected. He was to discover that Crook could stick like dirt too.

Daisy had already opened the door. Durward heard the loud, cheerful voice with its slightly cockney intonation asking for the master of the house.

"It's for you," said Daisy, glimpsing him on the stairs. Her voice and the glance she gave him instantly betrayed their relationship. Durward hid his annoyance and came down to the hall. "Good afternoon," he said.

"Afternoon. It's really Mrs. Durward I wanted. I represent her lawyers."

Not a muscle of Durward's face moved; the slightly diffident smile played round the well-cut mouth, his eyes were unshadowed.

"Oh, then hadn't you better come in?"

Crook charged past him into the hall. "This way," said Durward, indicating the living room. "I'm afraid my wife's not here at the moment. . . ."

"Ah! P'raps you can give me her address. My name's Crook, and I'm actin' for Entwistle. He can't do these country trips, got a lazy heart."

Durward looked troubled. He clasped his hands and swung them between his knees.

"To tell you the truth, I can't. I don't know it."

Crook's red brows lifted. "Travellin' around?"

"I believe she's with friends, but . . ."

"You'd better tell your Uncle Arthur about it," said Crook in his deplorably unprofessional way. "Lady not comin' back, perhaps?"

Durward stood up and walked across to the window; he remained there, staring out, for a minute before he answered.

"To tell you the truth, I don't know, I simply don't know. It must sound absurd to you, but the fact is I really know nothing.

I can surmise a little, but I've no foundation for anything I may think. I've been hoping against hope that she'd go and see her own lawyers, but obviously she hasn't."

"Any special reason why she should need a lawyer?" inquired Crook.

"Again, I don't know."

"Well, just for a change, tell me what you do know," Crook suggested.

"It doesn't amount to a great deal. We were married in the New Year and had been living here very happily ever since. The only fly in the amber was my wife's dislike of the house. There's a ghost story attached to it and she became anxious to leave. I had no objection; in fact, Dr. Howarth advised it, and for some time we've been looking round for something suitable. But, as I expect you'll appreciate, it's not too easy just now to find the right thing. Still, we hadn't given up all hope. There wasn't any very great hurry so long as we found something before the winter. That was the position when we went into Bridport on the 25th July."

"And what happened in Bridport?"

Durward turned to him in sudden passion. "I don't know. That's why I'm still in the dark. We used to separate for our shopping and meet at The Pigeons for lunch, and that day, as soon as I arrived, the manager met me and told me that my wife had fainted. He thought it was the heat—but he was wrong."

"Meanin' . . . ?"

"Agatha loved the heat. It was the cold that frightened her. No, it was something else, something or someone she saw that morning. She was happy enough when we parted just before twelve, but during the next hour something took place."

"But you don't know what?"

"No. Only that it was something that terrified her first into fainting and afterwards into going away like a thief in the night. Because that's what she did. I got her home and into bed, and later in the evening I took her up tea and an omelet and suggested she should try to sleep. As she wasn't very well, it was agreed I should sleep in the dressing room. I looked in on her about ten o'clock, and she seemed quieter, more settled. As usual I woke about six-thirty and went across the passage to see if she were awake and would like some tea. To my horror, when I opened the door, I found the room was empty. Agatha never got up at that hour, so I knew at once that something was wrong. I looked through the house, but there was no sign of her, but on the table in the hall I found a note in her handwriting. It was the most extraordinary letter I've ever received, and I'm still at a loss to know precisely what it meant."

"Got it on you?" suggested Mr. Crook.

Durward looked amazed. "No. Actually, I destroyed it as soon as I'd read it. Well, why not? It was quite private, and Mrs. Hart isn't too delicate about prying into other people's correspondence."

"The more pryin' she did in this particular case, the better. You should have hung onto that note as the heir to the barony hangs onto his mother's marriage lines."

"If you had any notion what was in it," said Durward rather stiffly, "your advice might be different."

"Whatever was in it my advice wouldn't be different," contradicted Crook. "Even if she was accusin' you of bein' a twister and a heartless Don Juan. What did it say?"

"So far as I remember it ran something like this, 'Don't blame me too much, and when you think of me, think of me as a woman who for a few months wouldn't have changed places with anyone in the world. But it's true that the past isn't dead. You think you've buried it and stamped it deep into its grave, but sooner or later there's a resurrection. I thought that, at last, I was going to be happy for the rest of my life. I was a fool. Edmund, believe me, I'm doing the only thing possible for us both, I'm going away. You'll never see me again. If I've given you an iota of the joy you've given me, our time together hasn't been wasted.'"

"Very flowery," was Mr. Crook's terse comment. "Did she generally talk like that?"

"I've told you she was utterly overwrought. If only she could have confided the truth to me. . . ."

"The truth?"

"What it was that actually happened in Bridport to drive her to such a strait. I blame myself more than I can say that I didn't insist that evening, but she was so white, so worn, I hadn't the heart. I thought after a night's sleep she might be more—amenable."

"A lot of husbands have thought that, but they've mostly waked to find themselves wrong," was Crook's not very sympathetic comment.

"I've been brooding on this ever since. What could there have been in her past that she was afraid to let me know? The fact is, we hadn't known one another long before marriage, and I knew nothing of her but what she had chosen to tell me. It sounded the familiar uneventful story of the down-trodden daughter who never got anywhere except her parents' home. But there must have been something. . . ."

"Sure there was something. And you still don't know what it is?"

"I've no way of finding out. It's clear thatshe's hiding somewhere, terrified of being run to earth."

"Earth, eh?" Many a true word, as Crook knew, is spoken in jest. Earth might be just the place where she would be found. "And since then you've been playing a waiting game? Didn't occur to you that as her husband you had some responsibility for her?"

"I went to London a day or two later and put through all the inquiries I could. But they knew nothing of her at her club— I spoke to the secretary—and her tenants at her flat hadn't heard from her either. There weren't many people I could try. I'd only once met a friend of hers and I hadn't got her address."

"And how long were you goin' to wait before you thought of gettin' into touch with her lawyers?"

"If it were something—shady—though it's hard to connect Agatha with such an idea—she might even want to avoid her lawyers."

Crook leaned forward and tapped his companion impressively on the knee. "I can see you're one of these independent fellows who like to do all your own work, but you take my tip—whenever you're in a jam a lawyer's a good investment. Well, stands to reason. What's a lawyer for? To get you out of messes. If human beings were less fallible, our employment would be gone. Lawyers can afford to be indulgent, make excuses; they get their living off the fools and the knaves. If Mrs. Durward really was up against it, she should have flown to us as the drunkard to his bottle."

"You forget, the laity haven't your advantages. I'm sure her first thought was to get away where she wouldn't be found. And yet, it still seems absurd. My wife was the gentlest and most law-abiding of women."

"All the same, she was human, wasn't she? Oh, I could tell you stories that would make your ears grow double their size. Suppose there'd been a little mix-up with Papa's medicine a few years ago. It does happen. Ask any doctor. And suppose someone had found out. You know what they say about the mills of God. And the number of chaps who make a living out of the other fellow's mistake 'ud fill a munition factory."

Durward put his head in his hands. "This is like a nightmare. I've thought and thought and no solution comes to me. I couldn't advertise for her; it might meet the eyes of the very person she wanted to avoid. . . ."

"What's wrong with the police?" Crook demanded. "We have the best body of police in the world, all the evenin' papers say so, and who are you that you shouldn't get your share of the rates?"

"If I shrank from consulting her lawyers, it's obvious I wouldn't go near the police," Durward protested. "That might be the very thing to precipitate a tragedy. There's no telling how a woman's mind may work. . . ."

Crook made a derisive gesture. "Don't trot out all that old stuff about the mystery of women," he implored. "It don't cut any ice with me. There's no mystery about it when you tell the story. She had a shock, she was afraid of her guilty secret bein' discovered, and she cut her lucky. Did she take any luggage?"

"One suitcase with just the obvious necessities. Her other things are still hanging up in her room."

"Has it occurred to you," asked Crook slowly, "that she may conceivably have taken her own life?"

"Don't! I can't bear to think of it."

"How was she off for money?"

"She had her own banking account, and she hadn't done much shopping on Friday. She generally went to the bank at once if she was cashing a cheque, as I happen to know she was that day, so she'd have five or ten pounds in cash."

"H'm. One more thing. You say you hadn't found a house. But how about these securities she'd sold?"

"We were almost prepared to buy one house we saw and, as you say, she actually cashed in on her capital for this purpose. But when she had the money she hesitated. It was a charming house but it was large, too large for us. So we decided to wait a little longer."

"I see. Well, you've been very helpful, but don't blame me if it does come to the police in the end. You can't go vanishing in this country and not expect any questions to be asked. And, after all, the poor lady must be somewhere."

"You think you can find her?"

"If she's above ground I'll find her. And if by any chance she ain't, then the police will have their turn. I must be gettin' along now," he added a little abruptly. "But I dare say we'll meet again. Y'know," he observed an instant later, sticking his head out of the window of the Scourge and fixing Durward with a small, lively, penetrating brown eye, "it's a pity Mrs. Durward has first call on my services. I could be a lot more use to you."

* * *

After he had driven off, Durward stood staring after him for a long time. "What the devil does he know?" he muttered. "And —were those last words intended as a warning?"

He wished he could answer his own questions.

II

Having taken his cheerful adieu of Edmund Durward, Crook drove the noisy little Scourge to the main road, where he turned left towards the village. It was easy to learn Mrs. Hart's address. She had been three days out of the Cottage Hospital, with instructions to be good to herself, but her natural energy was already at full stretch. Crook found her vigorously scrubbing away some intruder's footprint from her immaculate little front step.

"Mrs. Hart?" he demanded, swinging open the door of the car.

She gave him one knowing glance that comprehended his appearance, his ludicrous little conveyance, his general jaunty air.

"We don't buy nothing at the door," she said, rising and preparing to slam it in his face.

"Not even a job?" insinuated Crook, coming a little closer.

She scratched her black head and looked at him suspiciously. "Not even that," she decided, moving backwards.

Crook nodded. "Nice to have a husband to support you."

"If I was to wait that long I might 's well set up in a morgue," she announced.

"With Mrs. Durward for your first corpse?"

Instantly her manner changed. She set her hands on her hips and leaned her little ferret face towards him.

"Mean to say they've found 'er? Coo! It's what I've told 'Art all along."

"They haven't found her alive," Crook amplified solemnly.

Mrs. Hart stepped back with a cordial invitation to enter. "I knoo it," she said triumphantly. "It's what I've told 'Art from the first. 'E's the murdering kind. I know, I've seen 'em on the pictures. 'Ow about a cup of tea?"

"Nothing I'd like better, seeing the pubs don't open yet," said Crook.

"You're all the same, you men," shouted Mrs. Hart over her shoulder, scuttling into the kitchen and beckoning to him to follow. "Wonder what your wife says about you."

"Nothing," said Crook placidly, following her and taking the best chair.

"Garn!" Mrs. Hart's excitement was getting the better of her. She threw large thick cups and plates onto the table. "They don't make that sort of woman. Unless she's dead too," she added as an afterthought, putting a loaf on a china plate and diving into a larder for margarine.

"She never existed," explained Crook mildly, tilting his brown bowler onto the back of his head. Mrs. Hart noticed the gesture with approval. Now she was sure he wasn't a gentleman. Gentlemen took off their hats when they came in. This was either a reporter from a newspaper, which was what she hoped, or he was a plain-clothes man, and even that she didn't really mind. Honest people don't have no cause to be afraid of the police, she liked to say. Crook could have told her a different story, but why destroy illusions? They're the butter on the bread of life, and that's rationed pretty close these days, as it is.

"Didn't she?" she asked, dashing more things—two knives, some potted meat in a jar, soft sugar in a bowl—onto the table. "Well, you'll be caught one of these days. There, 'ow about it? Now then, sit down and tell me what 'appened."

She sat down herself and, picking up the brown teapot that had been brewing on the hob since lunch, poured out the dark, thick stuff it contained.

"That's like tea, ain't it?" she demanded proudly. "You always could float a hen on my tea. But that coloured water Mrs. Durward used to drink!" She threw up her hands. " 'Elp yourself to sugar. Still, the gentry's like that. Why people want to go on bein' so envious of them I couldn't say."

Crook took up the cup of tea and stirred it energetically. "Do you think she was afraid of him?" he demanded.

"What, 'er? Not she. She was soft about 'im. Fancy 'er giving 'im all that money, the daft thing."

"You don't miss much, do you?" said Crook approvingly.

"I knoo there was somethin' queer about that pair from the start. Well, what did 'e marry 'er for at 'er age with 'er looks? Proper old-maid type she was too."

"Perhaps she was afraid not to give him the money."

"Not 'er. Why, 'e didn't expect it. But she fair pushed it on to 'im. 'I know men don't like taking things from women,' she said. Coo, I could 'ave told 'er different. Let 'er be married to 'Art for three months. Then she'd know they'll take everything off of you except your skin, and they'd take that if it was any use to them. Tell me"—her voice sank to a hoarse thrilling whisper—"was she 'ole or in pieces when they found 'er?"

"They haven't found her yet," Crook explained. "That's why I've come to you. I think you can help. You saw her that last night before she disappeared."

"Quivering like an ashbin she was. 'Stay with me tonight, Mrs. 'Art,' she begged me with tears in 'er eyes. 'Don't leave me alone with 'im,' she said. 'I'll get someone else down tomorrow.' "

"And you resisted even that plea? For shame. Where's your womanhood?" gibed Crook.

"Where you'd expect it of a decent woman of a night. In me own bed. I wouldn't 'ave stayed in that place, not for a basketful of monkeys."

"But you didn't mind leaving her?"

"She'd married 'im, 'adn't she? Not that I expected things to 'appen all of an 'eap the way they did. You could 'ave knocked me down with a fevver next morning when I come and find 'er gone."

"What time was that?"

"Eight o'clock, same as always. When I got to the 'ouse, believe it or not, they wasn't neither of them there. 'Adn't 'ad no breakfast nor nothing. I got the kettle on the boil and set about putting things straight. After a bit I 'eard a creak—that must 'a' bin the woodshed door—and Mr. Durward came in. I was in the kitchen. I called out, 'O, there you are. Thought you'd both gone for a 'oliday.' 'E looked ever so queer. 'Ad a bit of a rough-and-tumble if you ask me. Said 'e slipped up and 'urt himself, cut 'is face. Well, I'll say 'e slipped all right." She nodded like a little gipsy mandarin till the gold rings in her ears seemed to swing all ways at once. " 'Is boots was all over mud too. Ever such a job I 'ad with them. As for 'is clothes . . ."

"What was wrong there?"

"For one thing, 'e looked as if 'e'd been pulled through an 'edge backwards. All bits of twig and prickles and I don't know what. . . . But there was more."

"Yes?"

She leaned towards him. Her little mouth pursed itself into a rosette. "Blood," she hissed. "That's what 'e 'ad on 'is suit —blood."

"How can you be sure? He might simply have upset a glass of beer over himself."

"You don't go washing away beer in a basin," said Mrs. Hart darkly. "And that's what 'e'd been doing. When I went up to the bathroom I could see at once—there was guilty stains."

"How could you tell?" inquired Mr. Crook, refusing to be impressed.

"I'll tell you 'ow. There's a little cloth 'anging in the bathroom to swab round with, see? And when I went up later on there was marks on that little cloth, red marks. Oh, it was blood all right." She tossed her head triumphantly. " 'Nother thing. When I went along to 'is room there was the soot lying on the bed. I went to take it up, and it was all damp, but before I got a chance to look at it proper, 'e called out, 'There's no need to touch that. I'm taking it to be cleaned.' One thing, I could tell you where 'e generally goes."

"If he's the monster you imagine, he might go to a different place this time," said Crook casually.

"Go on, you can trace it, if you like. Don't tell me."

"Anything else to add to your story?" Crook inquired.

"I've only just begun. Well, when 'e come in 'e went upstairs right away, as I said. Then I 'eard 'is door open again—'e'd just shut it, see?—and 'e called over the banisters, 'Don't bother about getting breakfast for Mrs. Durward. She's 'ad to go to London in a 'urry. I've just driven 'er in.' 'What?' I said, 'without 'er breakfast?' 'She 'ad a cup of tea,' 'e told me, 'and she can get anything else she wants on the train.' Well, if she 'ad 'ad any tea she'd washed 'er cup and everything before she went, and they was never that considerate as a rule. Any'ow, the things from the night before was there. I began to think right away something funny was goin' on."

"I wonder you didn't go to the police," suggested Crook.

Mrs. Hart looked supercilious. "Easy to see you ain't married. Why, 'Art 'ud bash me to a jelly if I was to go stickin' my nose inside of a police station. Still, there wasn't nothing to stop me thinking, and I tell you, I thought a lot."

"And what happened then?" asked Crook, swigging down another cup of the poisonous tea.

"I know she never took no train to nowhere. Why, 'ow could she without so much as a tooth brush?"

"Sure about that?"

"P'raps you think she carried 'er luggage in her 'andbag. Well, it was a good 'ealthy affair but she couldn't 'ave packed everything into that. Besides, they were there on the dressing table, 'er brushes and combs and all 'er creams and so forth."

"And she never wrote for any of them?"

"She's where she can't write," Mrs. Hart assured him solemnly. "I'll stake my davy on that. And she 'adn't 'ad no tea. That kettle stays 'ot for an hour after it's bin boiled, and when I come it was as cold as Christmas. There's another thing." She tapped him mysteriously on the knee. "She never slept in 'er bed that night."

"How can you be sure?"

"I'll tell you. She was a proper lady, mind you, and like all ladies, she 'ad funny ideas. One of 'ers was to sleep with 'er 'ead low. When she 'ad breakfast in bed—not that she did much—she used to 'ave a pink cushion pushed in be'ind 'er back. Well, she 'ad 'er dinner in bed that night—'e said so, and any'ow the table was only used by one, as I could see in the morning, and she 'ad the pillow same as she always did. But she never took that pillow away. See what that means?" She quivered with the intensity of her excitement.

"That she didn't sleep low that evening."

"She didn't sleep at all. She didn't even try. She went to bed all right, and she 'ad 'er dinner—I found the tray in my kitching in the morning—and then before she could settle, 'e must have come up and—p'raps they 'ad words. I don't know. But I do know she didn't sleep in 'er bed that night. That cushion was there when I come in the morning."

"And you never heard any more about her?"

"Never 'ad the chance. 'Bout 'ar-pars-twelve 'Is Lordship come in to say 'e 'as to join 'er in town and they'll be shuttin' the 'ouse for a week anyway, so not to come on Monday and 'ere's a fortnight's wages. I knoo what that meant. Gettin' rid of me, 'e was. Oh, it made my blood boil to think of what 'e must 'ave done to 'er. Mind you, for all 'er soft ways, I liked 'er. She seemed such a poor 'elpless sort of creature. And there was times she 'ad a funny look about 'er, as if she'd gone to sleep in 'er own bed and woke up in a cageful of tigers."

"What do you think really happened?" Crook asked.

" 'E done 'er in. I'm as sure of that as I am my name's Lizzie 'Art. But 'e forgot about the luggage and 'e forgot about the pillow. Oh, well, I suppose no one can't think of everything."

"You seem to have thought of a good deal," Crook congratulated her.

"Any woman what's bin married to 'Art for twelve years learns to keep 'er wits about 'er," said the resourceful Mrs. Hart.

"I suppose you realize you haven't an atom of evidence—or doesn't a little thing like that trouble you?"

"Evidence!" Mrs. Hart sniffed. "I don't know 'ow much more you want. I s'pose if you was to find a cat lyin' on the rug all covered with canary fevvers and the cage empty, you'd say that wasn't proof against the cat. Well, the canary might 'ave lent 'im the fevvers to keep 'im warm, but some'ow I don't think 'e would 'ave."

Crook nodded. "Very twopence-coloured, aren't you? Your husband must have a grand time."

"Oh, 'Art, 'e don't take no notice. If 'e was to wake one morning and find a spotted lion in 'is bed instead o' me, 'e'd only tell it to go to 'ell for taking all the clothes."

"Well, it's a very interesting story," said Crook. "You know, you ought to go on the B.B.C."

"If 'e didn't know she wasn't coming back, would 'e 'ave brought that piece of good-for-nothing rubbish down with 'im?"

"The housekeeper?"

"If she's an 'ousekeeper," retorted Mrs. Hart grandly, "I'm Snow White AND the Seven Dwarfs."

"You can't say fairer than that," Crook agreed. "Look here, don't go publishing this all round the village. Yes, I know you think it's true, but what matters is proof. Truth by herself is no more good than coal without a match. Take it from me, I ought to know."

After her visitor had left, promising to call upon her again if there should be anything she could do further, Mrs. Hart ran up and down, washing the cups and preparing her husband's evening meal. She was now more than ever convinced that the body of her hapless employer was locked in the woodshed or else removed thence and buried in the woods. In her lively imagination she saw Durward, that pleasant, handsome gentleman, taking a hurricane lamp into the shed, fastening the door on the inside and, with the wind howling at the lock and the trees crying in the storm, carving up the corpse, packing it in biscuit tins and ultimately concealing it among the undergrowth and thick clay of The Bottom.

"They'll 'ave to act quick if they want to find 'er while you'd still know 'oo she was," she shot at her husband the instant he came in. "You'll never guess 'oo was 'ere this afternoon."

"That Mrs. 'Arris, I s'pose. I've a right to ask that woman for rent."

"Oh, well." Mrs. Hart was indulgent. "I pay the rent and I don't mind. Makes a bit of company. But it wasn't 'er today." She nodded mysteriously and her voice sank to a blood-curdling whisper. "Copper. Not in uniform, though."

"Copper 'ere?" Hart looked thunderstruck. "And you let 'im in?"

" 'E come about Mrs. Durward. That's goin' to be a slap-up show, you take my word. Might find my face in the paper, 'e said."

"If you don't 'urry up with my tea, you won't 'ave no face to put in no paper," was her husband's spirited retort.

"Now then," his wife reproved him. "No need to be 'asty. It all makes a change and I'm sure things are quiet enough 'ere, whatever they may be like in other parts of the world. Any'ow, it's 'uman nature to enjoy a murder."

"You take care one of these days you aren't enjoying your own."

Mrs. Hart chuckled. "You are a one!"

Her husband sighed. She was a maddening woman, but she earned enough for the two of them; she hadn't saddled him with brats; she never wanted to know who he'd been with, and it wouldn't be any pleasure bashing her in any case, because she

101

was perverse enough to get a sort of pleased notoriety out of it. He could just see her being interviewed. . . .

III

Mr. Crook drove riotously back to town. Entwistle was waiting for him in an agony of nervous impatience.

"What did you find?"

"That no one has seen your client since the 25th July, and that, according to Mrs. Hart, who's probably the most unreliable witness who ever took the stand, she handed her cheque over to her husband without even being asked to do it."

Mr. Entwistle moved uncomfortably. "Oh dear! It looks to me, Crook, as though this is going to be a matter for the police."

"Durward thinks the police may be the very people she's tryin' to avoid." He repeated Durward's story.

Mr. Entwistle shook an emphatic head. "I'm quite sure he's mistaken. I knew Miss Forbes and I am convinced that nothing in her past could justify such a fear. No, no, I anticipate the worst."

"Might be worth advertisin' before you call in the police," Crook suggested. "Save our faces all we can."

"And then, if nothing turns up . . ."

"Or even if something turns up," amended Crook grimly. "Y'know, it's an odd story. Why should she have to go to London so suddenly and at that hour? She hadn't any relations and, in any case, she'd have waited till after breakfast. Another point—it's not likely the post could have arrived in time for her to get this urgent letter, whatever it might be. That disposes of his story to Mrs. Hart. But one assumes that was a fairy tale for her benefit. As for his yarn that she just disappeared—well, it could be, Entwistle, it could be—though even so you'd expect her to take her hair brush with her. No, I fancy it'll come to the police sooner or later. Miss Martin 'ull see to that."

Entwistle shuddered in a gentlemanly manner. "This is all most unpleasant. Such a nice, quiet woman—no trouble at all. . . ."

"Law of compensation, p'raps," suggested Crook. "One thing, you'll be a public benefactor. This is the kind of story the public will eat with anything Lord Woolton still lets 'em have for breakfast."

Entwistle winced from the vulgarity implicit in practically everything his companion said, and went away to draw up a suitable notice.

🦜 🦜 🦜

CHAPTER NINE

THE PARAGRAPH in question appeared in the leading newspapers the following day. It read:

> Will Mrs. Agatha Durward (*née* Forbes), reported missing from her home, The Haven, Maplegrove, Dorset, since the 25th July, or anyone who knows her present whereabouts, communicate with Messrs. Murdoch, Carbery and Murdoch, Bloomsbury Street, W.C.1.

It was seen by a man called Geoffrey Dale, who instantly sent a telegram to Murdoch, Carbery and Murdoch.

> Calling tomorrow reference your advertisement.
>
> Dale

The next day there marched into Entwistle's office a tall, lean man walking with a slight limp; he had the sallow complexion of men who have spent much time in the East, and he broke into his story without preliminaries.

"I believe I saw this lady for whom you advertise on the last day on which she appears to have been seen by anyone," he announced, "and what perhaps is more to the point, I'm convinced I recognized the man she was with. Saw him years ago, only he wasn't calling himself Durward in those days."

"Know anything about the fellow's past that might throw any light on his present?" inquired Crook, who had been hurriedly summoned for the meeting. Entwistle frowned. This was not the way in which business was decently conducted. Not for the first time he recognized that decency and Crook didn't live in the same street.

"A good deal, though, mind you, the coroner's jury found it was death by misadventure. This fellow—Durward he calls himself now, I hear—saw to it that no other verdict was possible. Matter of fact, when I saw the pair of them in The Pigeons at Bridport on the 25th July I said to my friend that we ought to warn that woman. I've met the fellow on two previous occasions, and on each of 'em he was involved with a lady. And each time the lady paid."

Crook drew a finger suggestively across his throat. Mr. Entwistle shuddered.

"Not precisely. So far as I know, the first one got away with her life though not, by all accounts, with much else. That was in Malaya twenty years ago. Durward was the pretty new assistant on one of the rubber estates, the sort of chap women fall for and

103

men feel they'd like to know a bit more about. He was popular enough; it's an isolated part of the world, and if you aren't going to know your neighbours you may as well retire to a Buddhist monastery. Anyway, he was good-looking and danced well, and was a general good-sort in a professional sort of way. Any unmarried man's a catch out there, and there was no kind of card he couldn't handle. There was a girl there, the manager's daughter —we rather expected something to come of that. But it didn't. We were sorry for her at the time because her feelings where Durward was concerned were distressingly clear, but now—well, some people don't recognize luck when they meet it face to face. Matter of fact, she was cut out by another woman, the sister of the assistant manager's wife. She was a widow, a Mrs. Barley, and she came on a visit, a big, smart, handsome woman full of the latest gossip from London and with a trunkful of clothes from Paris. Goodness knows what use she expected those to be on a rubber estate. Still, from the moment she appeared, it was obvious what she wanted—and that was Durward. He was calling himself Paul in those days, by the way. The pair soon furnished quite a lot of gossip for the neighbourhood. They went all over the place together. They'd motor into Ipoh to dine and see the pictures, and they went for a long week-end to Kuala Lumpur. Mrs. Barley's sister, Mrs. Hopkinson, got a bit sour about it. She said it was the woman who paid all the expenses and was being fooled by a rascal. Mrs. Barley didn't seem to mind. She was fascinated by the fellow. There was even a certain amount of betting that the two would marry. Then something happened—Paul vanished, just disappeared overnight. He left a note for Mrs. Barley saying he'd been sent to oversee a neighbouring estate during the manager's sudden illness, but that proved to be untrue. Mrs. Hopkinson spread the story that a good deal of her sister's money had gone with him. He'd fooled her with some yarn about needing capital to become his own master, and it was generally assumed that he had promised her marriage as soon as that happened. No one knew the actual truth; Mrs. Barley shut her mouth and cleared out, and that was the last Malaya saw of the fellow.

"It was several years later when I met Paul again. I had been in Kenya and was coming home on sick leave on the *Demijohn*, one of the A. & B. boats. Almost the first person I saw when I came on deck (I'd been down in my cabin for the first three days) was this chap Paul. He looked very little older and he seemed as popular as ever, the life and soul of the ship. He had got his wife with him—it wasn't Mrs. Barley, of course. This was a girl fifteen or sixteen years younger than himself, but I saw on her

104

face the same infatuated expression I'd seen a dozen years earlier on the widow's. This was their honeymoon, a real romance someone told me. The girl was the daughter of a rich coffee planter who'd died the previous year, leaving her all his money. I admit frankly I didn't like the position. What I knew of Paul proved to me he wasn't overscrupulous where women were concerned, but even so I had no notion that, as soon as he'd got his hands on the money, he'd drop the girl overboard. Which," he added in a lower tone, "is actually what he seems to have done."

"Anyone else ever make that interestin' suggestion?" queried Crook, his eyes as bright and intent as a rat's.

"I dare say the thought went through a good many minds, or would have done if they'd known about Paul's earlier history, but in fact he got nothing but sympathy from the coroner. The tragedy took place less than a year after the wedding, and I heard of it by sheer chance. I was glancing through an evening paper when I saw a headline:

Heiress Drowned in Bathing Accident.

When I read the full story there was no room for doubt. The heiress was the girl I'd met aboard the *Demijohn*. It was a perfectly straightforward story. Paul had taken his wife out for a sail on a rather choppy sort of day, and when they were some way from shore she decided she'd like a swim. She could swim like a seal, by the way. The whole of this story, of course, depends on Paul's own evidence. He saw to it there should be no independent witnesses. The current just there ran pretty fast, but even so it shouldn't have been too much for a girl like that. She was a marvel in the water. He didn't go in, partly, he said, because he wasn't anything like up to her weight, but chiefly because someone had to stay in the boat to prevent its being swept away. Well, she dived overboard and he waited for her to come up. He said he wasn't anxious for the first minute because swimming under water was one of her strong suits; but when a couple of minutes had gone by and she hadn't reappeared he began to think there was something wrong. He still didn't go in after her for the reasons I've given you. I must say it all sounded damned plausible. He waited another minute and then began to shout. He got the jury on his side from the start by saying: 'I had no idea whether people under water could hear voices from above and I nearly split my lungs. I couldn't see a soul to hail and, anyway, if there'd been anyone within earshot he must have heard me. It was appalling.' He was a good actor—he'd been rather a talented amateur at one time, I believe, and he certainly looked the part. He said he rowed a few strokes in this direction and then a few strokes in that and then he yelled again. It took most of his energy to keep the boat where she was; she kept going with the current. Then he began to think she, his wife, I mean, must have come up under the boat and hit her head, injuring herself so badly she'd gone down like a stone. In a sea like that you wouldn't notice any particular bump. Of course, if it was genuine, it was a ghastly situation for any man. I tried to think what an innocent person would have done. Even if he had dived and got her, once the boat was out of reach, they'd both be done for. One member of the jury did suggest that the average husband would have taken some such chance rather than stay safely where he was, but the coroner crushed him all right. He was on the husband's side all along. He said it was one of the most awful and tragic predicaments in which a man could find himself. Anyhow, Paul seems to have hung about for nearly half an hour and then he abandoned hope and returned to shore. He insisted on collecting some men and a rope and going out again, but naturally they didn't find anything. The body itself wasn't washed up for several days, and by that time any jury would be hard put to it to say how she died. It was a rocky part of the coast." Dale stopped abruptly.

"Are you suggesting that this man murdered his wife?" demanded Entwistle in incredulous tones. "Have you never heard of the law of slander?"

Dale met his anger unmoved. "Afterwards it came out that she had recently made a will, leaving him every penny. There were no relatives to ask questions—they were all on the other side of the world—and even if there had been it would have made no difference. The hotel proprietor came forward to say he'd never seen a more devoted couple. The whole affair was magnificently stage-managed. You, sir," he turned powerfully to Entwistle, "may say it was coincidence, but I doubt whether even her arm is as long as that. First, Mrs. Barley. Next, this girl. And now you have the same man marrying a middle-aged woman who vanishes without a trace. And I dare say he isn't the loser by that."

"Mrs. Durward had made no will," said the still indignant Entwistle.

"So far as we know," Crook reminded him. "Anyway, we haven't got a corpse yet. I suppose you are sure of your man?" he added, turning to Dale.

"I'll swear to it in any court. But it could easily be proved. He had an odd birthmark on the right shoulder blade, shaped like a banana. I felt at the time there was something wrong. The lady

was in a state of collapse. I asked the manager who they were
and he said they were a couple called Durward who lunched at
The Pigeons every Friday. He didn't know where they lived and,
in any case, it's a bit difficult to go up to a woman you've never
set eyes on before and tell her you believe her husband to be a
successful murderer. You admit yourself I wouldn't have a leg
to stand on. The coroner's verdict had been Death by Misadventure
without the smallest suspicion attaching to the husband."

"It's all very interesting," Crook agreed thoughtfully. "Y'know,
Entwistle, there are times when I feel British justice is almost too
magnanimous to the criminal. If anything unfortunate should
have ·happened to Mrs. Durward, none of Durward's earlier
history will be admissible as evidence. Jury mustn't be prejudiced,
y'see. Durward may have murdered half a dozen wives, but we're
only concerned with the latest—not countin' the plump bit he's
got at The Haven at this moment."

"If she's been missing for three weeks and no one's come
forward who has seen her in that time, isn't the inference obvious?"
Dale suggested.

"What the soldier said ain't evidence. One thing, if she is
still above ground, she can't be usin' her own name. We'd be
bound to have news of her if she were. We've been at war for
nearly two years. You can't buy an ounce of butter at the present
time, not a ha'porth of cheese or a lamb chop without bein' registered. And if you're registered someone's goin' to know your name."

"That seems to me additional proof she can't be alive."

"There's no proof except a corpse. And then you've got to
be able to show it's her corpse. Of course, she may have snitched
someone else's ration book. She may even have bought one. No,
of course it's not legal, but it can be done. Or she may be lyin'
in a hospital, playin' she's lost her memory."

"She may actually have lost it," suggested Entwistle crisply.

Crook nodded. "Game and set, partner. All the same, we'll
hope that ain't true. It would make things very difficult for us."

"What are you planning to do?" Entwistle asked. He saw
from the look in his colleague's eye that he was laying the foundation
of some plot whose details he'd probably keep to himself. The
worst of Crook, thought Entwistle, was his unorthodoxy. He saw
himself being dragged reluctantly at the tail of some fantastic pro-
cession organized by this red-headed brigand, who liked fantasy
for its own sake. Had he been a religious man, he would have
prayed in all sincerity that Agatha's body might be found without
delay, and Crook's guns spiked before they could be brought
into action.

During the next few days Crook worked mostly underground, testing Durward's story on every point, interviewing station officials at Bridport and the Hiawatha's secretary in London. He would have seen Grace Knowles, too, though, in fact, she couldn't have helped him but she was still away, no one quite knew where. Miss Randall, the secretary of the Hiawatha, said that of course she knew Miss Forbes, whose marriage was regarded as a wartime romance, but that she hadn't seen her lately. In fact, she didn't think she'd been in the club since the wedding.

"You're quite sure about that? She left her home in Maplegrove about three weeks ago and seems to have vanished into air."

"One of our members did say something about an advertisement," acknowledged Miss Randall. "I do hope nothing is wrong."

"Oh, well, you know what that novelist fellow says, 'Hope is not yet taxed.' All the same, I wouldn't like to bet on it. Is there any chance Mrs. Durward might have come in during that last week of July or the first week of August and you not see her?"

"She couldn't have come in during July because the club was closed for painting and cleaning, and our members were accommodated elsewhere. And I can assure you from my own knowledge she has not been in since."

"That seems to put the kibosh on things," Crook agreed. "Suppose someone had telephoned during that first week, was there anyone here to take messages?"

"We had one of the men staff at the hall telephone, but that was all. I was out of London myself during the last half of July."

"Any chance of seeing the chap who was in the hall? Just as a matter of routine, you understand."

Miss Randall sent for the man, who was emphatic in his conviction that no message had been received from Mrs. Durward since her marriage. Crook also saw Hassell, who was in charge of the dining room, and Mrs. Bones and Mrs. Bott from the cloakroom, from all of whom he elicited the same reply. Nor was he more successful at Bridport. The station master said there was no train to town before nine a.m. Crook nodded his satisfaction.

> *"The shroud is done. Death muttered, toe to chin.*
> *He snapped the ends and turned the needles in.*

"Now, Mr. Murdering Durward, let's see what you can make of this," he observed gaily to empty air, and took his way to The Pigeons.

It was a Friday and the place was pretty full. Nevertheless

Crook managed to find a small table unoccupied and ordered beer and the presence of the manager.

"The manager, sir?"

"Scotland Yard," said Crook, without turning a hair. "But don't give me away."

The manager came at a run. "My name's Crook," said the Criminals' Hope. "Have some of your own beer, won't you? Strictly in confidence, I'm investigating the disappearance of a Mrs. Durward, whom I think you know by sight."

The manager looked instantly sympathetic. "Certainly I do. She and her husband used to come here every Friday. He still comes—never misses—though now he comes alone. I did see something in the paper . . ." for, of course, it hadn't been possible to keep the affair out of the press. "Loss of memory, he was telling me. Very sad. They seemed such a devoted couple. Of course, she wasn't what you'd call a young woman, and there's no doubt about it this war does get some people down."

"It does," agreed Crook. "Right down. As low as six feet sometimes. Do you know if Mr. Durward's here yet?"

"It's a bit early—no, there he comes now."

"That's all right," said Crook. "He knows me." His manner dismissed the manager. "Morning to you," he added to Durward.

Durward paused in his stride. "Oh! Good morning."

"I thought it was a safe bet to find you here on a Friday," said Crook. "Have some beer."

"Not at the moment, thanks. It doesn't seem quite the time . . ."

"Any time's the time for beer. I was coming along to see you, but then I recollected this was your marketing day. Waiting for anyone?"

Durward shook his head.

"P'raps you'll lunch with me. What, my dear chap? Oh, of course you will. I shan't pay for your lunch, you know. It'll all go into the account."

A little reluctantly Durward accompanied him from the lounge to the dining room.

"Am I to take it that your presence here means you've learnt something fresh about Agatha?" he inquired, as the waiter took their order and left them.

"Only that two negatives don't make a positive. No one seems to have set eyes on her since she left The Haven on the 25th—26th, rather, since she went early that morning."

Durward moved restlessly. "What's the next step?"

"If we don't satisfy Miss Martin, she can exercise her citizen's right to go to the police."

ANTHONY GILBERT

"Her right?" exploded Durward. "What on earth is it to Miss Martin what my wife chooses to do?"

"Any citizen's got the right to go to the police and say he feels suspicious about a neighbour who's disappeared."

"But what affair is it of hers?"

"Miss Martin's a lady with a great sense of what she owes the community. She likes to take her share. If things are wrong, what's she there for but to put 'em right?"

"What evidence has she that anything's wrong? I should have supposed that if there was any mystery about my wife, I should be the person with prior claim to approach the authorities."

"So you had," replied Crook simply. "You had it for three whole weeks after the lady disappeared and you didn't use it."

"Did you expect me to put a private agent on to her?"

"No use asking me. I wouldn't know. But—well, look at the thing in its broad aspect. Suppose no one but a relative could inquire if the lady next door or the gent over the way vanished without a trace. Why, it's putting a premium on crime, simply askin' people to dispose of their families when they got a bit of a nuisance. Now, now, nothing personal, you understand. If Miss Martin does take this thing up officially, the first thing to happen will be the police 'ull come to ask if you've any information about the lady's whereabouts. You'll tell them the story you told me— at least, if you're wise you will."

"And then? Look here, Crook, I always understood that if an adult wanted to disappear and the police had no case against him or her as, of course, is the position here, this was a free country."

Crook tapped him warningly on the arm. "Don't try tellin' a lawyer that," he observed. "You believe it, if you like, though most likely you don't, but we know just how much freedom there is for the individual. Mind you, the average person has all the liberty that's good for him. Freedom's like beer or money— different people can stand a different amount. It's absolutely thrown away on some, just makes them sick, while others can't get along without it. Besides, there's the undeniable fact that our Miss Martin don't believe Mrs. Durward disappeared of her own free will."

"What does she mean to insinuate?"

"You don't want me to dot all the i's and cross all the t's for you, do you?"

Durward laughed harshly. "There's no need. Since you've been kind enough to ventilate this affair in the press, you'd be surprised at some of the unsigned letters I find in my box."

"It would take a lot more than obscene abuse to surprise me,"

110

Crook assured him. "LOOK here, I know you think we've been damned high-handed about this . . ."

"Well, haven't you?" Durward inquired.

"What would you do yourself, if you had papers requiring a client's signature and you couldn't find your client? You'd ask her husband's co-operation in unearthing her, wouldn't you? Well, that's all we've done."

"For a start," Durward sounded grim. "Don't tell me the matter ends there."

"And don't tell me you want it to. Good heavens, man, you're anxious about your wife, aren't you?"

Durward stubbed out a cigarette. "I'd like to know more about Agatha's trouble before I get the police on her track. You don't know my wife. I do. If she gets desperate she may do —anything."

"On the other hand, if she thinks you'll let her vanish into space without a word, she may not think that exactly complimentary, either."

"There's always the chance that she's lost her memory," hazarded Durward.

"Miss Martin's afraid she may have lost a lot more than that. And if that should be the case, we're still her lawyers. We're responsible for her estate. By the way, did she ever make a will?"

"She often talked about it—said as soon as she came to town she'd see Entwistle, but so far as I know she never did."

"Nor as far as Entwistle knows, either."

"Then the odds are she didn't. Do you mean to say the police will follow this up? I call that insufferable."

Crook leaned towards him confidentially. "Take my tip and don't be so damned high-handed when they do. There are quite a few people who think it odd you didn't approach the police yourself. Not delicate-minded people who'd appreciate your motives, but common blundering chaps who see something fishy everywhere. What you have to remember is that they're the majority, they're the kind of people you find on a coroner's jury— but perhaps you don't know anything about coroner's juries?"

"I haven't much experience," agreed Durward, not turning a hair. "Perhaps you'll give me some idea what I ought to expect."

"First of all the police 'ull tell you, very nicely indeed, that they've had inquiries about Mrs. Durward, and they'd like your assurance that she's all right. When you say you can't give them that, they'll start looking for their own assurance."

"Beginning with my house?"

"Well, it was her house too."

"Quite. But they can't be mad enough to think I've got her hidden there."

"In any case, you won't have by the time they arrive."

Durward looked really shocked. "I believe you think—my God, Crook! You can come along with me now, if you like, and look for yourself."

"Your suggestion, not mine," Crook pointed out.

"No sense giving the police an opportunity of saying I was forewarned." Suddenly he put his hands over his face for an instant. "You know, this seems fantastic. It's barely possible that this is happening to me. I suppose all chaps in my position feel that."

"They say so," Crook agreed. "You know, I think you're being very wise over this. Mind you, I don't expect to find a thing, but . . ."

"You won't be as surprised as I if you do." Durward pushed back his chair and rose a little noisily. As he looked round the room he seemed to realize for the first time that he had been a focus for interested curiosity. His colour deepened. "Come on," he adjured Crook. "The sooner this mystery's cleared up, the better. Who on earth could have guessed that things would turn out like this?"

* * *

The Haven was a small house, consisting of two floors, with very little cupboard space. You couldn't, reflected Crook, have hidden a good-sized baby there. In the wardrobe in the main bedroom hung a number of dresses and suits all of neat old-fashioned style, while the dressing table drawers contained a quantity of subdued, beautifully kept underwear. He closed the last of them and went to stand at the window, looking over the garden Agatha had made with such pride. The snapdragons were all out in the borders and the hollyhocks she had put in as small plants had opened their papery pink flowers.

"I used to make those as a kid," said Crook suddenly. "Pink crepe paper, doubled and pleated, or cut out in points, and secured with a bit of wire. Roses we called 'em, however they turned out. I was quite a dab at it." He looked with some surprise at his short thick fingers, as though he scarcely believed they had ever been capable of such finicking work.

"Agatha wanted to grow roses here," said Durward, "but the soil's not very promising."

Crook thought of the missing woman, who must have stood here often, planning her garden and watching it grow. Had she known at the end what lay just ahead? Had she gone down into the dark mercifully unaware of what was happening to her? Had she been afraid? Incredulous? It wasn't a nice thought. He moved abruptly.

"What's that shed?"

"That's where I keep our boxes—there's no lumber room, as you see—and the gardening tools; and I do a bit of carpentering there. I made that little book rest and put up those shelves for Agatha's shoes. If you want to go through that too—perhaps you better."

"I feel the authorities would consider the woodshed most important," agreed Crook gravely, and followed his host downstairs.

The shed, that was clearly kept locked, contained a number of boxes and packing cases and an old-fashioned black-domed trunk.

"I'll open all these for you," said Durward in a voice of deathly calm, "just to make sure my wife—my wife—isn't in any of them."

"On the small side, aren't they?" Crook spoke with deliberate offensiveness.

"All the same, there might be a hip joint." The man's voice was deathly in its quiet. With a sort of concentrated fury, he flung up the lids, disclosing the most bizarre and irrelevant of contents. Crook was impressed by the quantity and variety of them.

"Didn't know you'd been on the stage," he observed.

"I did a lot of amateur acting when I was out East. I was fool enough to let that out to Miss Martin, which is why she kept bothering me. If I'd had any sense I'd have told her I couldn't act for little apples, and none of this might have happened."

"If you'd had any experience you'd have told her the facts when she came inquiring for Mrs. Durward," Crook told him drily. "If you'd said, 'My wife and I have separated,' you'd have spiked her guns at once. Mind you, that woman won't stick at much, but even she would hardly have begun investigations in that case. It's an odd thing how often truth is the best policy and how seldom chaps realize it."

"I dare say, if I'd had a little more experience, I should have thought of that," Durward agreed. "As it was, I was still feeling a bit sensitive. . . ." He opened the big black trunk for his visitor's benefit. It was filled almost to the top with books. "I ought to have unpacked those. I've been meaning to ever since I got here, but you know how it is. One puts things off. I haven't opened the thing since I arrived."

Crook glanced casually at the top layer. Nothing of much interest there, he thought. A good many detective stories, an explanation of the fall of France, two or three historical novels, a travel book by Peter Fleming. He picked up the latter and glanced through it. Durward watched him as he bent over the trunk to replace the volume in his hand.

"Who did this belong to?" Crook inquired, still doubled over the box.

"Oh—my mother. No, she's not alive now. She died abroad at the end of the last war."

"And after that? Who had it after that?"

"Who?" Durward scowled. "Why, no one except myself."

"But you lent it to a friend, perhaps. Oh, come, my dear chap, you've forgotten. I'm convinced you lent it to a friend."

"I did nothing of the kind. It's never been used for anything but books for the last twenty years."

Crook straightened himself at last. "Be your age," he said. "When did you see a book wearing a gee-gaw like that?"

And he held out his hand, on the palm of which was a round clip-on pearl earring.

❦ ❦ ❦

114

CHAPTER TEN

I

THE MORON was waiting in the kitchen when Durward came back from seeing Crook drive away.

"Whatever did that man want?" she inquired. "I must say I should have thought it was your wife's affair if she wanted to go away."

"Apparently it's the affair of the whole country."

She shrank from his white set face, his blazing eyes that looked almost black now.

"Eddie, what do you mean? There wasn't really anything *wrong?*"

"Of course not. Or, if there was, Agatha didn't confide in me. But she's put me in the devil of a hole, sneaking off like this. Of course she'll turn up sometime. . . ."

"Then it isn't true what they're saying about her in the village?"

He caught her plump shoulders in his thin, muscular hands. "And what are they saying in the village?"

"That she—she killed herself. Mr. Field at the grocer's was ever so disobliging only this morning."

"I suppose they think I drove her to suicide. Or perhaps that I murdered her."

She tried to twist away from that pitiless grip. "I never heard them say that."

"You couldn't have listened hard enough." Suddenly he let her go. "Who would have thought that, after the kind of adventures I've had all my life, the risks I've taken, it should be a woman like that who'd ruin me?"

The moron gave him a wild, piercing look. "Eddie, you don't know where she is, do you? You don't!"

"If I knew where she was I'd drag her from there to here by the hair," said Durward, with quite appalling ferocity. "Getting me into a jam like this. The whole country's going to be talking of it in twenty-four hours."

Daisy touched him fearfully on the arm. "Eddie, why don't you take a bit of a holiday? Get away from all this. It's getting on your nerves; really it is."

"That's a wonderful suggestion," replied Durward brutally. "Cut and run and sign my own death warrant. Perhaps that's what you want me to do."

"Oh, Eddie, how can you say such things?"

She had no brains to speak of, but she had instinct, like an

115

animal, and she knew that he was afraid. This fact made her eager to leave before trouble developed. She didn't call it deserting a sinking ship—it was just self-preservation. She thought with bitter regret of her carefully hoarded hundred and fifty pounds; she didn't want to lose that. But she remembered Agatha Durward who, perhaps, had had money too, and was now probably only her husband knew where. She slipped upstairs and began quietly putting her things together. Here Edmund found her a little later.

"What do you think you're doing?" Edmund demanded.

"I thought perhaps you'd rather I went for a bit, Eddie," she faltered.

He looked so white—with rage? with dread?—she couldn't be sure—that involuntarily she stepped back.

"Well, if they're asking questions it mightn't look too good me being here." She could believe anything now, believe he had done his poor wife in. He looked as if in a minute he'd take her by the throat too.

"That's a fine idea," he exclaimed. "Let the whole world see that the women who come to live with me all vanish without notice. Perhaps next week there'll be paragraphs in the paper about you." He came a step nearer. She screamed. It reminded him of Agatha, who had screamed too. . . .

Downstairs a bell rang unexpectedly. They had been so much engaged in their brief passage of arms that neither had heard feet approaching.

"Go and see who that is," Durward ordered.

"Eddie, no, I—suppose it's the police?"

"Well, what have you got to hide?"

"Nothing, but . . ."

"But you think I have. Go on down."

Stumbling, rubbing the tears out of her pale, shallow eyes, she hurried down the narrow stairs. He thought, as he'd thought before, "Quite a little push 'ud do it." He heard the front door open, and listened intently. Damn it, it was the police. That fellow, Crook, was a fast worker. He stood rigid for a moment, wondering about the next move. He'd been in tight corners before, but none quite like this.

The moron's voice came nervously up the stairs. "Mr. Durward, it's—there's a gentleman to see you."

He fitted the mask of composure over his haggard features. "For me? Oh, good evening. You're . . ."

"Inspector Merton, sir." He offered his credentials. "There are just one or two questions I wanted to ask you, if you don't mind."

The examination followed the familiar ground. Durward played his part well, answering the questions clearly, but without the treacherous glibness that so easily arouses suspicions in the official breast. Now and again he paused for thought. He gave the impression of a man honestly trying to help the police, yet not altogether unaware that he might himself stand in danger.

Merton, making his report later, said, "He's either a damn good actor, or else he's as innocent as he'd like us to believe."

They came at length to the fatal presence of the earring in the black trunk.

"Did Mrs. Durward ever use the trunk for her own purposes?"

Durward shook his head. "It was packed with books and had been for a considerable time. I can only suggest that the earring got caught in one of the cross-straps of the lid (there was a variety of pockets and red webbing strapping on the inner side of this) and had stayed there unnoticed for years. As I told Mr. Crook, the trunk once belonged to my mother and this may easily have been hers."

"You don't positively identify it?"

"How can I possibly identify it? My mother died over twenty years ago. But it's a very ordinary kind of earring. My wife had some very similar, though there again I wouldn't dream of saying, 'I know this is one of hers.' Most ladies who wear earrings have a pair of pearl studs."

The inspector agreed that this was so. Then he asked for Daisy.

"You can see her, of course, but I'm afraid she won't be able to help you much. She only came down here after my wife left me."

"I'd like to see her just the same, as a matter of routine."

The moron, quivering with fear, crept into the room. No, she agreed, she hadn't known Mr. Durward long. She had met him in London, actually in a district train. She had dropped her handbag and he'd picked it up. She had said, 'Well, fancy, don't know what I'd do without that,' and he had said, 'No. You practically haven't an identity without your bag these days.' They had got out at the same station—Victoria—and he had offered her tea. After tea they went to the pictures. He told her he was very lonely as his wife had left him. She had no notion that the separation had been so recent, or she wouldn't have accepted his suggestion that she should come to The Haven as his housekeeper. She was a housekeeper by profession and had just given up a post, as the lady was going into an hotel and closing her flat. Durward had told her that he would soon be leaving The Haven and starting in business. She admitted she had fancied having a business of her own when she could raise sufficient capital, and he had suggested they should go into partnership.

"And it was on that understanding that you came down here, Miss—er——"

"Morris, Daisy Morris. He said we could discuss details, and he must have someone to look after him till the lease came to an end."

"Did he tell you what sort of business he proposed?"

"He thought of getting a house in a safe area and taking guests. He said there was a lot of money in it if it was properly run but, of course, it took a good deal to get started. We'd have to buy furniture and all and advertise."

"And you gave him money?"

"All I had, about a hundred and fifty pounds. The hundred was left me by a lady I'd worked for for eight years, and the rest was savings. Mr. Durward told me he had his eye on a house, but it was rather more than he could afford. He thought we might go round together and look for something suitable."

"He asked you for your money?"

"Well, not exactly, but he said it would look better if he wrote the cheque. He had some money in the bank, and he was selling some stocks, but, owing to the war, that took some time, and the sooner we started the better."

"So you handed it over of your own free will?"

"Yes. On the understanding it was for the house."

"Had you done anything about seeing one?"

"He said a man he knew was looking out for one for him, and as soon as he heard of anything likely we'd go and inspect it. He said we couldn't go driving round the country because of the petrol."

"He never spoke to you of marriage?"

"How could he? He had a wife, though she'd left him. But he said he'd do the right thing by me."

Merton nodded. He knew this vacuous type of mind. She'd been infatuated by Durward, of course, and carried away by his tale of desertion. Merton hadn't the slightest doubt of the position. He wondered how long Durward had intended to wait before he shook off this incubus also. He didn't imagine murder had been on this program. It wasn't necessary to murder women like Daisy Morris. Most likely he'd play the tea-shop game on her: leave her for a minute—these rogues were astoundingly unoriginal—and disappear by another entrance, leaving her to settle for the two of them at the cash desk.

"I'd like to go back to London," the moron was quavering. "I don't know anything about his wife, never set eyes on her, and I don't like this place. I'm not accustomed to this sort of thing."

By this sort of thing she meant Crook and the police, as the inspector well knew. "He ought to give me back my money, though. You're the police, you ought to make him."

"That's not our job. You handed it over of your own free will."

Daisy began to cry. "I don't like this house. I don't like the way things are going. I don't feel safe here for another night."

"Nothing 'ull happen to you so long as we've got the case in hand," Merton assured her.

"You can't keep me here. You've got nothing on me."

"We'll have to check up on your story," Merton told her. "If you've done nothing wrong you'll be all right."

"Of course I've done nothing wrong," she snivelled.

"Then what have you got to worry about?" He shut his notebook with a snap.

"Are you coming back?"

"That depends," said Merton crisply.

He drove off in the police car, taking Durward with him. He said he wanted his statement drawn up and signed at the station. When the coast was clear he returned with Mrs. Hart, in a condition of twittering excitement. She had been shown the earring, but would go no further than saying it was like one Mrs. Durward had worn, but earrings were all so alike these days she wouldn't definitely commit herself. This was a setback for the police, who would have had more to go on if they could have started with the premise that this bauble could have belonged to the missing woman and none other. Under police supervision, she examined Agatha's wardrobe and said at once, "What's 'appened to that curly gray coat she 'ad? And the suit she wore with it?"

"She must have taken them with her," suggested Merton.

"If you ask me, she won't want no clothes where she is. Besides, they was 'anging in this very cupboard the day after she'd gone. I 'ad a look. And where's 'er suitcase? That was in the corner there."

"Mr. Durward may have put it with the other boxes in the woodshed. Could you identify it?"

" 'Course I could identify it—if it's there."

But, confronted by the conglomeration of luggage in the shed, she found herself at a loss.

"It wasn't none of these I'll take my davy. Wonder if 'e sold it or give it to that—trollop 'e's got in poor Mrs. Durward's place. One thing, that dress she's wearing now is one of 'ers. Many's the time she wore it during that scrap of 'ot weather we 'ad in June. Like 'er imperence. But I could see the sort she was the minute I set eyes on 'er."

119

II

The result of all these inquiries was that Merton told Durward he was not satisfied with the position and, no further news of Agatha being received, he proposed to drag the various ponds in the woods.

Durward looked a little white. "You consider that necessary?"

"We can't leave anything to chance, and it's an odd thing that no one's heard anything of her. Anyway, if we find nothing, that'll be a relief to you, won't it?"

"And if you don't find her there, I suppose you intend to dig over the whole Bottom? You'll have your work cut out, won't you? I should think the war might be over by the time you're through." He threw up his hands in a gesture of despair. "Good God, man, do you realize that the lady you're talking about so cold-bloodedly is my wife? Do you imagine I'm made of stone?"

"I'm sorry, sir," said Merton civilly. "But you must be more anxious than anyone to have her found."

"I never dreamed you'd look for her—here."

"We've tried everything else—hospitals, mortuaries, everything. There's nothing more left."

Durward nodded. He knew it was true. Agatha had disappeared as though she had been a figure on a slate to be wiped off with a bit of damp sponge. Since her return to The Haven on the night of the 25th July no one had come forward who could vouch for seeing her.

The ponds were systematically dragged without bringing anything to light beyond some old boots, a couple of battered pans and a number of skeletons of small animals, probably cats. Inquiries in other directions were still in progress, but without result. The cashier at the Westmoreland Bank was interviewed, but refused to commit himself. The customer might have been Agatha, but it might also have been someone disguised as Agatha. The police had no choice. When the ponds had been dealt with, they began the heart-breaking task of looking for the body in the crowded woods of The Bottom.

"Durward's right," said Sergeant Ramsay to his superior officer. "He'll be a graybeard before we've turned all this over."

Experts were summoned to examine the ground for signs of recent digging, but the weather was against them. There had been quantities of heavy rain of late, amounting in places to floods, that had dislodged great masses of earth, and would certainly have blotted out any conceivable clue.

"This chap's got the laugh of us all right," Ramsay continued.

"This is the kind of job that's handed on from father to son."

"That'll be all right," said Merton heartily. "Just you see your son's proud of his dad's sticking power, that's all."

Durward watched them from the windows of The Haven. It had been suggested to him that he might prefer to shift to The Crown, but he had refused the offer. At no time an insensitive man, he realized to the full the feelings of the villagers, by whom Agatha had been quite kindly regarded. She was, of course, a stranger, and it took ten years before strangers were accepted, but then Durward was a stranger, too, and not a particularly desirable one. The notion that she might have come to a miserable end, with her husband for the instrument that encompassed it, spread far and wide. Durward was conscious of odd and antagonistic glances when he went out, and there were even times when he was grateful for the fellow who unobtrusively shadowed him wherever he went. Too late he realized that he had done himself an active disservice by bringing Daisy Morris to The Haven. No one believed in her housekeeping status, and more than one woman followed Mrs. Hart's example in saying that hanging was too good for the likes of him.

"You'd better be careful," Ramsay told the little cockney, "you're a lot too free with that tongue of yours and that's a fact."

"It's a free country," retorted the unabashed Lizzie Hart. "And why are we fighting this war if it isn't to keep it so?"

"If you don't look out you'll find yourself in court," the policeman warned her.

"And 'oo's going to take me there? Mr. Murdering Durward? Not likely."

On the whole Durward was better off at The Haven than he would have been elsewhere. The police were civil and noncommittal. The labourers, who had been engaged to assist with the digging, were told to keep their mouths shut. All the same, this war of nerves told on their quarry. Sometimes he couldn't sleep at night; then the moron would see him steal softly to the window, draw back the curtains and peer out. She began to catch the infection of his fear. Again she told Merton she wanted to return to town. A man who had done away with one woman, she said tearfully, wouldn't have much compunction in treating a second in a similar manner.

"Done away?" repeated Merton. "Meaning, you've been suppressing evidence?"

"I never," she protested.

"Then what right have you got to say he's done away with anyone? You be careful or you'll find yourself in court."

Durward, of course, was aware of the change in her. He knew that she watched his movements, and he contracted the habit of glancing upwards as he crossed the hall to see if he was being observed from behind the banisters. In a room he would switch round sharply, as though expecting to find her peeping through the crack of the door. Once he accused her fiercely of spying on him.

"I'm not doing anything of the sort, Eddie," she protested tearfully. "If you really think I'm like that, you'd better give me back my money and let me go."

But when she spoke of the money, Durward's face grew hard and sullen.

"I can't get hold of the money at present. I've told you that a dozen times."

"You said you were going to put it into a little business. Well, you haven't, have you?"

"Well, it's mortgaged, if you know what that means."

"That I can't have it, I suppose. Then what am I to do? I can't do anything without money."

"Then stay quietly here and don't drive me mad with your insane questions."

"There's no need to bite my head off like that. Anyone would think you really had something to be afraid of. But even the police can't find a body that isn't there."

Durward did not reply. Her face seemed to shrink and harden. "Can they?" she repeated.

"Of course not. What idiotic things you say, Daisy."

"Only—p'raps she is there. P'raps that's why you jump when anyone speaks. P'raps that's why you were so keen on me coming down here, because you didn't want to be alone with her."

"Stop it, you fool." All the suavity she had loved in him and that had charmed her life's savings out of her had vanished. "What are you trying to do? Hang me? And for God's sake, don't start about the money again. I've told you you can't have it and that's the end of it."

At that the moron lost her head completely. "You're nothing but a thief and a swindler," she shouted. "I wouldn't be surprised if you did kill her; I wouldn't be surprised if you'd killed hundreds of women and buried them all. . . ."

He caught her by the shoulders, shaking her furiously.

"You're damned lucky not to be underground yourself," he said. Suddenly he was quiet. "I'm sorry about that," he told her. "But can't you see I'm half crazy? I can't help believing now that Agatha is dead. If she weren't, she'd have come forward, if only to clear me of this monstrous suspicion. No, she's not buried in the woods, whatever you may think, but even if they find her and it's clear I couldn't have had a hand in her death, it'll be nearly as bad for me. They'll think I so ill-treated her I drove her to her death, with that damned Mrs. Hart revelling in the whole thing, creating false impressions all over the place." He looked to the moron for a word or expression of comfort. But she, leaning against the wall, well out of reach, only asked sullenly, "What happened to her money? Is that mortgaged too?"

Then he knew that he had no friends at all.

III

In public, however, he maintained an admirable surface composure. When the police wanted accommodation of any kind he was ready to offer it. He answered their questions again and again, refused to be intimidated by the glances of some of the labourers who were working in The Bottom, and on fine days would even take a deck chair and sit in the little garden Agatha had made with such high hopes, watching the men's figures moving in and out of the trees.

"He's got a nerve," commented one of the diggers. "Why, he may be sitting on her grave for all we know."

"Hell," said the sergeant, "so he may."

The suggestion was not without precedent. The following morning he told Durward they were proposing to dig over the garden. Durward looked shocked. "Is that really necessary? My wife took a great deal of trouble over it, and you can see for yourself it's not been disturbed."

"We won't do more harm than we can help," Ramsay promised him.

Durward went back to the house. It was a Friday and the moron had already departed for Bridport. He had watched her go from an upper window and wished to heaven she need never return. Now he had to put into action a plan made at the beginning of the police campaign. He had always known that if they began digging in the garden he must get away somehow. And the time was short. The garden was small and there were a lot of men. His only serious stumbling block was Miller. The fellow dogged him like a shadow. As a matter of practice, he had several times tried to throw the man off his trail, but never with success.

"Keep your head," he told himself. "The race isn't to the swift but to the cunning. And so long as you know more than the police, you hold the ace. It's when they know as much as you that you're sunk."

He had laid plans for this getaway days ago, and now he proceeded to put them into action. Too much depended on the next half-hour for him to make a mistake.

CHAPTER ELEVEN

THE HAVEN was now like a beleaguered fortress. Look in any direction and you saw a man in uniform; even in the garden the labourers dug under police supervision. There seemed as much chance for a man in mufti to walk out unaccompanied as for a British prisoner of war in a German camp to pass unnoticed between his guards. Nature, however, teaches the observant many lessons. In cold countries where the snow lies deep for many weeks at a time certain animals and birds change their coats from summer brown to the bluish white tinge of their surroundings. With these examples in mind, Durward planned his escape.

There was, he knew, no time to lose; and it was his good fortune that this should be Friday, when the moron was out of the way. Her inane questions were driving him mad; certainly she would have ruined such chances as were his had she been on the premises. In the garden the men sweated and dug; in the woods the police patrolled. In the grounds in front of the house Miller hung about, watchful for his quarry. Durward saw it all from an upper window and proceeded with his plan. A little later one of the ubiquitous police walked out of the side door of The Haven and round to the front of the house, where a police car was standing. This, fortunately, had been left unlocked. The policeman opened the door, stepped in and began to back the car for the turn into the drive. His heart was thudding like a piston rod, shaking him to pieces. Everything now depended on his own coolness. He had taken the first turn of the drive when he saw Miller like a lion in the way. Miller would almost certainly come down to ascertain the identity of the driver. It was an instant of crisis. It was lucky from the hunted man's point of view that a little earlier the rain had begun to fall, thin and fine, blurring the glass of the windows. The automatic wiper was in action, but the rest of the glass protected the driver's face from curious glances. With the coolness of desperation, he wound down the window and, putting out his head, called to the approaching man, "Look out for your fellow, Miller. He was slipping down in the direction of the woods and going damn' fast at that."

"He's got a hope," said Miller, but he hastened his steps. Surely, he was thinking, those chaps in the garden won't let him get through. Besides, there are men in the woods.

As he entered the house the first thing to catch his eye was an envelope lying on the hall table, addressed to Inspector Merton in Durward's writing. It was a characteristic hand, difficult to imitate. Miller, after an instant's indecision, slit the flap. Merton wasn't on the premises at the moment, having business elsewhere. The note said:

Last time you dragged the pond you drew blank. This time you may be more fortunate. Since you have taken from me my good name, my reputation, you may as well have my life to complete the work. Then perhaps justice will be satisfied.

"Very lah-di-dah," was Miller's unemotional comment, as he stuffed the note into his pocket and began to run towards the woods. He stopped to ask one or two of the men if they had seen Durward, but they all said they hadn't. There was no sign of a tall figure moving through the trees, and a faint stab of anxiety pierced Miller's breast. The pond was set very deeply among the trees, some distance from the house. Once a man drew near it, it would be difficult to distinguish him from the undergrowth. As Miller drew nearer, his feet began to slip on the muddy surface, rendered more untrustworthy than usual by the falling rain.

"If he was making for this, it looks as though he's got there already," muttered Miller apprehensively, putting up his hand to rub the fine needles of rain from his eyes. "How the devil did those chaps in the garden miss him? They know the chief's instructions. And why didn't that chap himself, whoever he was, pull him in?"

He reached the pond's edge and stooped to examine the ground about the edge. When he straightened himself again it was with a sigh of relief. His own footsteps were there for all to see, but he was prepared to swear that no other man had come this way since the rain started. All the same, his troubles were by no means over. If Durward had been seen coming in the direction of the pond, the odds were he had turned aside and struck into the denser part of the wood. There are more ways of committing suicide than by drowning. An uglier thought occurred to him. Had Durward fooled him by the simplest of all tricks? While Miller was making his way down to the pond, was the suspect moving in another direction, perhaps seeking some path among the trees as yet unknown to the police? The woods were so extensive that once he was in them he stood a good chance of making his escape. All the same, Miller was partly reassured by the recollection that Durward's hat had been hanging in the hall as he passed through. Surely he would not risk going into a town where he was known without so much as a hat to disguise his features?

"Don't be a fool. He's probably got more than one hat," he told himself angrily, plunging among the undergrowth. Here, where grass and moss grew quickly, and the shrubs barred every way, it was difficult to trace any man's passage. Searching frantically, he moved farther and farther from the house.

Meanwhile the man he sought had abandoned the car in a lane on the outskirts of Newchester and was making for the railway station. He knew that at this time a local train left for Kingsland, where it joined up with the Bridport-London train. If he met with no hindrances he should be able to catch it. By the time they discovered his subterfuge, as they were bound to do, he would be safely away from them all. He had the sense to realize that even London didn't spell safety, yet all his being yearned to find himself there. He would be, he knew, like a rat back in its familiar dockland precincts. And, at least, he told himself dryly, the authorities should have a run for their money. He had shaved off his moustache and this made some alteration in his appearance. He had also affixed a pair of very heavy dark eyebrows that he had used for similar purposes in other days. This was not, after all, his first brush with the police. He smiled grimly. Abandoning the car, he hurried into the town, blessing the rain as he went. Few people could hope to recognize an individual face in such weather, for by this time the rain was increasing in intensity, and his uniform would protect him from curious glances. At Newchester he booked a ticket to Kingsland, whence he would obtain a second ticket to London. He wanted to make things as difficult for the police as he could.

The train at Kingsland was packed as it came in with men in uniform, mostly Canadians. Durward had to stand in the corridor and soon became engaged in conversation with his fellow travellers For the greater part of the journey he let them do most of the talking. Presently they asked him questions and, since his knowledgs of police methods was not entirely negligible, he seldom found himself at a loss for an answer. When, however, his knowledge ran out, he drew on the resources of a fine and vivid imagination. London was reached without incident, and when the train stopped at Waterloo Durward instantly swung himself off, with a friendly nod to his companions who were making a more leisurely descent. They had kit-bags and all manner of gear to collect. As the fugitive strode away towards the barrier one of the Canadians stepped down onto the platform and stood looking after him with puzzled eyes.

"What's got you, Sandy?" a neighbour asked.

"I'm not sure," said Sandy. "But there's something wrong. I can't exactly fix what it is, but it'll come to me presently."

"Wrong with that chap?" The other seemed surprised.

"Yes." Sandy's brows furrowed.

"Don't think he belongs to the Gestapo, do you?"

Sandy laughed. "It'll come to me," he said, and then they surged off the train and the incident was momentarily forgotten.

As soon as he left the station Durward made for a cheap-jack tailor he knew of in Victoria Street. Here he demanded a ready-made suit of plain clothes.

"Getting married on Monday," he confided. "And I haven't bought a suit for three years."

"And they say you chaps are so careful," sighed the tailor.

"Three years since my first wife died," his customer continued. "I never meant to take a second chance."

"They say betting's the Englishman's favourite sport," contributed the tailor wittily.

Durward was beginning to enjoy himself. The recklessness that had carried him through so many dubious and perilous adventures was returning in full force.

"It's Providence, as you might say. I was satisfied enough. But one day I was walking through Earls Court when I met a pal of mine, who said, 'How about a drink, Jock?' Well, I was never one to refuse a good offer, so I said, 'Why not?' We went into a bar called The Ring o' Roses, and he introduced me to his wife and another lady. We got talking and it came out that she'd lost her first husband about two years before. We'd neither of us meant to marry again, so, seeing we had so much in common, we thought we might make a match of it."

By the time he had finished this spirited recital he was glowing with a sense of its veracity. He could even see himself stepping into the bar, being introduced to a lady in a black hat with roses on the brim. . . . He was aware that the man had brought him a suit and he proceeded to try it on. When he found one that fitted him he paid for it in one-pound notes and carried it away under his arm.

* * *

At the barracks assigned to them in London the Canadian soldier called Sandy suddenly smote his knee with his hand and cried: "I've got it. I knew it 'ud come to me sometime."

"Got what?" demanded the man next to him.

"What was wrong with that policeman on the train. I've been in England a year now, and that's the first time I've seen a police officer without a gas mask and a tin hat."

* * *

At The Bottom the labourers were wiping the sweat from their

foreheads and telling one another it was time to call it a day.
" 'Itler'll be in London before we find this perishing body," said
one, not for the first time.

"Or we'll be in Berlin."

"Oh, we shan't find it as soon as that. 'Ullo. Well, I'm jiggered.
Take a look at this, Joe."

His shovel had struck something that wasn't earth and wasn't
stone. He threw the spade down and began to dig with his hands,
like a dog. At about the time that Durward was swinging himself
onto the train for London, the police unearthed the suitcase from
the spot in the garden where Durward had buried it on the afternoon of Saturday, the 26th July.

Merton came in at this juncture and proceeded to examine
the find.

"That's hers all right," he remarked grimly. "Let our Mr.
Durward explain that away if he can."

The suitcase, which was a fair-sized one of black leather, with
a soft lid, bore the initials A.F.D. in gold, and had been buried
about four feet below the level of the ground. The earth had been
carefully smoothed above it, and though Durward hadn't, in fact,
placed his chair directly above the spot, he had always sat where
he could keep his eye upon it.

"It comes of being too careful," said Ramsay a little pompously.
"If he'd stayed indoors we mightn't have thought of looking here,
just under the windows as you might say."

Merton knelt down on the damp earth and examined the case.
Clearly it had belonged to Agatha before her marriage for the
letter "D" had been added comparatively recently. The first thing
they saw was the gray curly coat, and under that was a gray tweed
costume with a black line, the stylish suit Agatha had bought for
her first visit to The Haven.

"Our fine gentleman's going to have his work cut out explaining
them away," the sergeant remarked.

Most of the clothes in the case bore Agatha's name neatly
stitched in Cash's tapes. Everything was there, her creams and
powders, her toilet articles, her brush and comb set, sponge bag,
stockings, supply of handkerchiefs, a pair of house shoes—everything, said Merton, that a woman would need for a short visit.

"I think I'll have a word with the bereaved," he added grimly.
In his mind's eye he had a picture of the missing woman. All
through her slow, colourless years this must be the last fate she
would imagine for herself. He saw her, the thin, careful English
spinster, leaving the security of South Kensington for a strange
middle-aged romance. He had little doubt now of her fate. Not

that he underestimated the difficulties still ahead. The men had
dug over a fair proportion of the garden without finding a trace
of the body. Most probably Durward had buried the corpse first,
deep, deep in the black earth, and then, remembering the story
he was going to tell, had packed a case with her belongings and
dug this second shallower grave. Merton left the experts photo-
graphing the find as he hastened towards the house. As he entered
the hall footsteps sounded on the boards, and he discovered himself
face to face with the moron, just returned from Bridport. When
she saw him she uttered a little squealing cry.

"Oh dear, you did give me a start. I keep forgetting all the
policemen about the place. I'm not accustomed to this sort of thing."

"Very few people are," agreed Merton smoothly. "As a matter
of fact, I thought you were Mr. Durward."

"Oh dear!" repeated the moron characteristically, "Is he out?"

"I don't know. Didn't he tell you what he was doing?"

"He doesn't tell me anything these days. But I shouldn't think
he's gone out. His hat's still in the hall."

Something in the man's expression must have struck through
to her dumb mind. She came over to him, clutching his arm with
her plump hands.

"You've found something," she said. "I know you have. You've
got to tell me—you . . ."

"Keep your head," said Merton sharply. "We haven't found
a body, if that's what you mean."

"You've found something. I always felt you would. But you
can't drag me into this. I'm going back to London, never mind
about the money."

"You can't go tonight," Merton reminded her reasonably.

"There's a train."

"You've nowhere to go when you arrive."

"I can't stay here with him. I'll come back with you to
The Crown."

"Just at the moment I want Mr. Durward. I wonder where
Miller—oh, there you are. Where's your man? I'd like a word
with him."

Miller looked worried to death.

"He was seen going towards the pond nearly three hours ago,
but he must have turned aside because he never got there. We've
been hunting for him ever since."

"Who saw him?"

"One of the constables."

"Which one?"

"I couldn't see his face very well because of the rain. He was driving the car towards the road and he told me to look out for Durward. I came into the house and found this." He produced the letter he had taken from the table. Merton glanced at it and thrust it into his pocket.

"Find out if this man's back. I want to see him."

It appeared, however, that the mysterious constable had not returned. Neither had the car. Merton scowled blackly.

"You're marked for promotion," he assured Miller. "Your job is to watch one man—not an army, not even a pair—just one man, and you let him get away under your nose."

"I don't understand how . . ." Miller began, and then there was a fresh interruption in the shape of a car rapidly backfiring. A moment later there came chortling up to the door a little red abomination like a scarlet beetle, from which descended the last man on earth Merton wanted to see at that particular moment.

"I hope I don't intrude," said Crook sedately, "but my clients are gettin' a bit impatient, and they've asked me to give you the works. You know what women are," he went on in chatty tones, oblivious to the dark expressions on the faces all about him. "Afraid they're goin' to be cheated of their corpse after all the trouble they've taken to provide us with one."

Merton scowled yet more blackly. "You can tell them we haven't got one for them—yet. Do they suppose I keep 'em in cold storage?"

"I wouldn't be surprised," said Crook. "Must be tough luck to be a woman. Always expectin' more than there is in the world." No one answering him, he looked round. "Durward not showin' up at the moment?"

Merton hesitated. Miller began, "But . . ." caught his superior's eye and fell silent again.

Crook grinned in sudden comprehension. "Mean to say he's given you the slip?"

"That's just what he does mean," said the moron unexpectedly behind them. "Yes, I heard what you said about the policeman driving the car. I suppose Eddie bought him—with my money."

Crook slapped his knee in a deliberately theatrical gesture. "Not on your life. Our Mr. Durward don't put down good money if he can help it. Well, well, well, to think of him getting away with that."

The moron's eyes were like saucers. "You don't mean Eddie *killed* a policeman?"

"Love-a-duck! What fun you and our Miss Martin would have if you got together. No, no. Your Eddie was drivin' the car. Come to think of it, I saw the gear last time I was over."

Merton interrupted sharply to know what this was all about. Crook explained. "He said he'd been a keen amateur actor, and he'd brought a lot of his costumes with him here. And among them was a bobby's get-up. Well, I'll lay if you search Master Durward's room you'll find his nice pin-stripe suit hanging on the peg, but the policeman's uniform will be missing. Let's take a look."

Turning, he lumbered away from them, resembling a small elderly elephant of a ripe brown shade. Merton, with no choice, reluctantly followed him, looking as outraged as a professional actor when some amateur suggests that some direction he has just been given might be improved in this way or that. Crook, however, never had a thought to spare for the effect he was producing; clattering up the narrow twisting stairs to Durward's room he flung open the door. As he had surmised, the suit Durward had been wearing that morning was hanging in the wardrobe. All his toilet requisites were in their usual places. Durward was taking no chances. Everything he owned at The Haven had been examined by the police and might one day be identified; but if he bought cheap anonymous stuff in London he'd cover his tracks. One man buying a shaving brush looks remarkably like another and, as Crook could tell you, not one man in a hundred uses his eyes.

"On my word, I'm sorrier than ever I haven't got this chap for a client," Crook was mourning. "I do like a fellow with guts *and* brains."

"You might have your work cut out explaining why he buried his wife's clothes four feet deep at the end of his own garden," Merton prophesied.

"It's a schoolboy's trick, perhaps, but it's not a penal offence, Inspector, and you won't persuade an old bird like me that it is."

"Not burying a suitcase isn't," Merton agreed grimly. "When we find the body . . ."

Crook looked pensively out of the window. The men were digging with might and main, despite the gathering darkness. They looked like an army of extraordinarily vital fox terriers, flinging up earth in all directions.

"How long do you give them to find it?" he inquired.

Merton shrugged. "Today—tomorrow—it can't take long to dig the garden over. After all, when they bolt it usually means we're getting warm. Durward should have thought of that."

"I don't doubt he did," said Crook amiably. "Let me know when you find anything, won't you?"

Merton was struck by his tone. "What do you mean, Mr. Crook?" Like a good many other officials, he knew Crook's reputation and secretly respected it. "You don't think she's there?"

"I wouldn't expect it myself. You know, Inspector, you under-rate Durward. You're forgetting he's probably a chap with a lot of experience. Remember that old joke they used to try out at school? About T double O and T W O and the second day of the week? Nine chaps out of ten fell into the trap and said Tuesday before they stopped to think. Well, that's the kind of cunning Durward's displayed to date. He knows you'll assume that where the suitcase is there is the body also, and so you'll go right ahead turning the whole Bottom upside down, if necessary." He shook his head. "No, Merton, I don't think you're on the right track. That's why he went out of his way to draw your attention to the garden. The obvious thing for him to do would be to bury the body in the woods. Much less chance of finding it there than if he put it in the garden. But—if you find the suitcase in the garden, what happens? Look out of the window and you'll see."

"So you think the body is in The Bottom, sir?"

Crook shook his head. "Oh no, I shouldn't say that was at all likely. You see, there aren't any rosebushes there, either."

In Crook's office in Bloomsbury Street Mr. Entwistle was saying, "I simply cannot understand it. Allowing the fellow to sneak off under their very eyes. The trouble with this generation, Crook, is that it's inefficient. It's lazy, it's womanish."

"Go on," Crook applauded him. "In another minute you'll be saying, 'We could do with a bit of Hitler here to buck these chaps up.' Well, that may be all right for you, but my great-grandmother came from Whitechapel, and, take it from me, Hitler don't know a good thing when he sees one."

"Suppose, in fact, they never do find the body?" the fussy Mr. Entwistle continued. "After all, there was Landru . . ."

"They pulled him in just the same. Still, I wouldn't worry. They'll turn up the body any time now."

"You mean, you have a theory where it will be found?"

Crook looked at him in amazement. "Mean to say you haven't tumbled to that little trick yet? Really, Entwistle, you shake my faith in human nature, and that's not right, really it isn't. It's all in the Book we none of us read often enough, something about not quenching the smoking flax and no flax ever smoked more."

Entwistle took his hat and went out. Crook was a clever chap, if unscrupulous, though he hadn't known until today about that grandmother from Whitechapel, but really it was a pity he wasn't just a little more refined. It did give people a wrong impression. They expected lawyers to be suave, urbane—you only had to see theatrical representations of them. Whereas if you saw Crook you'd suppose he was a bookie's tout, vulgar brown bowler and all.

* * *

"Y'know, Bill," said Crook thoughtfully, "I wouldn't be surprised if a lot of people were goin' to have a bit of a shock in the course of the next day or two. Trouble is, so few of 'em are taught to use their eyes. If they were, this affair would have been a clear run from the start. But as it is . . ."

"Come off it," said Bill unemotionally. "You know you'd be as sick as mud if they did. How much longer do you give this case?"

"Couple of days," said Crook definitely. "We ought to have pulled both of 'em in by then."

II

Merton, an intelligent and painstaking man, was not slow to take Crook's hint. In fact, he kicked himself in private for not seeing for himself the significance of the thorns in the missing man's coat.

"What happened," he told Ramsay, "is that Durward knew he'd got to get rid of the body double-quick, and he knew that if inquiries were made, we'd do what, as it happens, we have done. We'd drag the ponds, we'd dig over The Bottom, we might even tackle the garden. Certainly digging over The Bottom's a tall order, but you never know your luck. We might hit on the very spot the first day, and though he might say he buried his wife's clothes for a joke and, as Crook points out, you can't pull a man in for that, a body's a very different affair. What we've got to do is find some place where there's a rose hedge or thicket or something of the kind. Crook's right. He didn't get those thorns in his coat out of The Bottom."

Thus it was that not long afterwards his inquiries brought him and his assistants to a large empty house called The Warren, where the gateway was barred by an overgrowth of climbing roses as dangerous as a spiteful cat. The house was off the high road and had been empty for a considerable time. It was one of the houses the Durwards had inspected in their search for a new home.

"Peach of a place," said Merton. "You might bury an army here and no one guess."

It was clear that someone had made a way through the thorny barrier at no very distant date. The tall grass of the lawn was heavily trampled. The whole of the grounds were unkempt and of considerable acreage. The flower beds were overgrown, untended, run to seed. A few marigolds sprawled in one of the borders. The lawns themselves were like paddocks; thistle and burdock grew everywhere.

"Someone came this way not so long ago," said Merton thoughtfully. "Look where the grass has been torn and stamped down. It was something heavy that did that. Otherwise, the grass would have sprung up again and left no trace."

The trail, such as it was, led round the side of the house where a broken window testified to the fact that someone at some time had made an illegal entry.

"Might as well look inside the house. It would be a good place to put a body," said Merton.

They made a thorough examination, even to the point of investigating the big open fireplaces, but they found nothing. It seemed probable that tramps or gipsies had slept here during the winter months, but of the body they sought there was no sign.

"He can't have gone very far," Ramsay objected. "He was working in the dark."

"We don't know that," said Merton. "He may easily have waited till daylight. It's an isolated road; he wouldn't be likely to meet anyone."

The search continued. In the garden at the back of the house was the well that supplied the water. Merton examined it with care. Creeping jenny grew across the lid, and "Someone's been tampering with this lately," he said. "There are signs of the stuff being torn up by the roots. Here, Smith, Durden . . ."

They came and tore up the lid. A fearful stench assailed their nostrils.

"Poison gas," said one.

"I doubt it," said Merton.

It was none too easy to fish up the unorthodox contents, but it was done at last. A hideous, misshapen thing, wrapped in sacking, lay on the path beside them. The atmosphere was mephitic. One man nearly fainted. The other, who had served in the great war and was less sensitive to horrors, helped to tear away the sacks. What was revealed was enough to turn the most robust stomach.

"How in God's name is anyone going to identify that?" demanded Merton gruffly.

"It's a woman," said the sergeant in faltering tones. "The clothes will help, of course. And—look here—there's the pair to our pearl stud all right."

"We'd better get this taken along to the mortuary. I wonder who's going to do the identification. Our Mr. Durward's the man, but he's not available. Oh well, we shall have to rely on Mrs.

Hart. Anyway, there's not likely to be more than one missing female in the neighbourhood at the moment."

Mrs. Hart, warned but undismayed, put on her best hat and accompanied the policeman to the mortuary.

"This won't be a picnic," the man assured her sombrely. "The body's been in the water three weeks. You'll have to go largely by the clothes. There's—not so much else."

"There's shoes," said Mrs. Hart, undaunted. "There was a case 'Art was telling me of a lady that 'ad bin buried four years and was no more than a skellington, but it was 'er shoes as 'ung the 'usband. Funny 'ow no one seems to think of everything."

At the mortuary they drew down the sheet to reveal the repulsive thing they had taken from the well. Mrs. Hart uttered a loud shriek.

"My goodness gracious me! *It's 'er.* Strewth! Oh, it's not what's left of the fice I'm going on, but—you couldn't forget a dress like that in a 'urry."

※　　※　　※

CHAPTER TWELVE

CROOK sat in his office telephoning to Cummings. "Hold everything," he said. "I've got a break for your Sunday paper that'll set every pressman since the Flood wrigglin' in his grave."

"Another body?" suggested Cummings.

"Nothing like a murder for amusin' the public, is there? You might have thought, with all the murder that's goin' on all over the world just now, one female more or less wouldn't be noticed. But, boy, are we going to knock 'em in the You-Know-What? Stop me on the street and ask me."

He took up the picture paper. All the war news today was on the back page. The front page had headlines inches high.

DURWARD MYSTERY SENSATION

WOMAN'S BODY FOUND IN WELL

The body of a woman identified as Miss Grace Knowles of Princes Gate, London, W., was found in the well of an empty house ten miles from The Haven, the isolated cottage occupied by Mr. and Mrs. Durward, both of whom have disappeared. The police have been searching for Mrs. Durward for several weeks. This discovery may well mark a new turn of events. A case containing Mrs. Durward's clothes was found buried in the garden of The Haven. Police are still searching for her body.

"Even you, Crook, will scarcely pretend that you anticipated this." Mr. Entwistle, larger, paler, more conscious of a weak heart than ever, loomed above Crook's tubby little form. "That poor woman! What a tremendous shock it must have been."

"You stand there, Entwistle, as large as life, and tell me you didn't know it was Miss Knowles they were goin' to find in the sack? Oh, you're stringin' me. Of course you knew."

"I did nothing of the kind," puffed Mr. Entwistle, "and nor, I am convinced, did the police. Why on earth should we anticipate such an anticlimax?"

"Then who the heck did you think it would be?"

"Mrs. Durward, of course. Well, naturally."

Crook shook his head. "You disappoint me, Entwistle, really

137

you do. Mean to say that after you got the central clue you still thought it would be Mrs. Durward?"

"What clue?" demanded Entwistle.

"The earring, of course."

"Naturally, I assumed that belonged to Mrs. Durward."

"Did you now?" Crook thrust his thumbs into the holes of his vest. "And will you tell me what a woman with pierced ears would be doing with a clip-on stud?"

Mr. Entwistle was like the Queen of Sheba. All the virtue was gone out of him. He excused himself by saying he didn't really like murder; complicated wills and mad old ladies with persecution mania were his cup of tea.

"I still don't see why you plumped for Miss Knowles," he protested half-heartedly.

"How many other women had been in the house? Mrs. Hart? She's still above ground. Miss Martin? She never got any farther than the step, and I take off my hat to Durward, I do really, that he didn't allow her to come farther than that. It's more than I've ever been able to do. Remember what Sherlock Holmes said? Eliminate the impossible and what remains, however unlikely, is the answer."

"But—there's no sense in it, Crook. What could Durward have against a woman like that, whom he'd only just met?"

"Dare say she learnt a bit too much and was proposin' to pass it on to her friend, Agatha, when they took down their back hair. So far's we know, she wasn't crazy about him, and it could even be that she saw through the gloss and glitter. She don't sound a particularly tactful woman, and I daresay she gave him no choice, though that won't help him when he's in front of the judge."

"And now," said Mr. Entwistle, as a parting shot, "I suppose you're going to tell me you could lay your hand on Mrs. Durward."

"I wouldn't say that," replied Crook seriously. "But I'll give you a hint. The clue to the mystery lies in the handbag."

II

The search for Durward was now widespread throughout the country. The police had established their contention that he would make for London, for a certain Mr. Joseph Levy of Victoria Street had come forward with the information that a man in police constable's uniform had come to his ready-made tailoring department with a tale of being married in the near future and had bought a brown suit for four pounds, cash down, no discount, and unequalled at the price. Mr. Levy was so anxious to vindicate his own character as a purveyor of Mayfair goods at Pimlico prices that, at this point, he jerked a professional card from his pocket and laid it before the officer who was taking down his statement.

"Any time you're wanting a suit, Sergeant, just remember my address. This card'll tickle your memory. You've a fine figure, and I could fit you so an ambassador wouldn't know it hadn't been made to measure."

"What was this man like?" demanded the sergeant.

"Tall, dark, thick eyebrows, clean-shaved, with a queer sort of scar at one corner of his mouth."

The sergeant smiled faintly. "This isn't the first time you've given evidence to the police."

"You get to look out for faces in my trade," said Mr. Levy, a shade obscurely.

"What did he do with the uniform?"

"Carried it off in a cardboard box and wore the suit I'd just sold him. Said he was going to see his young lady and get her opinion."

"How did he pay for the clothes?"

"In pound notes."

"Of course he didn't give you an address?"

"He said he lived in the suburbs." Mr. Levy waved a magnificently jewelled hand. "The suburbs!" he repeated. "That's no place for a man of taste that wants an elegant cut."

"Give me a description of the suit," said the sergeant.

A little later full details of Durward's altered appearance and change of attire were in the possession of all metropolitan stations. The next morning the story appeared in the press. But what so far no one realized was that Durward, wearing the brown suit, had gone first thing next morning to another job tailor and bought a blue one, and that it was in the blue suit that he left London for the greater protection of the provinces.

"He won't hang onto that uniform longer than he can help," said the police shrewdly. "He'll have to dump it somewhere, and we ought to know where within twenty-four hours."

Here, however, Fate was unkind to the righteous. On the same day that Durward left the city a parcel was delivered to the vicar of a dockside parish that had suffered badly during the air raids of the winter and spring. The war, plus overwork in one of the poorest of London's parishes, prevented Father Whelan from ever glancing at a newspaper, and in any case (and here Crook would have applauded him) he seldom believed anything he read; therefore he knew nothing of the Durward Mystery. It was left to a romantic lady visitor, who helped with the clothing club, to say, "What a very extraordinary thing to send us. I suppose we could put it into the theatrical box, though it's hardly suitable for the sort of mystery plays we put on in this parish."

"Wait a minute," said a colleague. "Didn't you read the papers? Don't you know they're looking for that man, Durward, who is supposed to have escaped wearing a policeman's uniform?" For the papers, naturally, had featured the story.

"Oh, but it couldn't be, Muriel."

"I can't see any other reason for it being sent here. I think we ought to tell Father Whelan."

"You know he hates anything to do with the police."

"Because he knows, if justice were done, a good proportion of his parish would be under lock and key for street betting."

"Well, there isn't any sense in having laws if people don't keep them. He's always saying that about church law."

After some soul-searching, the lady in question decided it was her duty to inform the vicar of her suspicions, which she did, with some trepidation that same evening.

Her fears were proved to be well-founded. Father Whelan, a stout little priest, full of the proverbial Irish ginger, fixed his devoted worker with a burning blue eye and said severely, "If ye ask me, Miss Twiss, ye'd be better occupied sticking to the job ye have in hand, than taking sides against a poor fellah that has all the police of the country against him anyway."

Miss Twiss was somewhat taken aback. "I thought, as a citizen . . ." she faltered.

The little man threw up his hands. "Glory be to God, what's being a citizen to do with it? Ye're a woman, aren't ye, and since when has it been a woman's duty to hound down a fellow creature? We don't know the half of the story."

"He's killed a woman," whispered Miss Twiss.

"That's what the police say. For meself, I'd be glad to hear his story. There never were people like the police for fixing a murder on the handiest chap. It's the easy way out."

"He's supposed to have done away with his wife too," whispered Miss Twiss in curdling tones.

"And, if he did, hasn't he trouble enough with all those interfering bobbies on his track, without you making it worse for him? I tell you, you and me are the lucky ones. All our troubles are under our own umbrellas. If God Almighty had seen fit to give us the vocation to matrimony, we might be fleeing from the fellies ourselves. I've been working in this parish forty years now," he continued, warming to his subject, "and in that time I've met a power of wives would be the better for a little murdering. No, no, you let the poor fellah be. Why, if they were to get him and hang him, ye'd be as bad as the man himself, and without the excuse. Let the police, that are paid for the job, get on with it, and do you remember the law of charity and thank yeer Maker for the chance that's kept you out of their way."

* * *

In the meantime Miss Knowles's body had been examined and a verdict of death by strangulation given by the police surgeon. Inquiry showed that no one had seen the poor lady since a certain day in June. The housekeeper at Elegant Flatlets said that she had received no instructions from Miss Knowles about forwarding letters, and had assumed she was still visiting among her friends. No, she agreed, it was unusual for her to be away so long, but she was a very refined woman, who kept herself to herself, and her long absence had aroused no particular comment. She appeared to be one of those women, among whom Agatha had once numbered herself, who are able to disappear from life without attracting any comment. Further inquiry showed that her bags had been sent from Bridport labelled "To Be Called For" and were still at Paddington Station. It seemed obvious that Durward was responsible for this, though, until he was located, no definite statement could be made. The Durward case was now a first-class attraction, and a number of people made open and adverse comments against the policy of the governors of the B.B.C. for not retailing the latest developments over the air at the end of the news.

"The instant I set eyes on him I knew he was a monster," said Miss Martin vigorously and quite inaccurately. "That poor woman!"

"It's awful to think that at this very instant he may be rubbing shoulders with decent ordinary people like you and me," contributed Miss Grainger.

"Or murdering yet another victim," amplified Miss Martin. "After all, he got rid of two women here in six months. He must have had a lot of practice."

"When I think of poor Agatha Durward and what she must have suffered, I thank God for keeping me single," exulted Miss Grainger.

"I don't believe in throwing all the responsibility onto Providence," her friend rebuked her. "I'm single because I didn't choose to marry. That showed my good sense."

Marriage is an enthralling topic to women of all ages. They had a lovely morning.

In public houses, in factories, on doorsteps and on the tops of busses people discussed the Durward case. Two bodies were better than anyone had dared to hope. It cheered up numbers of people who had left London because they didn't care about air raids and found themselves bored and exasperated by the idleness of their new existence. Landladies had comfortable half-hours debating this point and that with their lodgers. A certain Miss Bumble of King's Herring got up all the details and offered them to her newest boarder, who was a bit cast-down, poor thing, owing to being bombed out of her home some time earlier.

"To think of that poor thing married to that awful man," she said juicily. "Going to him as innocent as a new-born babe, never dreaming she'd only leave the cottage done up in a sack. Well, my dear mother used to say there's more to marriage than you'll read in the story books and so you'll find out, my girl, but the Lord preserved me from such a fate, and here am I at sixty-six letting my room and my burial money laid by, and there's she, twenty years younger, lying somewhere in a stinking ditch with her throat cut, as like as not, and all her nice clothes being put in mould or worn by that hussy that's taken her place."

Miss Faulkner, who was certainly very jumpy since her grim experience, tried feebly to turn the conversation.

"I can't bear to think of it," she whispered.

"Now it does me a power of good thinking of it," said Miss Bumble. "There's times I say to myself, Maria Bumble, you've worked hard and honest all your life, and here you are marching onward to the tomb and what have you ever had? And then I read a story like this and it starts me counting my blessings. I expect you're glad, too, Miss Faulkner, to be preserved from such awful perils."

"You don't have to be murdered just because you're married," her lodger offered.

"You're a lot less likely to be murdered if you're not married," Miss Bumble proclaimed.

"And you don't know that he did murder his wife."

"If she's not dead, why hasn't she risen up to testify against him?" demanded Miss Bumble, with awful joy. "No, no, Miss Faulkner, dear, you take my word for it, she's lying somewhere, waiting, maybe, till the sea shall yield up the dead that are in it, to sign his death warrant."

"Surely the—the other body will do that."

"Still, it 'ud be a pity not to have the two of them while they're about it. My lodger on the top floor, Mr. Graham, was saying that most likely the country's littered with bodies of this man's wives. Why, he says she may not even have been a wife. She sounds a daft sort of creature at that."

"I don't see how she could be expected to know whether he was married or not," Miss Faulkner protested with some show of spirit.

"It's what I say," agreed Miss Bumble, whisking the crumbs off the table with a little brush, "marriage is a snare and a delusion. Let this be a warning to you, Miss Faulkner, if you had any such idea in your head, with all these soldiers about and all."

"Oh, that's ridiculous, Miss Bumble."

"You'd maybe have thought it ridiculous for this creature to marry at an age when she'd better be thinking of her latter end, but she did. And what's the result? That her end's overtaken her before her time. And to think of that man being at liberty to raven upon the rest of us. Why, no one knows where he is at this minute. There might come a ring at the bell and I'd go to open the door and there'd he be and I'd never know—not till it was too late."

The front door bell pealed loudly and both women started.

"It's like the Finger of God," said Miss Bumble reverently.

"It's more likely the butcher," said Miss Faulkner.

"I'd best be going," the landlady agreed. "If that Jessie once gets to the door she'll be there gossiping till the Huns march into the sea."

She slapped the tablecloth back into the drawer, took up her crumb scoop and vanished.

"If it's anyone for me," called Miss Faulkner desperately, "I'm not well enough to see visitors."

"You didn't say you were expecting anyone," said Miss Bumble severely, reappearing for an instant in the doorway.

The bell rang again.

Miss Bumble went down. On the step stood a fat, cheerful little man with eyebrows like a thicket, and a bowler hat atop.

"Is Miss Faulkner in?" he inquired.

"Are you the gentleman she was expecting?" Miss Bumble's voice was cold. She was not at all taken by her caller's appearance, that she privately thought common and pushing.

"Her lawyer," said Crook glibly. "Down from London. She in?"

Miss Bumble unbent a little. Lawyers generally meant money, and seeing poor Miss Faulkner had lost everything, simply everything, it was to be hoped he'd come down with something in his pocket for her.

"Well, she is and she isn't, if you know what I mean," she replied.

"I'll wait while she makes up her mind," said Crook cheerfully, stepping into Fernlea's unambitious little hall. "How is she these days?"

"Well, she's what I'd call a bit low in her mind," said Miss

Bumble cautiously. "Mark you, she had a bad time of it, bombed out like that."

"I'll say she had a shock," agreed the high-spirited Mr. Crook. "She's lucky to have got in here."

"I always say you have to do what you can; and there was plenty of them homeless after that raid. Seems as though, now they're tired of going for London, they're just keeping their hands in, as you might say, coming to little places like this. Why, she hardly seemed to know who she was and where she'd come from. The bombs take them that way sometimes, the doctor says. I had to show her her handkerchief with A.F. on it, before she could so much as tell me her name."

"Bad raid?" murmured Crook, cautiously examining "The Monarch of the Glen" hanging on the wall by the kitchen door.

"Just two or three as slipped through, you know, but they did some damage. A whole row of houses come down and twelve killed. I tell Miss Faulkner to be glad she got away with her life, if she did lose all her things. Lucky she had her bag with her and a bit of money, and I went with her to the town hall next day and saw about her identity card and ration book. People are very good here, I'll say that. Well, we've been lucky most of the war. But I'm glad you've come. You'll be able to settle things up for her. She must have some friends, but the shock seems to have driven things out of her head. Why, she won't even read the papers."

"I can't say I blame her," said Mr. Crook cheerfully. "Nothing very bright there."

"I've been trying to get her interested in this Durward murder. Ever so exciting I call it."

"That," said Mr. Crook judicially, "would give anyone an appetite. I think I'd better come up. She's quite right, you know. She hasn't got any friends or relations."

"No? Well, she's missed a lot of trouble. You have to look on the bright side. That's what I'm always telling her."

The fugitive, sitting with locked hands in a chair turned away from the window, started as the door opened and her landlady came in, followed by a man the self-styled Miss Faulkner recognized instantly.

"Here's your lawyer come to see you all the way from London, Miss Faulkner, dear," announced Miss Bumble happily. "He's brought you good news, so you must cheer up a bit."

She closed the door and went righteously away. She wasn't one for listening, however strong the temptation.

"Well, well, well, Mrs. Durward," said Crook, depositing his bowler hat on the sideboard. "I'll say you've given us a good run for our money. Now, suppose you tell me all about it."

But Agatha had risen and shrunk farther back against the wall, her hands twisting nervously together.

"I don't understand . . ."

"Come, come, you don't suppose you were going to stay buried forever? Not with Arthur Crook on the trail."

"How did you find me?" Agatha whispered.

"Oh, we get around. And once I knew you were still in the land of the living—what put you wise to Durward, by the way?"

"How did you know?"

"You weren't all of a piece with your friend, Miss Knowles? I didn't, till we found the suitcase. Then I was sure."

"The suitcase?"

"Don't you ever read the papers?"

She shook her head.

"Not even when it's about yourself? A film star could teach you a lot, Mrs. Durward."

"I didn't want to see them. There was one heading—Police Search for Mrs. Durward. I thought—it was ostrich-like, I suppose —that if I didn't read the papers they were less likely to find me."

"Why didn't you want them to find you? I don't say the police is the same as the angel choir, but you could be a lot safer with them than going about on your own."

"Oh, don't you understand?" Agatha's voice came in a desperate cry. "I thought it was me they wanted—for murder."

Crook looked frankly puzzled. "Her murder?" he inquired.

"No, no," moaned Agatha. "Oh, don't you understand? For his murder, my husband's. I thought I'd killed Edmund."

"Take it easy," said Crook. He pushed forward a chair and persuaded her to occupy it. "The bad time's over. Just get that into your head." He put one huge freckled paw over those shaking hands. When he spoke like this you understood why he was so successful; his tone would have coaxed a hippopotamus out of its pool during a heat wave.

"Edmund isn't dead, is he?" she whispered.

"Not he. At least, if he is, the police don't know it. And mighty sick they'll be if he has escaped them. They want to ask him a few questions about Miss Knowles."

Agatha lifted a ghastly face. "I'll never forget her. I see her still in my dreams. I hear her call me, as surely she must have called that night, and I never heard, I never heard. Mr. Crook, have you seen her?"

Crook twisted his big mouth into an expression of wry disgust. "For my sins, I have. Don't go on thinking about her. The doctors say it must have been very quick, and I daresay she didn't cry out at all."

"I misjudged her so," Agatha continued. "I believed everything Edmund told me. It wasn't till afterwards that I realized what must have happened."

"Suppose you begin at the beginning," suggested Crook sensibly.

"That means, I suppose, the day Grace died, the last day she was with us. I hadn't been very well, and I sent her and my husband out together. I knew she'd like that. I could see she was very much attracted by him, as women always were. I couldn't help noticing it, but I didn't mind. How could I be jealous when I had so much and Grace had really nothing at all? She was so pleased to be going with him alone. After lunch I went to lie down and presently I must have gone to sleep. When I woke it was just after four o'clock. I listened but I couldn't hear anything, so I came out on the landing and called to them. But no one answered. I had looked at my watch and it was 4.15, and I thought they were running things rather fine. I went back and looked out of my window in case they were coming in by the back way, but no, there was no one there. I got tidy and came downstairs, and as I reached the hall the clock chimed half-past four. I remember the time particularly because I knew Grace was to leave by the 6.30 train, and I'd hoped to have a little time with her before she left. Then I went into the garden; I don't know why specially, but I went. You know the house is supposed to be haunted by the ghost of a woman who once lived there and drowned herself in the big pool. It was a queer misty sort of evening, and as I came through the gate into the woods I saw the ghost. I did really. I've always been terrified of ghosts. Grace knew that and so did my husband. When this one began to come towards me, wailing in the most dreadful manner, and waving its arms, I thought I was going mad. I shouted to it to keep off. Then I began to run towards the house, calling to my husband, and I suppose I caught my foot on something. Edmund said it must have been the rockery. Anyway, the next thing I remember was my husband bending over me, and the doctor was there too. I didn't remember quite at first what had happened, but gradually it came back, and I was terrified again. I don't think either of them understood how terrified. You can't realize, because you weren't there and, anyway, you're probably one of the sensible kind who wouldn't be scared by an army of ghosts." She looked up at him imploringly.

"Take your time," said Crook. "How about a cup of tea?"

"No, no. I've only just had a meal. Oh, I dare say I sound crazy to you, but with the dark trees dripping and the cottage black and empty behind me, and that white thing stumbling through the wood and moaning as it came—I understood then how people go mad. When Edmund and the doctor began to ask questions I told them. I didn't expect them to believe it, but they were very, very kind. Edmund got me to bed and promised not to leave me, and the doctor said he'd come the next day. But somehow I couldn't forget. I was afraid even to be alone in a room in case it came back. Edmund was right, you see. He told me, if I didn't throw off this obsession, I'd really go queer. And when the branches tapped on my window I did think they were the fingers of the ghost. And every time I heard a sound I thought it was her feet. I even heard her voice sometimes, her hands feeling over the outside of my door. I told Edmund we must go away."

"And he agreed?"

"He didn't say anything for a day or two, then he told me I wasn't crazy; I had seen something. I'd seen Grace Knowles dressed up as the ghost, for a joke, he said. Oh, but, Mr. Crook, Grace would realize it wouldn't be a joke to me. I couldn't believe she could do anything so cruel. But Edmund said he'd caught her carrying the sheet she'd been wearing. He said there'd been a fearful row, and he'd told her to get out at once, he wouldn't have her in the house any longer, and he'd driven her to the station. He said he'd told her she needn't write, we never wanted to have anything to do with her again. Oh, he thought of everything—everything." She put her hands over her eyes.

"I suppose, actually, he'd been the ghost and Miss Knowles had come up at the wrong moment and threatened to tell you, and he couldn't have that, of course. . . ."

"Yes, I'm sure of that now. I know Grace would never have done such a thing. But if Edmund wanted to—to lay hands on my money he'd have to find some excuse for leaving the house, and he'd know that would drive me out quicker than anything else. And I suppose he realized I'd hand the money over to him."

"If you hadn't he'd have charmed it out of you. What did he tell you about Miss Knowles not writing after she got back to town?"

"He said there'd been such a scene—oh, he was terribly clever —he used to urge me to write, but in such a way that he simply worked up all my feelings against her."

"Well, it would have been awkward if you had written and it had come out that she never reached London."

"And I believed everything he said, Mr. Crook. I was such a fool. He was so kind, so gentle, so understanding about it all. He agreed about a new house and helped me to look for one, and when he found it was so dear he said we must find something smaller. Even when I said I'd sell out and buy it myself he wouldn't let me, not right away. He said I must sleep on it. How could I guess he never meant to buy the house at all, but just keep the money?"

"So that was his game, was it? How did you find out?"

"It was that day at Bridport. I suddenly felt I couldn't hang on like this any longer. I told myself that men don't appreciate the way women feel about things; they're content to let them slide. I wanted to hurry Mr. Ainslie up. So, while I was waiting for Edmund, I telephoned and he read me the letter Edmund had sent, saying we weren't interested in the house. I couldn't believe it at first. And then I began to think and—if he hadn't taken the cheque I mightn't have been so frightened. But suddenly everything seemed to fall into place. It was like all the lights going out, and I was in the dark, but I could see, like a cat, just what Edmund's plan had been. He'd never meant to buy that house—he'd never meant to buy any house. It was just an excuse to lay hands on the money. He must have known I'd give it him."

"Of course he did. He's a good psychologist, you know. He played Miss Knowles for a sucker too."

"Poor Grace! Of course, he meant to separate us. He meant to isolate me absolutely from everyone and everything I'd known. I don't say he meant to kill Grace—I don't think he did—but she got in his way, and he was quite merciless. I didn't know whether he meant to kill me or not—I didn't see what he would gain, if he did—but I was sure he meant to go away with my money. He made a ridiculous excuse to go up to the village, leaving me alone in the house. He knew I couldn't bear being left alone, especially since the ghost episode."

"Did you object?"

"That night? No. I wanted him to go. I thought it was my last chance. I felt he had gone—and for good. . . ."

"Without any luggage?"

"I never thought of that."

"And with the chance of the whole place talking and drawing their own conclusions?"

"Would that have mattered?"

"You have got a lawyer," Crook reminded her. "Even if you'd forgotten that fact, I doubt whether your husband had. What did you do?"

"I knew I couldn't spend a night alone in that house. I'd go mad. I was terrified of it. I felt I'd rather be out in the dark woods, in spite of ghosts or tramps or—or wild beasts, only, of course, there aren't any wild beasts in those woods. So I dressed quickly and came down. And then something—something I can't explain—made me stop when I got to the woodshed. I felt I had to know what his secret was. By this time I thought of him as a monster, though, of course, I still knew nothing about Grace. I thought of poison gas; I even thought he might be in German pay, have a secret radio set there. Oh, I was mad, I expect, but I told myself I'd got to see what he kept there. But I never guessed —oh, God, I never guessed."

"It was a damned brave thing to do," Crook applauded her.

"I knew where the key was and I found it and opened the door. Mind you, I was sure Edmund wasn't coming back. I couldn't see anything sinister, just packing cases and our luggage tools and a sack or two on the floor, and Edmund's carpentering and a big spade and fork, the sort of things you'd expect to find in a shed. Most of the packing cases were uncovered and empty, but there was a trunk, with its tray leaning against the wall, and I lifted up the lid—I don't think I really expected to find anything there —and then I saw her—I saw her."

"I know," said Crook steadily. "We've seen her too."

"She'd been my friend," whispered Agatha. "We'd done such a lot of little unimportant things together. And I'd been hating her for weeks. And all the time, when she didn't write, it was because she couldn't, because she was *there*. Her head had been pressed back, and she seemed to be staring at me with her dreadful darkened face and her tongue lolling out and her eyes—her eyes . . ."

"Easy," warned Crook. "Easy. Don't tell me you're a weak woman, Mrs. Durward. The average dame would have been in an asylum ever since."

"I just stared and stared. I couldn't take my eyes away. I said over and over again, 'It's Grace. It's Grace, who was my friend.' Edmund had said something about accepting our hospitality, and so she had, and so she did still—inside that trunk, dead, horribly, foully. I knew there was nothing I could do but get away, to save my own life. A man who's killed one woman won't hesitate at killing another. I was less sure now he wouldn't come back. He wouldn't leave *that* where anyone could find it. I ran out into the dark, leaving my little torch shining on the shelf. And then I heard him. He had come back and he'd come too soon. I heard the front door close and then his footsteps in the hall. It was a flagged hall. I used to think that was one reason why the house was so cold. They rang like—it sounded like a death knell to me. I prayed that he'd go upstairs first, but he didn't. I heard him come along the passage and I thought: 'History's going to repeat itself. She there and I here—and by tomorrow we'll both of us be where no one will think of looking for us.' I was quite sure of that. Then he came into the garden and he saw me there, with the door of the shed open behind me, and my torch on the shelf shining straight onto that face, bathing it in light. Mr. Crook—Mr. Crook . . ."

Crook's arm was round her shoulders. "You're doing fine," he said. "I couldn't ask for a better witness. But go right on. No one's going to hurt you. My clients don't get hurt. They pay me to keep 'em safe. Now then."

"He came down the path very quietly, came quite close before he spoke. He looked over my shoulder and he saw the trunk open. And something moved in his face, just for an instant, as a shutter moves in a camera. I knew in that moment he'd made up his mind I'd got to die. And I knew I was going to die because I couldn't help myself. I backed away from him—into the shed. He came nearer and nearer. He began to speak, said it was a pity I'd been so curious. He practically told me he'd meant to kill me, but—not like this. It was to have been painless. And then he said: 'It's always a mistake to be too curious. She was too curious. She knew too much. You do understand, don't you?' I think it was then I realized that, of course, he'd been the ghost, not Grace, and she'd found him out and accused him, and he'd killed her so she shouldn't tell me. Or perhaps he wanted to make out I wasn't sane—I don't know that, I suppose I'll never know."

Her face was so ravaged it was like the face of an old woman. Crook thought of it—all those weeks knowing what was in the shed. He must have had a nerve of iron to play his part so naturally. No one had suspected the truth. He must have been waiting for an opportunity to dispose of the body, but he'd done himself a disservice by pretending to be the ghost. The result was Agatha would never be left alone after dark, and it was only after dark that he'd dare bury the gibbering thing in the woodshed.

"He seems to have thought of a good deal," he said aloud.

Agatha's shining face, shining with sweat and terror, nodded uncertainly. "Yes, but there was one thing he forgot. He forgot I wasn't dead yet. I went back till I could feel the wall behind me, and when I looked away from his face I saw hers and I thought, 'In a minute I'll look like that, I'll look like that.' And suddenly my foot touched the big spade, and before I could think I'd swung it up and struck out at him. He wasn't expecting that. It caught him on the side of the head and he went down like a log. I saw the blood. I didn't stop to see anything else. I thought, 'I've killed him. I've got to get away.' Oh, I know if I'd been rational I'd have stayed, or at least I'd have told the police and faced the music, but, you see, I thought I'd killed him, and there was so much death there, so much death. . . . I grabbed up my bag—some instinct made me clutch that—but I forgot about the torch till I got to the garden gate, and then I couldn't have gone back for it to save my life. There was no moon and everything was as black as—as death. I kept slipping and sliding and clutching at the trunks of the trees. And every step I took, I could hear something moving round me; the leaves rustled and the rain dripped off the branches and I didn't dare look round because I knew he'd got up with his dead, bloody face and was coming after me. Once I felt his hand on my shoulder and I shrieked, but it was only a branch; and once I saw something moving, but it was just a shadow. I got out of the wood at last into a field, and I hid under a hedge in the hope that he'd go by without seeing me. I don't know how long I stayed there—it seemed hours—but I crept out at last through a gap onto the road. It was still dark and it seemed very cold. I didn't think anyone would recognize me by that time. I was clotted with mud, and my hat was drenching, and there was mud on my face and hands, where I'd crouched in the ditch. I heard a little bus coming along the road—they run a late bus for the factory workers—and it stopped and I got on board. I felt everyone must be staring at me but, of course, it was very dark, and there were scarcely any lights in the bus. The bus went to Newchester and everyone got out, and I got out too. I didn't know where to go. There was a church there with a wide porch. I'd seen it before when I drove over there. It was rather a famous church with a crusader tomb. I went and hid in the porch and wondered what I was going to do, and how soon they'd find Edmund—and Grace. I supposed Mrs. Hart would give the alarm and I'd be arrested for murder. And perhaps for Grace's murder too."

"What's your motive for murdering Miss Knowles?" Crook inquired sensibly.

"I was long past being logical by that time. But a lawyer could have made out that I was jealous of Grace, that there'd been a scene. I couldn't argue it out even to myself. I knew I shouldn't be able to hide long; I hadn't very much money, and I didn't know how I'd get any more. There was some in the bank but I wouldn't dare show myself there. I heard the church clock strike twelve, and almost immediately afterwards the sirens sounded. I could see flashes in the sky where our own shells went up, and then came a bomb—I knew what they were like because of the bombs in London. I'd been there until the beginning of the year, and we had as many in South Kensington as in a good many other places. People began to pour out onto the roads, and it seemed to me this was my chance. Anyway, I couldn't stay in the porch. The church might be hit at any minute. I came down into the road and no one paid any attention to me. They were all dressed in the oddest clothes, some in nightgowns with only a shawl or something thrown round them, and wardens and the police were herding them into shelter trenches. I went with the rest. There wasn't anything else to do."

"You certainly made a night of it," Crook agreed dryly. He took a small flask from his pocket. "Take a swig of this. No, you don't want to dilute it. The government's done all that for you."

Shivering, she did what she was told.

"And you've been here ever since?"

"Yes. When the raid was over they came down and began to ask our names and said they would fix us up somewhere else until the houses were fit to live in again—those that weren't absolutely destroyed, I mean. I gave them a lot of trouble because I didn't know what name to say. I had my identity card in my bag and I was terrified they would ask for it, but then Miss Bumble came in. She was splendid. She said she had room for a lodger, and she looked at me and picked up the handkerchief I'd dropped and asked me what my name was. I just stared, so she pointed to the initials. It was one I had before my marriage, and when I saw the initials 'A.F.' I said Alice Faulkner. She didn't ask a lot of questions; she said I could come along at once. There were several others in a state of collapse too, but mostly it was shock from the bombing. I hadn't been hurt by that, though I was in a worse mess than ever. The next day she went down with me to the town hall and got my card and ration book for me. There was such a rush on that they weren't too particular, and I overheard what another woman said about a whole row of houses being down and said I'd lived there. I couldn't believe it when they gave me my emergency cards and let me go. It was like a miracle."

"And how long did you imagine this was going on?"

"I didn't know. I just lived from day to day. At first I used to read through the paper looking for news about Edmund. But there wasn't any. I didn't know what had happened. I just waited. Then one morning about three weeks later I saw a headline. Police Search for Mrs. Durward. It didn't occur to me it was my body they were looking for. I thought it was me myself."

"It would have saved us a lot of trouble if you'd dropped Entwistle a line," Mr. Crook suggested dryly.

"How did you find me?" Agatha wanted to know.

"Oh, we get around, as I said before. And when I'd seen the contents of the suitcase I began to think the police were well in front of the hounds. You see, after that I was pretty sure you were alive."

"Why?"

"Your handbag—it wasn't there. Everything else, but no handbag. It wasn't in the house either or the shed or the ponds, and it wasn't likely Durward would dig a special grave for it. On the other hand, he wouldn't leave it lying about if he wanted to suggest you'd hooked it on your own account. No, I argued that you and your handbag would be found together, and it seemed reasonable that you were the person who'd removed it from The Haven. So I got a chap on the trail and we asked a question here and a question there. The black mackintosh helped. Your Mrs. Hart remembered there used to be one hanging on the door, but it wasn't there the day after you disappeared. It happened that someone a bit more observant than the rest remembered the black mackintosh. And then we went a bit farther, and a lady in a black mackintosh had been buying 'essential garments' as the officials put it, on special clothes coupons issued to the bombed-out. Well, one thing and another, we put our man to work and he came to the conclusion that Miss Agatha Forbes and Miss Alice Faulkner were the same person. It was you who went up to the bank on the 8th August, wasn't it, and drew out your balance? I thought so. There was a suggestion it might be your husband disguised, but he was always in Bridport on a Friday—never missed. And he wasn't the sort of chap to trust eighty pounds to anyone else."

"I had so little money and I had to get more. I was terrified of being recognized. But there'd been nothing in the paper about Edmund then, and I felt I better get it before they were openly looking for me. I tried to get a strange cashier, but I wasn't lucky."

"No one would absolutely swear to you. And there were plenty of people who believed it was your husband in disguise." He looked at her curiously. "Were you going to lie low for the rest of your days?"

"I don't know what I was going to do. I was terrified of Edmund discovering where I was and attacking me again, so that I shouldn't be able to give evidence against him."

"No law on earth can make you testify against him if you don't wish to," Crook told her dryly. "Still, he's going to have his work cut out explaining how the body of Miss Knowles got into the well. If he can cut his way out of that tangle, I'm a Chinaman."

✢   ✢   ✢

CHAPTER THIRTEEN

THE DURWARD case was now drawing to its astonishing close. The reappearance of Agatha staggered people all over the country. There were even those who were disappointed at being cheated of their second corpse. The inference was that it was inartistic on Agatha's part not to be lying in a wet ditch with her throat cut. On the other hand, there was a party who blamed her severely for remaining hidden so long. When her husband was being hounded for his supposed murder, a loyal wife, they declared, would have come forward to clear him. And there were a few sane and normal people who thought her behaviour quite natural in the circumstances. It cannot, these urged, be pleasant to find that your husband is a murderer.

After the missing woman's spectacular resurrection the authorities held an inquest on the body of Grace Knowles. Durward was still missing and Agatha was the chief, indeed, the only witness. Her story made a very strong impression on the jury, who returned a verdict of Wilful Murder against Edmund Durward. When Crook saw that he chuckled.

"Some of those fellows are going to eat their hats in the near future," he warned Bill. "Why, there's no evidence against the fellow at all. They can't even prove he put the body in the well."

"Some circumstantial evidence is very strong," quoted Bill solemnly, "as when you find a trout in the milk."

II

Edmund Durward, sitting in the lounge of his provincial hotel, read the finding of the coroner's jury and, going to the desk, informed the clerk that he had had a sudden summons to the deathbed of an aunt and would require his bill immediately. Since the police had given the public a detailed description of him, including the tell-tale scar at the corner of his mouth, he had worn a neat, dark moustache. He was travelling at his ease round the country, spending one or two nights at each hotel where he stayed. He gave out that he was engaged on private government work as soon as he arrived, and this appeared to engender instant confidence. When he heard of Agatha's appearance at the inquest he knew he had received his cue to resume his own identity.

Merton was discussing the situation with a couple of subordinates when Durward came into the station.

"I believe you are looking for me," he said, "in connection with a death that took place at my house some time ago."

He offered obvious proofs of identity and was immediately warned that anything he said might subsequently be used as evidence against him. Durward courteously acknowledged the forethought of the authorities, adding that he had nothing to say until he had consulted a lawyer. In conformity with the jury's decision he was then arrested for the wilful murder of Grace Knowles and allowed to send for his legal adviser.

Mr. David, Durward's solicitor, was a tall, thin man with a curiously shaped skull; it was very flat and broad above the ears; the nose was large and dominating, the mouth long and shrewd. He had a habit of cupping his long stubborn chin in his long, wrinkled hand while he spoke; this had a rather odd effect of which he himself was unaware.

He was surprised to find his client quite composed and not apparently much concerned with what, presumably, lay ahead.

"This is a bad business," he said abruptly. "You shouldn't have gone into hiding, you know. It doesn't make a scrap of difference to the facts, but it'll impress the jury. Their idea is that an innocent man gives the police every conceivable assistance. To clear out is always consistent in their mind with guilt."

"I'm not sure they haven't got something on their side," Durward agreed. "All the same, there's a greater loyalty than loyalty to the police."

David looked at him questioningly. "Loyalty to one's wife," Durward explained. "So long as Agatha stayed in hiding I couldn't come forward. Why, I didn't even know what story she was going to tell."

His solicitor frowned. "Don't say things like that in the box, will you?"

Durward smiled. "I know you're a model of discretion." Then his smile, so frank, so charming, faded and he looked troubled. "In fact, I'm going to rely a lot on your discretion. My position is a very unusual one. That's why I wouldn't make any statement to the police. I want your advice."

"Admit anything that can be proved," said David at once. "Once you're caught out in the smallest taradiddle, where the police are concerned, you're as good as hanged. As for what they can't prove, that's another matter."

"This case is going to make history," said Durward in thoughtful tones. "The point is—they can prove nothing. Neither side can prove a thing. You can't prove I'm innocent, but that doesn't matter. You don't have to. The point is they can't prove I'm guilty, and if they can't the case will go by default."

"This isn't Torquemada's crossword," said David drily. "And for heaven's sake don't indulge in wisecracks in court. Let's have your story."

"It begins with the visit of Miss Knowles to The Haven at my wife's invitation. She was, you might say, the only intimate friend my wife had. While she was with us she and Agatha would some-times talk about the ghost who was supposed to haunt The Bottom. I used to laugh at them for they both declared that if they saw the ghost they would be terrified. I told Agatha that if she did see it, she wouldn't collapse, she had too much good sense and too much courage. Perhaps Miss Knowles really wanted to put the matter to the test; perhaps she was—shall we say?—jealous of my wife. She gave me the impression of being very repressed, a little unbalanced. Her interests were incredibly narrow. All her talk was of this woman and that at her club, and how A wasn't speaking to B; and how C had intrigued to get D off the Harmony Sub-committee, and so forth. I suppose there may have been a time when my wife also was interested in that kind of thing, but if so it was in the past, and she'd put the past behind her. She simply wasn't interested in that kind of triviality any more. I don't mean," he added quickly, "that the new things that interested her couldn't be called almost equally trivial, but that's beside the point. They were no longer Miss Knowles's trivialities; and I certainly got the impression, when I was alone with our guest, that she resented the inevitable change in Agatha that marriage had made. I go into all this detail to try to explain what must have happened on Miss Knowles's last day with us."

"You mean, you're not sure what happened?"

"I can't be sure because I wasn't actually on the premises. My wife had had a bad headache and asked me to entertain our guest, who was catching a late train, leaving The Haven about six o'clock. Miss Knowles and I returned from sightseeing at about four o'clock. Agatha, who had been lying down, was still asleep. I had been a little troubled about some small discrepancy in the way my car was running, and as I was going to drive Miss Knowles to the station that night I thought I'd better take a look at the engine. Miss Knowles said she was going to gather flowers, and I recom-mended her to get them from the woods by the big pond. Then I went out. The garage is a little distance from the house and I heard nothing of what, according to my wife, subsequently occurred. The next step, so far as I'm concerned, was my return to the house at about a quarter to five. My wife and her guest were both in the hall. Agatha was leaning against the table with a look of absolute horror on her face. Miss Knowles, to my amazement, was crumpled at the foot of the stairs. I thought for a moment that she had fainted. I began to speak, but my wife turned to me babbling—there's no other word—about the ghost. I gathered that she'd seen the ghost. In fact, for a moment I thought they had both seen it, and Miss Knowles had collapsed in consequence. I only wish that were the truth, but the fact was far more tragic. I realized almost immediately that something appalling had taken place. My wife pointed to Miss Knowles and said something again about the ghost. Then I saw, crumpled in a corner of the hall, a white sheet, and began to understand what had happened. Our guest, either as a joke or as a piece of malicious mischief, had impersonated the ghost and driven Agatha almost out of her wits. Apparently she had come in and taunted my wife for being afraid. Agatha had leaped at her, half crazy with genuine terror, and had attacked her. She must have caught her by the throat, using more strength than either of us would have believed she possessed. For one instant more I thought Miss Knowles had fainted, but when I knelt beside her, trying to revive her, I realized what had happened. Agatha came and leaned against me, whispering, 'She is not dead, is she? People don't die so easily as that. She's just play-acting again. And then, when I said nothing, she went on, 'It was wicked, wasn't it, Edmund, quite wicked to try to frighten me like that?' I can't begin to make you you understand how I felt. For one thing Agatha didn't seem like the woman I'd married. She was a stranger, and a deranged stranger at that. I don't think she could take in the implications of what she'd done. She was mainly concerned with Miss Knowles's really quite brutal conduct. The fact that the woman was dead— for she was, though the body was still warm and flexible—didn't seem to strike through to her consciousness."

"But surely, her appearance . . ." objected David.

"Oh, there was no question about the appearance. The face was dark with blood, the tongue protruding. It was terrible. I realized that whatever Agatha had done it had been in a moment of frenzy. Normally, she wouldn't have struck a kitten. I knew, of course, she was very highly strung, and quite early in our married life she spoke to me of an aunt who had spent several years in a private asylum, suffering from delusions. She seemed at one time to be troubled with considerations of heredity, but I must say I didn't pay a great deal of attention. Most of us have some sort of skeleton in our cupboards, and it wasn't as if we had the next generation to consider."

He stopped, drawing a long breath and looking anxiously at Mr. David.

"It didn't occur to you to get the police, I suppose?" suggested David dryly.

"I see now that it was the obvious thing to do, but, in the circumstances—well, what would you have done yourself? Agatha was my wife. If the police were called in she would certainly be arrested for murder, and the best that could happen would be detention at His Majesty's pleasure. It might be even worse than that. There had never been any sign of madness, or even of eccentricity during our life together, and it didn't seem very likely that anyone else would come forward to suggest a mental taint. I saw my wife being sentenced to penal servitude for life—I don't think I thought they would hang her—and I couldn't do it. If anyone else had found her—but I was her husband. I'd always thought of her as someone to be looked after—she wasn't one of the shrieking sisterhood who know they're as good as you are and a damned sight better. And, faced with that horror on the floor, and my wife, half out of her mind, begging me to protect her, I did a criminal thing—I became an accessory after the fact. Once that happened, all the rest followed."

"I wouldn't have believed you'd be such a fool," said David.

"Fool or not, at the time it seemed to me the only way out. The first thing to do was to get rid of the body. I hadn't realized how heavy quite a small woman can be when she's dead. I had to get Agatha to help me. Together we lifted her up and got her into the shed. The trunk was empty at the time—I filled it up with books afterwards—and we crammed her into it and shut down the lid. It must have been about then that Agatha seemed suddenly to realize what she'd done. She had a violent fit of hysterics and began to run and caught her foot and fell. It was a good thing really, because she knocked herself completely out. That gave me a minute to think. I knew, of course, it wouldn't be advisable to leave the body in the trunk long, but first of all I had to see to Agatha. I picked her up and carried her into the house—she wasn't nearly so heavy as Miss Knowles—and then I remembered the luggage in the guest's room. It would be a mistake for the guest to disappear and the luggage to remain. I had to get the doctor for Agatha, who was still unconscious, so I put Miss Knowles's gear in the car and drove it to the station, where I labelled it Paddington—To Be Called For. On the way back I called in on Dr. Howarth. I had to think up some story to account for Agatha's collapse, and it seemed to me, up to a certain point, it would be a good thing to tell the truth. I said, therefore, that we had had a guest staying with us who was a keen amateur actor, and she had thought it a good joke to dress up as the ghost. When Agatha did come round she didn't remember anything of what had happened. Shock, I suppose, had blurred her mind. All she knew was that she had seen the ghost and was simply terrified. She kept begging me not to go away, not to leave her. The doctor gave her a sedative and promised to come in the next morning."

"Do you mean," interrupted David, "that your wife really believes the story she told at the inquest?"

"As to that, you must judge for yourself when you've heard the rest of my story. What I am convinced of is that for some time afterwards she honestly had no recollection of what had taken place. She was very nervy and cried very easily for two or three days and, of course, she insisted that the ghost was a genuine spectre. I'd taken Howarth partially into my confidence and presently he told me he thought it would be wise to tell my wife the truth about Miss Knowles impersonating the thing. I wasn't sure but I felt I should be guided by him, and did so, with the result I had anticipated. My wife at first wouldn't believe me; then, when she did, she exclaimed that she never wanted to have anything to do with her friend again, wouldn't write, wouldn't see her, would never forgive her. But still she didn't appear to recall anything of what had really happened. In a way it was a good thing she felt so strongly because she didn't worry when no letter came from Miss Knowles, and she stubbornly refused to write to her. We agreed we must leave the house; she said she would never be happy there again, and after what had happened you can imagine I had no particular wish to remain."

"What about the body?" asked David.

"I was in a bad quandary about that. Had my wife recalled the circumstances I could, of course, have buried the body in The Bottom, and it was long odds against it ever being found. But digging of that sort can't be done by night, and during the day my wife practically never left my side. I couldn't let her see the body, so long as her memory remained clouded, in case she really did go out of her mind. All I could do was hope an opportunity would present itself."

"You were taking a lot of risk, weren't you?"

"I accepted the risk when I hid the body. For the time being it was safe enough in the woodshed. No one but myself had the key and, as I had always kept the place locked, it didn't arouse any comment that I should continue to do so. All the same, I began to feel pretty insecure. If Agatha went out alone to the village, Mrs. Hart would be on the premises, and by the time Mrs. Hart had gone, Agatha would be back. Then came the incident at Bridport. I don't know what happened, but I imagine that some chance word, some trivial occurrence, was enough to readjust my wife's memory, and in a flash she recollected everything. The shock, naturally, was terrific. Indeed, she fainted."

"Did she tell you this afterwards?"

"She didn't speak of it, but she muttered about 'the ghost' and showed an extraordinary aversion to returning to the house at all. I can think of nothing else that would account for the lightning change in her. Besides, what happened later that evening bears out my theory."

"What did happen?"

"I got her home and into bed. Later I took up her supper, and then, finding myself out of tobacco, I asked her if she would mind my going as far as old Bannerman to get some. She said she would be all right. As a matter of fact I had to find some place where the body could be hidden and where it wouldn't be likely to be found, and I had to do it quickly. Now that Agatha was, as I believed, halfway to recollection, there was no time to lose. She might endanger both our necks at any moment. It was unfortunately a wet kind of night, and in any case I couldn't dig a grave at that hour. I did consider dumping the body in the pond, but if inquiries should be started that was the first place the police would examine. Then I remembered The Warren. Agatha and I had been over the place when we were looking for a house, and it seemed to me a body might remain there for months, if not years, without being found."

"And when it was, it mightn't be recognizable?"

"They can always tell a good deal by the clothes, can't they? Anyway, I didn't dare look very far ahead. I came back, determined to get rid of the body that very night, and found my worst suspicions justified. My wife had left her bed and had crept downstairs. She must have known where I kept the key of the woodshed for she had found it and opened the shed, and when I came into the garden she was standing by the open trunk, staring down at—at the body. I came up to her and told her she should be in bed, tried to take her away. And she began to scream and say that I'd murdered her only friend. I don't think she was play-acting. I think her memory had only partly returned. She recollected helping me to put something into the trunk, without remembering the earlier part of the story."

"Very convenient for her," growled David. "Did she take any notice of you?"

"By this time she was over the edge of sanity, I'm convinced of it. She fought herself free from me with a strength I wouldn't have believed she possessed. I understood that night how she could have strangled Grace Knowles. It had always puzzled me till then. She began to shriek like a mad thing—it was lucky there was no one near enough to hear her—and suddenly she snatched up a spade and lunged out at me. I wasn't prepared for that. I went down like a stone. The next thing I knew was that I was still in the woodshed, with Agatha's little torch shining straight on the trunk and its ghastly burden, and you can take my word it did look pretty ghastly after three weeks. I wasn't surprised that the sight of it had done for Agatha's sanity. My first thought was for Agatha. I didn't believe she had gone away without even a torch. She hated the dark. But when I staggered into the house there wasn't a trace of her anywhere. I had no idea where she had gone. In that state of mind she would be capable of anything. But I did realize that the first thing for me to do was get rid of that body. I washed some of the blood off my face, and then I went down and tied up the corpse in old sacks"—the sweat came out on his forehead at the recollection—"and somehow I lugged it into the car and drove to The Warren. It all took much longer than I expected, but at last I got it shoved down the well. When I got back I could scarcely walk, but I didn't dare rest. I had to refill the trunk with books. I didn't want people to come examining it."

David didn't ask him why. It was too hideously obvious.

"I seemed to spend hours coming to and from the house bringing books to fill the trunk, but at last it was done. I felt so exhausted I couldn't go up to bed. I just dropped onto a couch in the living room and dozed a bit there. When I woke it was all like a nightmare. I had to go out to the shed to make sure the body had gone. Well, it had. And so had Agatha. The only woman who hadn't gone was Mrs. Hart, who arrived as cheerful as dammit and started to make inconvenient remarks. I could see she didn't believe my story about Agatha having been called to town, but until I had some news of her I didn't know what to do. That afternoon I realized that, to give some semblance of truth to my story some of Agatha's clothes should be missing, so I packed the suitcase and buried it that evening. I hoped Mrs. Hart hadn't noticed she had taken nothing with her."

"That type of woman doesn't miss much."

"On the other hand, no jury would dare rely on her statem•nts. Any counsel could tie her in knots. Well, there's the story. I'd like your opinion on it. Which of us will be believed? Agatha or I?"

III

David leaned against the wall, hands in pockets, and stared at his client.

"Are you telling me that's the story you're going to offer the court?"

"You said yourself it was better to stick to the truth."

"Truth? Do you think a jury's going to swallow that? Why, you can't prove a word of it."

"I know. But, on the other hand, they can't prove that I killed Grace Knowles. After all, they've got to declare publicly that I'm guilty *beyond all reasonable doubt*. Don't you think, in the circumstances, they'll feel there is reasonable doubt?"

David considered. "Yes," he said at last. "They probably will. It'll only be a skin-of-the-teeth verdict, all the same. Not too satisfactory from your point of view."

"A damned sight more satisfactory than hanging by the neck until I'm dead," said Durward dryly.

David moved restlessly up and down. "It's asking a good deal of the average Englishman to believe that a woman like Mrs. Durward, not very young and not, so far as appearances go at all events, very robust, could strangle a woman. It's not a female method of murder."

"It's not without precedent," Durward urged. "And at least it proves there was no premeditation. Then, too, you have to consider the other woman. Miss Knowles was older than my wife, a small, rather nervy woman, given to talking of her own indifferent health. She brought a number of bottles of tonics and globules and so forth with her. And—though I suppose it's unchivalrous of me to labour the point—the jury will know that my wife had admittedly made a murderous attack upon me with a spade. In fact, she says she thought it was fatal, and it did knock me out for some considerable time. I suppose the truth is that when she was really up against it, over the edge, as it were, she had a measure of strength that normally she didn't possess. Don't they tell you that lunatics can perform prodigious feats that, in their sane hours, would be utterly impossible to them?"

"You're suggesting that your wife is actually insane?"

"I wouldn't like to go so far as that, but I do urge that at such moments as the one when she attacked Miss Knowles, and again when she dashed at me with the spade, she didn't know what she was doing."

"There's only one place for people like that," returned David dryly, "and that's an asylum. By the way, can you back up your theory at all? I mean, had she ever showed signs of abnormality or acute nervous strain before this?"

"Actually, she hadn't. I knew from the outset that she was rather highly strung. Perhaps coming to marriage comparatively late in life, after a very—er—abstemious and celibate existence—would account for it. But that's not precisely the same thing."

"Not precisely," David agreed in his dry way. "Was she ever under a doctor before the night of Miss Knowles's death?"

"So far as I know she never saw one down at Maplegrove."

"We can check up her London record, of course. But she seems to have lived alone and gone about at her club, etc., without ever exciting comment or arousing any sort of suspicion. On the other hand, we can probably produce evidence to the effect that she was terrified of the supernatural and had been heard by several people to say that if she ever did see a ghost she would go crazy." He stroked his cheek. "There's another point. There's no proof, from the prosecution's point of view, that Miss Knowles did dress up as the ghost. We've got to account somehow for her extraordinary behaviour. Do you seriously think she thought it was a good joke?"

Durward looked a little embarrassed. "Honestly, I don't. The impression I got of her was of a woman with a grudge against life. She hadn't minded so much when she and Agatha were, so to speak, on the same level, but—well, I suppose it's natural in a woman to want her own home and—and admiration and protection —and Miss Knowles had never had anything of the kind—and she was jealous. It's an ugly thing to say, but I'm convinced that was the truth. I think Agatha thought so too. That's why she sent us out together sometimes, and—well, perhaps I was indiscreet."

David looked horrified. "You're not trying to tell me you were fool enough to make love to the woman?"

"Of course not. Anyway, there was no temptation. But—I was rather proud of Agatha and, after all, we'd only been married six months. I rather sang her praises to her friend, said how plucky she was . . ."

"And Miss Knowles thought she'd show you that everyone has his heel of Achilles? Yes, it's a possible story and you're probably right about the verdict. All the same, it's got to be very carefully handled. Your wife has, unfortunately, developed the strongest possible feeling against you."

Durward knitted his brows. "I suppose if she really thinks I murdered her friend, that's easily understood."

"I'm afraid it's more than that. Mrs. Durward's got it firmly into her head that *you* were impersonating the ghost."

Durward nodded. "I gathered something of the kind. But,

frankly, will any jury believe that? What conceivable motive does she suggest I had? She had told me repeatedly that she'd go out of her mind if she did see anything supernatural. What sense would there be in my taking such a risk? Suppose she really had gone mad, permanently mad? I should still be responsible for her, and no man wants a lunatic for a wife."

"That's true. That's a point we can make for the defence. Though, as to motive, the prosecution will suggest that you wanted to lay hands on your wife's capital and, owing to the terms of her father's will, you had to adopt rather unusual methods."

"Meaning that I had to furnish some strong reason why she should want to get out of the house—knowing it wouldn't be possible to rent anything and that my own capital wouldn't be sufficient for the purpose?"

"You seem to have a remarkably clear view of the position," David complimented him grimly.

"I've had plenty of time to think about it. You know, I call that a bit far-fetched. I didn't know she was going to hand the cheque over to me."

"The suggestion will be that you intended to get hold of it, and Mrs. Durward will certainly say she would have given you that or anything else she had at that time. Did she, by the way, ever render you financial assistance prior to that date?"

"She made a contribution towards the housekeeping once or twice," Agatha's husband acknowledged. "But there was nothing formal about it, and neither of us thought it anything out of the ordinary."

"As a loan?"

"There wasn't any question of repayment. She'd have been furious at the idea."

"Did you ask for the money?"

Durward hesitated. "I suppose the prosecution could say so. As a matter of fact, she and I were on such excellent terms that . . ."

"Quite," David interrupted. "The Crown will say they were so excellent that she had no suspicions of you, that you played your cards in a masterly fashion and had completely won her confidence. No, we don't want more of that in the witness box than we can help."

"But, look here"—Durward sounded agitated for the first time—"if I had had any such fool idea as impersonating the ghost, common sense will point out that I shouldn't have taken such a risk with a third person on the premises. I had plenty of opportunity . . ."

"Ah, but suppose she had suspected human agency? It was always possible, and in that case you'd have been able to throw the suspicion on Miss Knowles, and the odds are she'd have taken your word against her friend's."

"Still, that's mere supposition. I don't see how counsel will dare bring that into court. No one can produce a tittle of evidence that I had the remotest idea of terrorizing my wife. On the contrary, everyone will tell you we were a devoted couple."

"An argument like that is like Baker Street Station, it goes all ways at once. It might merely be further proof of your cunning."

Durward shook his head decisively. "No good, David. The fact is there isn't a scrap of evidence on either side. I say that Agatha strangled the poor woman in a fit of panic; she says I did the same thing from a different motive. I can't prove that she's guilty and she can't prove that I am, and I'm damned if I see how the court can prove anything either. It's her word against mine. I admit I helped to conceal the body; Agatha says she doesn't remember anything of that. She claims to have been completely 'out' between four-thirty and six-fifteen. I say she didn't catch her foot and collapse until a few minutes after five. Again, there's no proof either way. Howarth can tell the jury that she was unconscious when he arrived, but from the prosecution's point of view he arrived an hour too late."

"From the defence's point of view too," David reminded him in his grim way.

"At five o'clock we were shifting the body," Durward insisted. "I remember hearing the clock chime, and Agatha gave a little scream, thinking it was a bell. That clock sounds remarkably like a bell sometimes. And I remember stumbling over a flower basket I'd lent Miss Knowles—she said she was going to pick flowers to take back to town—and Agatha giving another little scream as the corpse lurched. It's pretty difficult, isn't it? I mean, you can argue all round the clock and meet yourself going to bed and get no further."

David abandoned that point and passed to the next. "There's something else we've got to remember. At the present moment, you're something of a national hero. You've let yourself virtually be accused of your wife's murder, and you've lain low on her account. People like you for that. I suppose it won't be necessary to point out that by coming into the open you'd have been forced to reveal the fact of Miss Knowles's death and the circumstances attending it. The average person won't think that out for himself. But when you come forward with this story and clear yourself, or attempt to do so, at her expense, the general feeling will be that you're trying to put her in the dock in your place."

Durward gave him a rueful smile. "This legend about the

chivalry of the male has its inconvenient side," he confessed. "I was very fond of Agatha and I don't think I could be called a bad husband to her, but even so I don't want to hang just to save her feelings. Actually, there can't be any question of her being held on a murder charge on my evidence. No magistrate would allow the case to go to court. If I were guilty and she had fainted at four-thirty, as she says, what a grand chance for me to saddle her with the responsibility. She admittedly remembers nothing. No, I don't fancy her neck's in any danger. If she can't prove that I killed Miss Knowles, I certainly can't prove that she did."

David eyed him gloomily. "The probable upshot of this will be that the general public will assume it's a policy of mutual defence."

"But, good heavens, man, they'll have to prove motive surely. Oh, you mean they'll say I was the ghost-and she found out and threatened to tell Agatha, so I strangled her. But that doesn't hold water either. If my wife had fainted, I only had to swear when she came round that Miss Knowles had worn the sheet, and she certainly would have believed me, as you yourself have already pointed out. No, that cock won't fight."

David considered. "There is, of course, the fact that Mrs. Durward made a murderous attack on you on the 25th July, but the Crown will urge self-defence."

"I hadn't laid a finger on her. There was no question of an attack. I simply wanted to get her away. I could see that the realization of what had happened, her discovery of Miss Knowles's body had tipped her off her balance. That, incidentally, is why I was playing a waiting game about the house. I naturally agreed when my wife suggested leaving The Haven. She had been very melancholy after the affair of Miss Knowles's death, though I honestly don't believe she remembered what had happened. The doctor was very anxious for her to go; he thought the site un-healthy, but I don't think it was unnatural in me not to be too anxious to tie myself down to a large and costly house with a woman who might develop homicidal mania in my own direction at any time."

"You didn't suggest your wife seeing a doctor?"

"It was a bit difficult," his client demurred. "She'd have asked at once what for. Besides, it would have to have been a mental specialist. No, I simply didn't know what to do. I couldn't confide in anyone."

"That's plausible enough," David admitted. "By the way, I suppose the cheque she gave you is still—er——"

"I'm prepared to hand it to her representatives at any time."

Durward blessed his forethought in restoring the money to the bank before taking his story to the police.

"I don't think I've ever had a case quite like this," David agreed. "So far as I can see there isn't a scrap of evidence either way."

Durward nodded. "Legal stalemate; and any jury in the land would be bound to agree. But all the same," he added grimly, "it's not exactly an enjoyable situation, look at it any way you please."

IV

Sir Aubrey Bruce, K.C., was giving himself a rare evening off when his telephone rang and David's voice said, "Doing anything tonight, Bruce? Fine. There's something I'd like to discuss with you. Be round in twenty minutes."

Twenty-two minutes later he was unwinding his muffler and marching up and down the K.C.'s study.

"It's this Durward case," he explained. "It's one of the most astounding defences I've ever struck—but is there any chance it'll hold water?" He plunged into details. Bruce listened, enthralled, while he drew his familiar fish all over the blotting paper. A handsome moustachioed fish for Durward; a sturdy, pot-bellied fish for Crook (whom he knew and whose skill evoked his reluctant admiration); a slender, silvery fish for the elusive Agatha; a poor, gasping little fish for the unfortunate Grace; an elegant, elderly fish for David himself.

"Well?" said the solicitor belligerently, winding up his case.

"Suppose you were on the jury?" said Bruce. "I take it no new evidence is likely to be offered. What would you say?"

Mr. David considered. "In my own country—Not Proven."

"And in the alien south—Not Guilty. And you'd be right. There's no direct evidence."

"Circumstantial evidence has hanged plenty of men," David reminded him.

"Not when it points both ways, as it does here. Whatever information is laid before the court can tell equally against Durward *or* his wife. No, if he's a murderer he's an experienced one. Mrs. Durward's the one witness the Crown can call, provided she's prepared to give evidence against her husband, and all she can say is that she infers he's guilty, since it's a choice between the pair of them and, naturally, she's not going to implicate herself."

"If she's telling the truth, she can't. She swears everything went blank."

"Much her best defence. I wouldn't be surprised to hear Crook put her up to it. It's his favourite defence. I didn't see, I don't remember, everything went blank—and actually it's a pretty good one. It throws all the responsibility on the police. Even the most cantankerous judge won't expect a witness's memory to return under cross-examination. But if it's a good defence for Mrs. Durward, it's a first-class one for Durward too. He's got a witness to prove his point about her being unconscious. Therefore, there's no one to contradict his story or back up hers."

David looked gloomy. "That's what Durward insists. There's no proof anywhere."

"Except that Durward was popular and apparently an excellent husband. I'm told there's a letter written by the unfortunate Miss Knowles to a London friend, Miss Wharton, saying that Mrs. Durward seemed divinely happy and that the husband was utterly devoted."

"That's Mrs. Hart's story too. Though actually I wouldn't care to have her in the box. She puts a sinister interpretation on his devotion. Then, too, there's the fact that Mrs. Durward told Mrs. Hart that Grace Knowles had impersonated the ghost. Oh, Durward's defence may be as fantastic as something by Walt Disney, but there's one chance in a hundred it's true, and that one chance is going to save his neck. If the jury's properly instructed it'll know that the question before it isn't who killed her if Durward didn't? But can we say beyond all reasonable doubt that this man is guilty?"

"That's very encouraging for Durward," was Bruce's dry comment.

David flung him a sidelong glance. "Frankly and unprofessionally, Bruce—what do you think?"

"Frankly and unprofessionally," said Bruce, "I think he's as guilty as hell, but I don't think he'll swing for it for all that."

❀   ❀   ❀

CHAPTER FOURTEEN

IN HIS PRISON CELL Durward sat considering the story he would tell the magistrate in the course of the next forty-eight hours. It differed in no particular from the story he had already offered to his solicitor. He went over it in great detail, but he could find no flaw. People could talk as much as they pleased, and talk they certainly would, but a court demanded proof. And there wasn't a living soul able to provide it. Agatha's fortunate collapse was his trump card. During that missing hour and a half anything might have happened; she wasn't in a position to deny anything. No, he told himself, his moment of real danger—and how real that had been—was two months old. If Agatha had suddenly regained consciousness while he was struggling with Grace Knowles, then he might indeed be a lost man. But as it was, she was in no better position to establish her innocence than he. He blessed the British system of justice that demanded weight of evidence for a conviction. It might not be a popular verdict, but already he knew it was a certain one.

II

There had been some difficulty in deciding on the best plan for Agatha while matters were in the melting-pot. Clearly she could not return to The Haven; Miss Bumble would probably refuse to keep her, after what she regarded as wilful deception, and in any case the notoriety would be too distressing; while London was large and vague, and Agatha's only friend, Grace Knowles had done with London for good and all. Eventually Miss Martin came forward with a suggestion.

"Why not let her stay with us for a bit?" she asked Crook. "She'll be safe there. You don't see any reporter getting past me or Violet, except as chicken feed."

Crook thought she was probably right. But "Go there?" exclaimed Agatha. "Why, I hardly know them."

"Then they won't presume to lecture you. Only friends and relations do that."

"I don't feel I could stay in the neighbourhood," shuddered Agatha. "I should see the ghost of Grace every time I went out."

"Oh, you won't be going out much," said Crook callously. "That is, not if you're wise."

"But—Edmund's under lock and key. I'm safe from him now."

"I wasn't thinking of your husband, but of people generally. You take my tip and stick to the house."

She looked at him incredulously. "Mr. Crook, you can't mean . . ."

"Now, now, now, don't you try and tell me what I mean. What you have to remember is that your husband's had a lot of experience at pulling wool over people's eyes, and you know yourself what a nice sympathetic manner he's got."

Agatha shuddered. "You mean, people believe his story? They think he was shielding me?"

"It's a charming touch, you must admit that. How often do I have to tell you amateurs that truth's what you can persuade the other chap to believe? And I'd say your husband was first-rate at winnin' people round to his way of thinkin'."

She was looking at him, aghast. "You mean, they may really think I'm guilty, may try to arrest me?"

"Oh, it won't come to that," Crook assured her. "There's no evidence against you, except his story."

"Which isn't true."

Crook sighed. "There you go again. You leave this to the experts, Mrs. Durward. I can promise you no one will take you for the murder but, things bein' the way they are, you stay comfortably at The Buddies and don't go for any nice long walks on your own."

As it happened, the arrangement was the best Agatha could have made. She had no conception of the feeling locally; Durward's story had been told with so much hesitation, so much surface chivalry, that even those who had been loudest in their condemnation of the man while the search for Agatha was in progress now made public recantation of their suspicions. The general view was: If she was innocent, why didn't she go to the police and tell them she'd batted him over the head with a spade? And, if she really hadn't known about Grace Knowles's death, why did she keep so precious quiet about it after she did find out? It wasn't loyalty, it wasn't cricket, and no one can say more than that. Durward, on the other hand, had displayed loyalty all through. He had tried to cover Agatha at every turn. He hadn't even accused her of attacking him. Yet she had been prepared to see him arrested on suspicion for her own death. Public opinion was hot against her.

The Buddies had never troubled themselves much about public opinion. They believed, and said in round, clear voices, that if you had a job of work to do you'd much better give your time to that, instead of discussing something you knew nothing about.

Anyway, they weren't going to be asked to say which was innocent, which guilty. Whatever the law decided they would accept. Of course, there was always a chance the law would be wrong, but there was even more chance that outsiders would err. The law was paid to be right, anyhow, and it mostly was. Thus The Buddies, common-sense, unemotional women, wrapped up in the concerns of their cats, hens and rabbits, the majority of whom were, as always, in an interesting condition.

But if The Buddies were determinedly indifferent, there were others who still found Agatha a focus of interest. She hadn't been twenty-four hours on the premises when Merton swung open the gate and asked to see her.

"I'm sorry to bother you again," he said civilly, "but now that your husband has turned up, there are a few points we have to check in connection with Miss Knowles's death. Now, can you remember the precise time when you saw the—apparition?"

Agatha considered. "It was a little after four when I woke. I didn't get up quite at once, but lay listening for sounds of movement in the house. It would be about a quarter-past, I suppose, when I came onto the landing. I couldn't hear anything, and I went into Miss Knowles's room. Her suitcase was there, but she wasn't. I thought they were running it rather fine and that perhaps the car had broken down. I went back to my room and just got tidy and came down the stairs. I remember hearing the clock chime the half-hour as I went into the garden. And it would be a minute or two later that I saw the ghost."

"And how long after that that you fainted?"

"Naturally, it's not very easy for me to say." Agatha's voice was sharp with intolerable strain. "I don't suppose it was more than a minute really, though I seemed to stand there watching her—it—for ages. Then I ran towards the house and caught my foot . . ."

"And when you came round . . . ?"

"I was in my room—I've told you all this before—with my husband and Dr. Howarth beside me."

"Have you any notion what time that was?"

"It must have been a little after six. I remember the doctor saying something about having missed the news."

"So that for approximately an hour and a half you were completely 'out'? You remember nothing of what happened in that time?"

"I've told you I don't," cried Agatha desperately. "Oh, why must you come asking me the same questions again and again? I shan't change my story, and I'm not likely to remember anything now that I didn't remember before."

171

"Of course not, Mrs. Durward. But you must admit that his story throws a slightly different complexion on the case. Now, I've only one more point to raise. You've told us that the 25th July was the first day that you became apprehensive about your husband?"

"After I telephoned Mr. Ainslie—yes. After that, I was terrified. I felt I couldn't stay in the house with him any longer."

"And at about seven o'clock that evening you heard him leave the house after he had brought you a meal in bed?"

"Yes." She stared at him dumbly. Whither were all these questions leading?

"And immediately you decided to leave too?"

"I felt I had to get away before he returned. I couldn't be found on the premises. I felt that perhaps my very life depended on it."

"You were in such haste you didn't even pause to pack a bag or collect your toilet things?"

"I felt every instant was important."

Merton's face seemed to harden. "Then, Mrs. Durward, how was it that, feeling as you did, you deliberately returned to the house, after leaving it, searched for the key of the woodshed and opened it, although you had no idea what it contained?"

"I—that was just it—I had to know."

"You realized that your husband had only gone as far as the village and might return at any moment?"

"By that time I'd come to the conclusion that the tobacco was just an excuse. He had gone for good. And before I left I had to know what was in the woodshed."

"You hadn't felt particularly curious about it up till that time?"

"N-no."

"You had had other opportunities of examining the shed when your husband was not by?"

"I suppose I had, but it never occurred to me . . ."

"And the shed hadn't been mentioned between you since your telephone call that afternoon?"

"Certainly not."

"Then—I don't understand, Mrs. Durward. You felt your life was at stake, that everything depended on your getting away at once, and yet your curiosity was so overwhelming that you were prepared to take unparalleled risks to know why your husband kept the shed locked?"

Agatha clenched her hands. "I can't make you understand how I felt about it. I had to see what was inside, I had to, I had to."

"Yes, Mrs. Durward, I realize that. But should I be far wrong if I suggested that you had to see inside the shed because you knew what was in it and couldn't keep away?"

Agatha's mouth fell open; her face turned greenish white. "I knew? How can you suggest such a thing? As if I'd have stayed a night in the house if I'd known. I believed Grace had been back in London for weeks. . . ."

"And yet you never wrote to her."

"After what my husband had told me, I didn't feel I could have any more to do with her."

"You didn't think it strange she didn't write to you?"

"I accepted my husband's word that there had been such a scene between them she wouldn't dare write."

"And when you did learn the secret of the woodshed, it didn't occur to you even then to go to the police?"

"How could I? No one could have killed her but Edmund and —and I thought I'd killed him."

"You could have pleaded self-defence."

"Oh, it all sounds so simple now," cried poor Agatha, "but at the time I didn't feel like a sane person. The world was breaking up all round me—no, there aren't words to explain. It was like being caught in a quicksand and knowing you can't save yourself."

"You'd never felt like that before, of course?"

"Never. Except, perhaps, on the afternoon I saw the ghost."

Merton nodded. "I see," he said. "Thank you, Mrs. Durward. That's all I want for the moment."

He had a word with Miss Martin on his way out.

"That chap thinks Agatha may have done it," Evelyn Martin confided to her friend later. "Brain storms—you know."

"I hope to goodness she won't have any while she's here," said Violet Grainger sincerely. "It would be too bad if she upset Josephine just now. You'd better warn her not to come upstairs more than she can help. There's no reason why Josephine should suffer because Agatha's unbalanced."

III

"This is a nice thing for me," grumbled Mr. Hart ferociously to his wife. "Getting yourself in the papers and all. Why you must work for murderers I don't know."

"I wasn't to guess they were murderers," retorted Mrs. Hart in her usual spirited tones. "And their money buys as much as anyone else's, don't it?"

"None of your lip. You were always telling me 'e was a wrong 'un."

"So 'e was. I could see the shadder of the gallows on that 'ouse from the first."

"It's a wonder you stayed."

"I was sorry for 'er. Poor thing, I'll never believe she done it. Why, she wouldn't 'ave the guts. No, 'e planned all this and now, if 'e does get off, it'll be a crool shame and a blot on the fair fame of British justice."

"If she give 'im 'arf as much tongue as what you give me, I don't blame 'im if 'e did mean to send 'er to join the one in the well," exploded the harassed Mr. Hart. "As for this picture of you in the papers, it's a disgrace. . . ."

"It isn't me, if you want to know," returned Mrs. Hart, defiantly. "It's my sister, Lil. I sent the wrong photo by mistake."

"Just what you would do," said Mr. Hart disgustedly. "Now, most likely they'll pull me in for bigamy."

"Coo!" whispered Mrs. Hart. "I never thought of that. Any-'ow, I'll do the thing in style next time. When I go into Bridport tomorrer I'll drop in at Polyfoto and 'ave meself took in forty-eight positions."

IV

Miss Martin came back from her weekly excursion to Bridport and called softly to her friend. Miss Grainger had been left behind for once, less on Agatha's account than on Josephine's. Both spinsters felt that Agatha would be a disturbing influence for their pet in a crisis, and both, as usual, had hopes that this time Josephine would "pull it off" as they expressed it.

"Violet—you there? Oh, yes. I say, they've discharged that husband of Agatha's—insufficient evidence to go to a jury. What do you make of that?"

"Will they take Agatha now?"

"I shouldn't think so. If there isn't enough evidence against him, there's even less against her."

"Then no one's going to swing for Miss Knowles? It seems a bit unfair somehow. If I were murdered I should like to think some-one besides me had to suffer for it. What about Agatha now?"

"I don't know, I'm sure. She's still his wife."

"You're not suggesting she should go back to him?"

"Well, my dear, I shouldn't think he'd want her. After all, she has done her best to slice his head open with a spade."

"That's true. Well—oh, the woman must have some friends."

"I doubt it. Goodness knows what'll become of her."

"You're not suggesting she shall stay here for good?"

"Oh, no. She wouldn't want it, either. Surely there are places where solitary women can be some use. Couldn't she go to live in a convent guest house?"

"It sounds a bit penitential."

"Oh, I don't think so. My Aunt Maggie lived in one for years. She and the Reverend Mother hit it off like anything. She used to arrange the flowers on saints' days."

"It'll be a bit of a change after living with dear Edmund."

"Take care. I hear her."

Agatha, who had been trying to make herself useful in the garden, came nervously in, carrying a letter that had just arrived.

"Oh—Evelyn—I thought I heard you. Did you—is there any news?"

Miss Martin told her. Agatha turned rather paler than before. But before anyone could speak there was the violent clang of the telephone bell and Miss Grainger went to answer it. "Hallo! Yes, all right. You can dictate it to me. Pencil, Evelyn. Yes, I'll tell her. Go ahead." She scribbled busily. "Yes, I'll read it back. 'Expecting you twelve o'clock tomorrow. Crook.' Right." She hung up the receiver. "It's for you, Agatha. I expect your lawyer wants to make suggestions about the future." She nodded cheerfully and went out.

"Oh, yes." Agatha looked vacant. "I can't imagine—I mean, I couldn't go back to London—the Hiawatha . . ."

"You mustn't be hypersensitive," Miss Martin told her firmly. "Just remember we're in the middle of a war involving millions of men, and history's being made every day. No one's going to pay much attention to the individual in the circumstances."

"That," said Agatha, with gentle irony, "will be a nice change."

Miss Grainger's voice sounded from the stairs, low, enchanted, athrill.

"Evelyn! Evelyn! You must come up. Josephine . . ."

"You don't mean . . . ?"

"Yes. Four. And not a tail among them."

Miss Martin stumbled excitedly up the stairs. A door closed. Agatha stayed where she was in the hall. She could hear an excited buzz of voices from the floor above. It occurred to her that there might be something quite cosy about a grave.

❦ ❦ ❦

175

CHAPTER FIFTEEN

MR. CROOK sat behind his office desk, very stiff and solid, looking like a rather ugly little idol expectant of incense.

"He's done us brown, Bill," said he grimly. "Not a loophole anywhere. I always said I'd like to be on his side. He's the sort of client that does a man credit." He drew a long breath. " 'The Man Who Diddled Arthur Crook.' What an epitaph for a tombstone."

"How about Mrs. Durward?" asked Bill.

"I've told her to come and see me at twelve o'clock. We must fix her future. Hallo, there she is."

Bill went out and came back, escorting Agatha. She looked bewildered and lost. Her husband was a murderer (though unconvicted), she hadn't enough money to live on, she was too old (she thought) to work. Unless, of course, she could be her own employer, and now that Edmund had her capital that was out of the question. At the sight of Crook, however, so serene, so bumptious, so clearly master of his fate, some of her courage returned.

"Take a pew," said Crook. "How's tricks?"

Agatha murmured that she was quite well.

"How are The Buddies?"

"They've been very kind," Agatha agreed.

"Not much of a life, though."

"It suits them. I believe that sort of thing would suit me. Flowers. Vegetables. A house and garden."

"Well," said Crook cheerfully, "why not?"

Agatha looked startled again. "I intended to write to Mr. Entwistle. I must, of course, make some plan for the future, and it must be something unconnected with the past."

Crook looked at her approvingly. "You'll do. All the past things are past and over. The deeds are done and the tears are shed. Used to have that hanging over my bed as a kid. About Entwistle. He's handed you over to me. You're not his cup of tea any more. Entwistle likes his clients to stop short of serious issues. And he draws the line at murder."

"So do I," said Agatha drily.

"Yes? Well, it's meat and drink to me."

"Perhaps you've never been suspected of it," Agatha suggested.

"I haven't, and that's a fact. And if I were it 'ud be a disaster. Why, do you realize I wouldn't be able to call myself in to clear myself?"

Agatha folded her hands on the edge of the desk and leaned forward. "Mr. Crook, I wanted to consult you—since Mr.

Entwistle doesn't care to be troubled with my affairs any longer—. about my future."

"Quite right," nodded Crook. "Got any ideas?"

"Sometimes," said Agatha passionately, "I wonder what future I can hope for. There are hundreds of people, I know, who believe Edmund's version, who think of me as a murderess, or worse, as a madwoman. You know, Miss Bumble refused to have me in the house for another hour after she heard Edmund's story. She said she'd never sleep quietly in her bed, and I dare say there are thousands who feel the same."

"Your husband's in the same boat, and he still seems pretty bobbish," Crook reminded her.

"That's different. He is a murderer, even if it can't be proved."

"Thought about your future relations with him?" inquired Crook callously.

Agatha stared at him in horror. "You cannot mean to suggest that I should go back to him?"

"If you want to convince the world that your mutual accusation was a put-up job, I can't think of a better way. Besides, not to put too fine a point on it, he mightn't be too keen. Still, you've got to live and your present income's about a hundred a year."

"Edmund ought, at least, to return my capital. I know it won't be worth what I was getting from it, but at least I shouldn't starve."

"Put it there!" said Crook heartily. "That's the way I feel too. That's why I've asked him to join this little discussion."

Agatha leaped up from her chair. "You can't mean that you've asked him here?" She had turned white at the mere suggestion.

"Take it easy!" said Crook in kinder tones. "Even your precious husband can't get away with murder under my nose."

"I cannot meet him," declared Agatha, with finality.

"Then you shan't. Bill will establish you all nice and cosy in the other room. But, mind you," he wagged a thick finger in warning, "you're not to come in till you're sent for. Understand?"

"I certainly should not come in so long as he was on the premises," shuddered Agatha. "Perhaps you think me a coward, Mr. Crook, but I'm remembering that night in the woodshed, the look on his face, his soft voice, his stealthy approach. I don't think I'll ever forget. Why, I feel half crazy at the thought."

"Look here," said Crook severely, "you can't afford to go mad again. I've got my work cut out as it is. Here, Bill."

The door opened and Bill Parsons came in, a tall, unsmiling man with a ruined face and a slight limp where a police bullet had caught him in the heel several years before.

"Give Mrs. Durward the morning paper and tell someone

177

to get her a cup of tea. And as soon as Durward arrives, shove him in."

Agatha had not long withdrawn before her husband put in his appearance. He entered with his old easy grace, though the long suspense had left him a little pale and drawn.

"Good morning, Mr. Crook," he said. "I understand you want to discuss my wife's position."

"Got it in one. As, of course, you know, she's in a bad way financially. Entwistle was against her sellin' out the stocks, but she insisted. Now there's no question of your settin' up house together—I take it you're no more keen than she is—am I right in thinkin' you'll hand her back her cheque?"

"Well, as to that," said Durward, "the money was a free gift, and I've been involved in considerable expense. . . ."

"You know your way about, don't you?" said Crook admiringly. "All the same, you'd much better hand that cheque across. There's goin' to be no end of talk if it comes out that you've hung onto it."

"And you think it's going to?"

"I wouldn't be surprised." Crook lighted a ferocious-looking cigar. "Ever hear of a paper called the *Sunday Echo?*"

"I—think so."

"Well, if you haven't, about five million people have. There's a chap called Cummings at the head, and you'd escape a skunk more easily than you'd separate Cummings from a scoop."

"And what do you suggest your friend, Cummings, can do?"

Crook looked at him thoughtfully. "I don't believe you half appreciate the interest the public still takes in you and your wife. You're a hot penny at the moment; and your wife's got a lot more sense than you realize. She knows this is the minute to strike, even if you don't."

"I'm afraid I still don't understand." Durward was courteous but his glance was very wary.

"Power of the press, my dear chap, power of the press. Cummings is prepared to pay your wife a very healthy sum for the inside story of The Haven Mystery. And, of course, if she finds herself short of cash, Mrs. Durward's got to accept." His thick fingers sifted casually through some papers lying on the table. "She's just gone, as a matter of fact. We've been runnin' through a few of the instalments. 'Mrs. Durward Tells the Facts.' "

"She can only repeat what she's already said, and she'd better be careful at that. I've been acquitted, remember."

"Not you," said Crook. "You can't be acquitted without a trial."

"It's rather late in the day for my wife to produce fresh information. She might even have trouble with the police."

"Not with me behind her she won't," Crook assured him confidently. "Here's rather a nice one. 'The Ghost of Bell's Bottom Walks Again.' And here's the best of all. 'Something Nasty in the Woodshed.' Oh, believe me, Durward, the public's going to eat this. We begin, y'see, with 'How I Met My Husband.' Ever noticed that woman's second blooming is always a fascinatin' subject? Well, take it from me, young love isn't in it. Then we get 'My Life at The Haven.' Instalment three. 'The Shadow Darkens . . .'"

"Even the most foolhardy editor won't publish those," said Durward fiercely.

"You don't even know what she's said."

"If she's accused me . . ."

"She hasn't. Didn't you hear me say these were the facts of the case? Listen to this." He selected a typescript and began to read. "The clock struck four-thirty. The house seemed uncannily still. Yet it was not the stillness of tranquillity. Rather did it seem the stillness of death. Outside, a sinister wind moved among the trees. Impelled by some mysterious force I left the house and began the long, dim climb towards the road. Perhaps it was some primeval instinct for companionship, for some reassurance of my oneness with humanity—or perhaps SHE summoned me. Be that as it may, my feet were drawn away from the house where all my hopes were centred, towards the living, pulsing world that would never again be hers. As I approached the garage I listened for the noise of human activity, but I listened in vain. The stillness was round me like mist, like fog, choking and blinding me. I wanted to go back to the dear familiar rooms, the kettle on the hob, the fire leaping in the grate, but in my brain a voice whispered insistently: 'On, on.' And then I saw her, moving between the trees, threatening, beckoning, irresistible, devilish, a figure of Death bidding me follow her into the cold valley of the shadow where no living thing can dwell."

"If the rest of Agatha's articles aren't more accurate than that, they won't have much value," commented Durward scornfully. "If she'd come anywhere near the garage I'd have heard her. Anyway, the ghost didn't come near the front of the house. It came up from the pool at the back."

"That does sound more in keeping with the legend," Crook acknowledged cordially. Then his voice changed. "But—I say—how did you know?"

Durward's recovery was instantaneous. "Because Miss Knowles had gone out the back way. I saw her myself from an upper window, carrying a basket. She was going to pick some flowers, but I suppose she changed her mind."

"Ah, yes," murmured Crook. "That would be the basket you nearly fell over in the hall when you were carting the corpse out to the woodshed."

"That's it," said Durward shortly. "Why, what's up?" For Crook was frowning.

The lawyer leaned over and laid one big freckled hand on his visitor's arm.

"This doesn't make sense," he said. "You know, you'd much better leave the story to your wife. She saw the ghost. You didn't."

"In any case, I object to all this publicity. The affair should be regarded as closed. My wife's a very unreliable witness. She was asleep when Miss Knowles left the house, and she was unconscious afterwards and remembers nothing of what took place."

"D'you remember what time it was that you saw her go?"

"We got in just after four. I went up to my wife's room, found her asleep, as I said, came down and told Miss Knowles she wasn't to be disturbed, and fetched her the basket. I went upstairs again and saw Miss Knowles leave the house. That would be about 4.10 or 4.15. I went out to the garage and came back at about 4.50 as near as I can remember."

"According to Mrs. Durward, she saw the ghost at, say, 4.35. Well, it could be done, given one condition."

"What's that?" Durward's voice was clipped and wary.

Crook leaned yet farther across the table. "*When you saw Miss Knowles going down towards the pool, was she carrying a sheet?*"

"Carrying a sheet?" Durward stared.

"That's what I said. The ghost wore a sheet, you remember. It was found later, folded in the hall and identified as a sheet off Miss Knowles's bed. By the way, you didn't see her go upstairs between 4 and 4.10?"

"Actually, I didn't, but that's not to say she didn't go up while I was getting the basket."

"It's very difficult," murmured Crook. "She couldn't have carried a sheet without your noticing it, I suppose? And no sheet is so small that it will get into a flower basket. Yet, if she was the ghost, she must have carried the sheet with her down to the woods. Sheets don't grow on trees."

Durward thought. "I suppose she just waited till I was out and then sneaked back, left the basket in the hall and fetched the sheet."

"It could be, Durward, it could be," agreed Crook cheerfully. "How far did you see her go?"

"Just through the gate at the foot of the garden and into the woods. Say about three minutes."

"And three minutes back. That brings us up to, say, 4.18. Yes, every minute counts now. According to Mrs. Durward, she came out of her room not later than 4.15 and called to you both. You must just have been out of earshot, and that tallies with your story. But Miss Knowles couldn't get back and fetch the sheet and be out of the house again without Mrs. Durward seeing her. Besides, she says she looked out of the window and there was no one in sight. Now, she must have seen Miss Knowles comin' or goin'. And if Miss Knowles didn't come, then she must have taken the sheet along with her the first time. And she didn't do that, because you watched her go, and she was only carrying a basket. Besides, if she didn't come back, how did the basket find its way into the hall? Baskets ain't like centipedes; they've no legs of their own. How d'you explain that?"

"It's not my job to explain it," returned Durward curtly. "I know nothing about the murder. I've told you that before."

"Well, well, we'll have to leave it to the *Echo's* readers. Cummings might make a competition of it. Prizes will be awarded for the best answers to the following three questions:

1. How did the basket get back to the hall?
2. How did the sheet get down to the pool?
3. How did Mr. Durward know that the ghost came from the back of the house and not the front?

You see, Durward, we're back where we began."

"I've nothing to say," said Durward.

"Then I'll make one or two suggestions. You couldn't *know* the ghost came from the back unless you saw it. But you couldn't have seen it because Miss Knowles was dead when you re-entered the house. By the way, where do you assume your wife was standing when she saw the ghost?"

"According to what I gathered from her later—you must remember all my information necessarily comes from her—she had gone through the garden and as far as the entrance to the woods."

"And then"—Crook flicked through some more papers—"she lost her head and turned and ran from the house, shouting for you. She caught her foot on the rockery and fell and lost consciousness."

"That doesn't square with the fact that someone strangled Miss Knowles in the hall."

"My point precisely. Now your version is that she walked into the hall and waited for the ghost to follow her in. Now, whatever your wife may have thought when she stood outside all alone among the shadows and the eerie influences and what not, no sane man is going to believe that when she was in her own hall with the ghost within striking distance, she didn't realize who that ghost was."

"I'm convinced she did," said Durward.

"You mean, she knew it was Miss Knowles she was attacking, not a ghost?

"I don't say that. I think by that time she was so panic-stricken that, when she found herself face to face with a sheeted figure, she struck out desperately. I dare say at that moment she didn't realize it was Miss Knowles, she didn't know who it was. Yes, I said just now that she must have known, but how can we tell what a terrified woman knows? She saw something that spelt danger to her, physically and mentally, and she lunged at it with a kind of superhuman courage."

"Suppose Miss Knowles had walked in with the sheet over her arm and her fingers to her nose, saying, 'Yah! Who's afraid of the Big Bad Wolf?' do you think then your wife would have attacked her?"

"I'm certain she wouldn't," said Durward without any hesitation at all. "She would have been furious at her friend's heartlessness; it would, I am convinced, have broken their friendship, but I'm sure it wouldn't have ended in Miss Knowles losing her life."

"Well, you can't say fairer than that," Crook agreed. "Then we'll take it Miss Knowles was wearin' the sheet when she came in."

"I think we can safely say that. After all, Agatha's own testimony goes to show it must have been the case. At no time has she said, 'Miss Knowles came in dressed as a ghost,' she simply said, 'I saw the ghost.'"

"Very lucid argument. But it does raise another point and that is—who took the sheet off Miss Knowles? I mean, you're not suggestin' that when she finished choking the poor dame, Mrs. Durward carefully removed the sheet and folded it in a corner? But if she died wearin' the sheet, why wasn't she wearin' it when you came in? You said yourself she wasn't."

Durward rose angrily. "Do you think I don't understand what you're trying to do?" he inquired. "You want to get me utterly confused, and then you'll declare I said something damning, lift it out of its context, go running to the police. Well, I shall deny everything, everything . . ."

"Take it easy," Crook besought him. "I'm quite an old bird, y'know, much too old to go to the police and say I think you admitted this or that, without offerin' them proof. As a matter of fact, I think they'd be damned interested in our conversation, open up a new aspect of the case. I don't think they ever thought about the sheet."

"I've admitted nothing about the sheet," said Durward quickly. "Actually, Miss Knowles probably did bring it back over her arm and taunted my wife. and Agatha was so furious she went for her. . . ."

Crook looked dubious. "That isn't what you said just now."

"It's what I've said all along," said Durward clearly.

Crook shook his head. "Your memory's not much more reliable than your wife's." He pressed a button beneath his desk. "What you actually said was . . ." He paused and a voice could be heard saying: "If the rest of Agatha's articles aren't more accurate than that, they won't have much value. Anyway, the ghost didn't come near the front of the house. . . ."

Durward turned sheet-white. "What's this?" he demanded thickly.

"My dear chap, I'm a lawyer. Always have a witness when important statements are to be made. I wouldn't be surprised if the police were quite interested in that record."

"Oh, you wouldn't?" Durward's face had now lost every vestige of the smooth, sympathetic manner that had brought him so much in the past. Now it was distorted, greenish white, the lips stretched, the eyes burning. "There's one thing you've forgotten, though. I've still a shot left in my locker. . . ."

Through his speech came the sound of words he had spoken earlier in the interview as the machine went pitilessly on. "I saw her myself from an upper window, carrying a basket. She was going to pick some flowers, but I suppose she changed her mind."

"Give me that record," said Durward, "or . . ." He whipped out a revolver. "You damned fool!" he said.

"Oh, you'll make me? And then you're goin' to try and persuade the world you ain't a murderer. It can't be done. Durward, I believe in miracles as much as anyone, but it can't be done."

"This doesn't make sense," said the voice on the machine. "You know, you'd much better leave the story to your wife."

"You've asked for it," said Durward, raising his arm.

"No, Edmund, not that way." The voice was a terrified shriek. Durward glanced instinctively over his shoulder to where Agatha stood, terror-stricken, in the doorway. That second of hesitation proved fatal. Instantly a book whizzed from Crook's table in the direction of the doomed man; the revolver clattered to the floor. Agatha put her hands over her face and screamed. The main door of the outer office opened and Bill flung himself at the weapon, reaching it a second before Durward. Behind Bill stood a tall man in plain clothes.

"Mr. Durward?" he said. "I'm Superintendent Marsh. There are one or two questions I'd like to ask you, if you'll be good enough to come with me."

Bill stepped deferentially back, loosening his hold on the revolver. The next instant, before any of them could move, there was a resounding report. Durward knew the game was up and had taken the only way out. As he died he hoped his ghost might haunt Crook forever and ever.

❧ ❧ ❧

184

"But I *don't understand*," exclaimed a shaken and bewildered Agatha, after the unpleasant preliminaries of removing the body had taken place. "Oh, I know about Edmund, of course. I heard what he said. . . ."

Crook suggestively cupped one hand round his ear. "Ever been on the stage, Mrs. Durward?"

"I—oh, no. Just amateur theatricals, you know,"

"You couldn't have come in better on your cue if you'd been the star of the Haymarket for forty years. Well, your husband's saved the country five thousand pounds. That's what a murder trial costs."

"But I'm still in the dark," Agatha protested. "I mean—I never heard of a man called Cummings, and even if I had I wouldn't have written up the story of my married life for anything he could offer me."

"Sure you wouldn't," agreed the affable Crook. "But—I had to get your husband to open up somehow. This case has given me several kinds of a headache and, believe me, I couldn't think of any other way."

Agatha looked shocked. "And that article you read him—you knew I hadn't written it."

"You mustn't mind about that," said Crook kindly. "No one can do everything."

"You seem to have done a good deal," commented Agatha. "I'm sure Mr. Entwistle would never have thought of such a thing."

"Entwistle has one kind of conscience and I have another. I've no doubt he's a very honourable gentleman, but it isn't always the Hon. Gents. who get out of the mulligatawny. It's a question of the type of conscience."

"I always thought lawyers had a very high standard."

"So they tell you, but when you come down to brass tacks you generally find it's their own reputation they're beefin' about, not their clients'. Accordin' to himself, every lawyer's middle name is Galahad. Well, I've always thought he must be a pain in the neck to live with. Now my conscience works differently. It tells me I'm bein' paid to prove my clients' innocence."

"But—suppose there is no proof?"

"Then manufacture it. What else is a lawyer for? The labourer is worthy of his hire, but he's got to earn his hire. My job in this case was to shove the blame onto Mr. Edmund Durward. Well, as you see, it worked."

"That policeman . . ." began Agatha uncertainly.

"Policeman? Oh, you mean our Superintendent Marsh? He's not a policeman, honey, just a part of the Arthur Crook service. The trouble with tyros," he added earnestly, "is that they don't show enough enterprise. They say 'Give me the facts.' Yes, but what they don't understand is that facts are like coloured beads. You can arrange them in any pattern you please. Now, if I'd been working for Durward, sooner or later the whole world 'ud have known he was innocent."

"But he wasn't." Agatha looked horrified.

"Sure he wasn't, but if he'd been my client he would have been," replied Crook simply. "I only work for innocent men. I'm goin' to have that put on my tombstone. You've got to choose your road and stick to it like glue, and that's mine."

II

Arthur Crook stood beside his desk glancing through a temperance tract that had come by the midday post. It was called "The Evils of Ignorance."

"One of these days, Bill," he said, "I'm goin' to write one called 'The Virtues of Ignorance.' If Durward hadn't been ignorant of the law he'd have known I hadn't got a thing on him. I couldn't have brought any of that evidence into court. Why, hell, it wasn't evidence, just a bit of supposition on my part and fencing on his. But it touched up *his* conscience and that was all I wanted. By the way, when did you turn that dictaphone off?"

"When he said, 'You've asked for it.' No need to drag our spurious Mr. Marsh into the case, not as usurping the rights of Scotland Yard, that is. Actually, he's a witness of Durward's suicide, which is all to the good. Just a client waiting in the outer room. You think of a good deal, don't you, Crook?"

"I wonder if Mrs. Durward really saw her husband's body," speculated Crook. "I never moved so fast in my life as when I tried to get between the two of them. That was a nasty piece of work altogether, Bill. Swindlin' women with a weddin' ring is one thing, but murder's another cup of tea. I wouldn't say Miss Knowles was the first he's put under ground, either."

"The good work goes on," said Bill dryly. "Look at this."

He held out a copy of a well-known weekly.

III

The advertisement read:

WIDOWER, aged 52, independent means, wishes to meet WIDOW, similarly situated, view matrimony. Business experience preferred. No children or other ties essential. Write Box . . .

In her comfortable home at Brixton Mrs. Bessie Dean read the insertion. She had been a widow for twelve months and didn't care about the estate. Her business was flourishing nicely, her home was her own, but she did feel she wanted a man in the background. Taking up pen and paper she began to write.

THE END

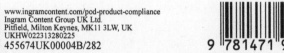